Different Paths

Books by Judy Clemens

The Stella Crown Series
Till the Cows Come Home
Three Can Keep a Secret
To Thine Own Self Be True
The Day Will Come
Different Paths

Other Novels
Embrace the Grim Reaper

Different Paths

Judy Clemens (signature)

Judy Clemens

Poisoned Pen Press

First Trade Paperback Edition 2009

10 9 8 7 6 5 4 3 2 1

Library of Congress Catalog Card Number: 2008923133

ISBN: 978-1-59058-631-0   Trade Paperback

Poisoned Pen Press
6962 E. First Ave., Ste. 103
Scottsdale, AZ 85251
www.poisonedpenpress.com
info@poisonedpenpress.com

Printed in the United States of America

*For all who have loved and supported Stella
from the beginning. May you find the love, loyalty,
and integrity she finds central to living a good life.*

Acknowledgments

As always, I couldn't have written this book without the help of many people. Well, I could've written it, I guess, but it wouldn't have been nearly as good.

Paula Meabon has been with me all the way with this series, and her first-person accounts of farming events and mishaps have enlivened the books from day one. She also takes the time to proofread the manuscripts, to make sure I'm not making too many glaring errors about dairy farming, and I appreciate it immensely.

Detective Randall Floyd of the Telford Police has been another faithful resource. Without him Detective Willard wouldn't have been half as smart, and Stella would've gotten herself into much more trouble.

Lorin Beidler, MD, first gave me the idea for Nick's illness, and Tami Forbes helped to make it realistic. Dr. Beidler also helped with other medical details in this book, which I won't name here or it would give things away.

Pastor Philip Clemens discussed Scripture and religious issues with me, pointing me toward relevant Biblical passages and current events.

Ron Baldridge, DVM, helped make sure Carla's veterinary supplies and activities were correct.

Identification Officer David Hammond of the Lima Police Department made sure I knew what I was talking about when it came to fingerprints.

Lee Jay Diller shared his knowledge of large trucks and their tires.

The Poisoned Pen Press crew—made up of Rob, Jessica, Marilyn, and Nan—is wonderful, and I thank them for all they do to make writing and publishing a book a joyful experience. Having Barbara Peters as my editor is an honor and a privilege, and not something I will ever take for granted.

Phil and Nancy Clemens, besides being great parents, are my trusted first readers, and I thank them for reading quickly and critically.

Steve, Tristan, and Sophia allow me the privilege of having a job I love. I could not do it without their support.

And thanks to Mike Grieser for the joke. There aren't very many jokes Stella would find funny. This was one of them.

We all of us have taken different paths now; but in
This the first great fragmentation of my maturity,
*   I feel the confines of my*
Art and my living deepening immeasurably by the
*   memory of them.*
                    —Lawrence Durrell, *Justine*

Chapter One

"That is *so* unfair!"

I stared at Nick's little sister, my hand in the air, hovering above the stacks of colorful cards.

Nick continued playing, flipping his cards over in threes, searching for another match to lay on one of the Dutch Piles. "What is?"

"Are you kidding me?" Miranda glared at him. "That Stella's helping you. This game is supposed to be about the speed of one person. Not a *team*."

Nick's mother clicked her tongue. "Miranda Jane, you know Nick needs help. He can't play Dutch Blitz like he used to."

I reached to lay my blue seven on a middle pile. "And believe me, having me as a teammate in this game doesn't really help. I'm more of an obstacle."

Liz, Nick's older sister, slid her own blue seven onto the pile before I got there.

I pulled back my card. "See?"

Miranda stuck out her lip. "Well, I don't see how Nick having MS is going to make him worse at this game."

Now Liz stopped, slapping her cards onto the table. "If you'd pay attention once in a while, maybe you'd understand. His body's not working right. His eyesight. His nerves. Have you forgotten everything we've told you?"

"I'm not an idiot. Of course I remember. But Dutch Blitz—"

"Girls, please…" Nick's mother looked from one to the other, her eyes darting back and forth behind her glasses.

I tipped my head to the side and scratched my ear, looking at the dark clouds visible through the window. My truck sat in Nick's driveway, the Virginia rain washing off the last of the Pennsylvania dust I'd brought with me two days earlier.

"I wish Lucy had never given Nick this dumb game," Miranda said. "'*A Vonderful Goot Game!*' I mean, how lame is that?"

Lucy, my farmhand, passing on some of her Mennonite heritage through a simple card game last Christmas. I swiped my finger across the fog on the window and wondered if it was raining at home. If Lucy was wet from milking even wetter cows.

Liz took a deep breath, then let it out in a huff. "What are you, Miranda? Sixteen again? You've regressed a few years now in maturity? Blaming everything on Lucy?"

"Not everything, just this game, and Nick cheating."

"Girls, will you please—"

"Blitz," Nick said.

We turned to look at him, and he smiled. "Gotcha."

It was true. His Blitz Pile—the stack of ten you try to eliminate—was gone. Without my help.

"Oh, that's just great." Miranda shoved her chair back from the table and stomped to the refrigerator, where she made a commotion out of filling her water glass from the automatic dispenser.

Nick glanced sideways at me, his cheeks filling with air. I made a face. Miranda was nothing if not dramatic, and Nick's recent diagnosis had brought her emotions into full bloom. Liz hit the nail on the head when she'd implied their little sister had turned back into a teen-ager. And speaking of hitting, I wished I could bop Miranda on the head a good one.

"Do you want to play again?" Nick's mother asked.

Nick laughed, while I tried to figure out if she was serious. Miranda ignored her, and Liz scooped up the cards and began putting them back in the box.

Nick's mother folded her hands on the table. "No, I guess not."

"I was actually thinking about lying down." Nick stretched his arms above his head, letting go with an exaggerated yawn, and I had to stifle a laugh.

"It's only one-thirty," Miranda said. "We just had dinner."

Liz stood up. "A perfect time for a little rest. I'm sure church wore Nick out this morning."

"But—"

"Stella's here. We can leave Nick in her hands."

As if he wouldn't be okay on his own. But I wasn't going to complain. Nick's family had been hovering over him from the first day of his illness, and I wasn't the only one ready to scream.

Nick cleared his throat, his face a mask of patience. "We'll be fine."

"If you're sure…" His mother gazed at him with that adoring-worried-disbelieving look only mothers can give.

Miranda set her glass on the counter with a snap. "Fine. Like *Stella's* been here every day taking care of him since he got sick. Like *she* knows anything about it."

"Miranda!" Nick's mother fluttered a hand against her chest.

"Ignore her, Mom," Liz said. "She's just being—"

"Herself," Nick said. "She's just being herself."

Miranda squinted at him, obviously unsure how to take the comment, but Nick smiled at her and held out his arms. She hesitated, then stepped into them for a hug, resting her cheek on his head for a brief moment before turning away.

Liz scooped up her keys from the counter. "Nick, you had some files to give me?"

"Right. Let me get them."

He got up and went into the next room, where he kept his computer and most of the paperwork for Hathaway Construction and Development. Liz followed him.

Nick's mother rose from the table, smoothing her blouse, and gathered up her purse. "How long are you staying this visit, Stella?"

"Till tomorrow. I'll head home in the afternoon."

"Why don't you come to my house for lunch? I'll make something for the three of us." She paused, then reached over to pat my arm. "Thank you for helping out with our Nicky."

Nicky.

"I'm glad to be here. You know that."

"Yeah," Miranda said. "Here for a few days, then back to your *cows*."

I took a deep breath through my nose and clamped my teeth together. "It *is* how I make my living."

Miranda rolled her eyes. "Whatever."

Yup. She'd definitely returned to life as a teen-ager. An annoying one.

"Besides," Miranda continued, "if you were smart you'd realize that as long as you're with Nick you don't *need* to make a living." She looked at me. "Oh. So maybe you'd better keep your job, after all."

Nick's mother inhaled sharply, and Liz came back into the room, interrupting whatever response I could've managed. She held a stack of folders under her arm. "Ready, Mom? I'll drop you off at home. I promised Robbie I'd cook him dinner tonight and I need to get working on it."

"Oooh, supper?" Nick leaned against the door to his office, his grin wicked. "So, sis, when are you going to take the plunge and start cooking for him *every* night?"

Liz laughed and swatted him gently on the shoulder. "Never."

When Nick raised his eyebrows she laughed again. "He'll do at least *half* of the cooking."

Nick smiled. "Well, it's good to hear you've been discussing it, at least."

"Like you should talk."

Liz turned her teasing eyes to me, but I couldn't help feeling Miranda's smirk even more. I lifted my hands in self-defense. "Don't look at me. I'm a terrible cook."

Liz guffawed, and came over to give me a hug. "Come down again soon. We're always glad to see you."

"Yeah. Me, too."

Nick's mom gave me a peck on the cheek, and Miranda skirted the far side of the room, glaring at me before following her mother and sister out the front door into the rain. Nick came up behind me and put his arms around my waist as we watched Liz back her car out of the driveway, their mother in the passenger seat. Miranda left next, her Lexus spinning its wheels on the wet pavement.

I leaned my head back against Nick's chin, my shoulders relaxing as Nick's little sister drove away. "Whew. I wasn't sure what was going to come out of Miranda's mouth next."

I felt Nick shrug. "She's having a hard time with it all. With me being sick. You having a place in my life."

I turned around in his arms and placed my hands on his shoulders. "Doesn't it drive you nuts?"

"She's freaked out. And she's never handled change well. Not like Liz. Or even my mom."

"Your mom really is amazing with it. Especially after your dad…" I stopped, Nick's eyes darkening from what I was sure was the memory of his father's death from cancer only a year earlier.

Nick patted my hips. "Enough about that. I didn't kick them out so we could talk."

"That's right." I grinned. "You said you were ready to lie down."

A smile tickled his lips and he pulled me against him, his hands on the small of my back. "Yeah. It's not my fault they thought I meant alone."

The look in his eyes was anything but tired, and my breath caught in my throat. "I don't think we put anything past Liz, but she's a big girl." He laughed quietly, and I slid my arms further around his neck. "And you're a big boy."

He laughed louder this time and lifted me off the floor, finding my lips as he lowered me against him. His fingers had just found their way under the back hem of my shirt when the sound of the Tom Copper Band filled the room.

The river rages
The waters flow
Past twinkling lights
The Schuylkill's show

Nick groaned. "My new ring tone."

I kissed him some more. "Don't answer it."

But tell me baby
Tell me true
Can you feel our love
The way I do?

Nick set me all the way on the floor and spoke, accenting each word with a point of his finger. "Don't. Move."

I sighed with resignation and let him go. "Hurry up. Tell whoever it is that it's not a good time."

He grinned and flipped open his phone. "This is Nick." His eyes flicked to me. "Hey, Lucy. Sure. She's right here." He held out the phone and I went over to get it. He held it above his head until I gave him another lingering kiss, then lowered the phone into my hand. "Make it quick."

I eased my arm around his waist and held him close. "Oh, I will."

He gave me the phone but kept me against him, and I angled my head away to speak into the receiver. "Hey, Luce, what's up? It better be good."

"It's Carla." Her voice was brittle as she said the name of my veterinarian and long-time friend. "She's in the hospital."

"What? What happened?"

A sob came down the line. "Her truck. It was…she was carjacked, Stella. And they're not sure if she's going to live."

Chapter Two

I pushed the speed limit all the way home, my fingers crossed that the cops wouldn't be out to get a single woman in a rusting truck. My luck held, and four hours later I pulled into the driveway at home, gravel spitting under my tires. My collie, Queenie, raced around in circles, barking, while Lucy's nine-year-old daughter Tess stood goggled-eyed as I jumped out of the barely-stopped truck. I jogged to the barn, where Lucy was swabbing Sleeping Beauty's udder. Queenie followed me, panting noisily, and I laid my hand on her head while I waited for Lucy's report.

Lucy stood and rested an elbow on the cow's sizable haunch. "Carla's out of the woods. She's stable, but they're keeping her in the ICU for observation. She got a good whack on the head they want to monitor."

I sagged into a squat, Queenie offering support to keep me from falling. With shame I thought of my earlier wishes to smack Miranda on *her* head. "Am I allowed to visit her?"

"Don't know. I suppose. I'm sure she'd be glad to see you."

I rubbed the sides of Queenie's neck, her long fur warm and soft. She sniffed at my face, her eyes betraying her heightened anxiety as she felt my own.

"It's okay, girl," I told her. "It sounds like it's going to be okay." I stood. "All right if I head over to the hospital, then? She's at Grand View?"

"Yup. Go ahead. Zach's here to help."

I glanced up, only now seeing our teen-age assistant further down the row. He tilted his chin my way, but otherwise ignored me.

"Give Carla my love, will you?" Lucy said. "Tell her I'm praying for her."

"Will do." I gave Queenie one last pat. "You know any more details about what happened?"

Lucy leaned back down, giving the cow's teats a last swipe with her cloth. "Just that someone surprised her. Came up from behind in the parking lot of the Roy-El Diner and took off with the truck, catching Carla's shirt in the door. Luckily she wasn't wearing her coveralls, since she'd taken them off for lunch."

"Why'd she have the truck? She doesn't usually work on Sundays."

"She was on call. Had to go out to the Moyers', check one of their horses. Anyway, her shirt ripped off almost as soon as the guy took off—"

"She's sure it was a guy? She know who?"

"She didn't really see him, but her impression was a male. Tall, in a ball cap and jacket. He took off and she banged her head on the pavement. Knocked her out. Some folks pulling into the parking lot found her. Don't know how long she was lying there. Couldn't have been too long." She pulled the milker down and slid the hoses onto Sleeping Beauty's teats.

"Thanks for calling and letting me know."

"No problem. I figured you'd want to come back, just in case…"

We let that thought go, and I turned to leave.

"Nick?" Lucy asked. "How is he?"

I looked back. "He's fine." An image of his face, furrowed with concern as I stuffed dirty clothes into my duffel bag, rose before me. Our afternoon delight had obviously been postponed. Not for too long, I hoped, but we didn't have a date set yet for our next visit. It was his turn to come up to PA, and it was hard finding a time when his doctors and family were willing to let him travel so far away.

"I'll give him a call when I get back to let him know how Carla's doing."

Lucy nodded, already on to the next cow.

Grand View Hospital was busy, but I had no trouble finding Carla's room. I'd been afraid they wouldn't let me in, not being actual family, but the nurse was friendly and helpful, glancing at my tattoo only briefly before telling me Carla's room number.

The door eased open with a quiet whoosh, and I caught a glimpse of Carla before she knew I'd arrived. I swallowed a gasp and stared at my friend's face, already black and blue. Her arm was wrapped in gauze, and her nose had swelled to twice its normal size. I took a deep breath and entered.

"Stella!" Her eyes lit up and a smile spread across her puffy face.

I made my way toward her, stopping suddenly at the sight of another person in the room. A man.

He stood quickly, his eyes flicking toward me. Tall and thin, his brown eyes bored into mine as his hands grasped a magazine rolled into a tight cylinder.

Carla waved an arm, strapped with tape and an IV, toward him. "Stella, this is Bryan. Bryan, Stella. Stella's known me for...well, forever, I guess. At least all the time that matters."

"Hello." He rolled the magazine even tighter, and twisted it in his hands before shifting it to his left hand and holding out his right.

I nodded, studying his blue cotton shirt and combed-back hair as I shook his hand. Pointy cowboy boots poked out from under his jeans, and a shiny NASCAR belt buckle adorned his waist. Super. I hoped he didn't want to talk about Dale Earnhardt, Jr., or any of those other guys, because I knew nothing about them. Didn't have any interest in them, either, as far as that went.

"Um..." He let go of my hand and cleared his throat. "I guess I'll go to the cafeteria. Get something to eat. If that's okay." He looked anxiously at Carla.

"Of course that's okay. Take your time. I've got some catching up to do with Stella, here."

"Okay. Great. I'll be back. If you're sure." He stepped toward the door, hesitated, and held the magazine out to Carla.

She smiled. "You take it. Read it while you're eating."

A smile flickered on his face, and he ducked his head briefly before exiting through the whooshing door.

"Who," I asked, "was *that*?"

Her smile grew. "Bryan. I told you."

"Yeah, but—"

"My new boyfriend."

"New boyfriend."

"Why do you sound so skeptical? Think I can't get one?"

"Stop it. It's just I hadn't heard about him."

She tried to sit up straighter and winced. I reached out, but she waved me away. "Push that green button."

I jabbed it with my thumb, and the head of the bed rose, putting her at a better angle for talking. "I told you he's new. I haven't had a chance to tell you."

"You met him where? The OK Corral?"

"Ha, ha. Very funny."

"Well, the cowboy boots, the belt buckle…"

"Yeah, yeah, make fun. I just so happened to meet him country line dancing."

I stared at her. "*What?*"

"I assume you've heard of it? The *Boot Scootin' Boogie*? The *Tennessee Twister*?"

"Of course I've heard of it. I just didn't know you—"

"Could do it? I might be a little rounder than you, but that doesn't mean I'm incapable of some fancy footwork."

"I know that. I didn't mean—"

"Bryan asked me to dance about, oh, three weeks ago, at the VFW in Souderton. We hit it off, and he's been hanging around ever since. He's been fantastic today after…well, since I got mugged."

I stepped closer. "Speaking of that…"

"Yeah, it's something, huh? You like my new face?"

"It'll be back to normal in no time."

"I guess."

I studied the IV in her arm. "So why are you still here? In the ICU?"

She waggled her eyebrows. "Subdural hematoma."

"Which means…"

"I've got a skull fracture. A vessel in my head tore, and they want to make sure the tear isn't expanding, bleeding all over the place in there."

"They didn't do surgery?"

"Don't need to for this, apparently, unless it gets worse. It's basically a concussion. I had an awful headache—but I'm on drugs now, so I'm okay—and they did a CT scan. Now they keep me here and watch me. I'm hooked up to monitors they're keeping an eye on." She pointed out the various wires attached to her body.

"For how long?"

"Till they're sure the tear is healing."

I grimaced.

"Yeah, I know, it sounds awful. But you know the worst part?"

"What?"

"I'm not allowed to eat anything."

I laughed. For Carla this was the hardest doctor's order possible. "Should I sneak you in some ice cream?"

She groaned. "Don't tease me."

I pulled a chair to the side of the bed and sat. "So tell me what happened."

"You haven't heard?"

"Just the basics, from Lucy. She sends her greetings, by the way, and her prayers."

"Good ol' Lucy. Couldn't have anybody better praying."

"Anyway, you don't know who it was?"

She laid her head back and looked at the ceiling. "Just that it was a guy. At least, I'm pretty sure. He wasn't real small or anything, and it wasn't a wimpy shove. But the clothes looked like a guy."

"And he came up from behind and stole your truck."

A shadow crossed her face. "My poor baby."

"No sign of it yet, that you've heard?"

She tilted her head toward me. "Detective Willard was here about an hour ago. Took my fingerprints in case they find my truck and need to eliminate me from the evidence. They haven't found it. I'm not real hopeful they will."

"I'm sorry."

Carla's truck was her life. Or her job, anyway. The Ford F250 was outfitted with a Port-a-Vet, which held all the tools of her trade. Many of the instruments belonged to her, personally, and not to the practice.

"You didn't see the guy's face?"

"You mean as I was caught in the door and slammed down onto the blacktop?"

I winced. "Well, when you put it that way…"

She lifted a hand. "The tiny glimpse I had was after the door was shut. I didn't see much of anything. If I saw any details, I forgot them. A ball cap is about it. And I don't even know what team. I sure hope he wasn't a Phillies fan, or I'll lose all my trust in human nature."

"Willard able to give you any hope?"

"Not really. They have nothing to go on. At least not yet. By the time my truck got into the system as a stolen vehicle the guy was long gone."

Her eyelids suddenly drooped, closing for a long moment before opening again.

I pushed the chair back and stood up. "I'll let you get some rest. I just wanted to come by and make sure you were okay."

"It's these darn nurses." Her voice was quiet, and a bit slurred. "They won't let me sleep."

"That concussion."

"Yeah, I know. And heaven forbid you let those vitals go without checking for more than two minutes." She closed her eyes again, and seemed to sink further into the pillow.

I reached out, then let my hand fall back to my side. "I'll be back."

But she was already out.

Chapter Three

The woman at the nurses' station smiled. "May I help you?"

"Carla Beaumont fell asleep. Is that okay?"

"Sure. We'll let her go for a little while before waking her up."

"All right. Thanks."

I found the elevator at the end of the hall and pushed the down arrow. When the light went off and the doors opened, Carla's new boyfriend stepped off. His eyes widened. "You left her alone?"

"Uh, yeah."

He jerked a look down the hallway, like I'd deserted my friend while she gasped her last breaths.

"She's fine," I said. "The nurses are keeping an eye on her."

He fidgeted with the still tightly-rolled magazine. "Yeah. I know."

A light caught on his belt buckle and I held up a hand to keep from getting blinded. "You met Carla dancing?"

He nodded, a corner of his mouth tilting up. "Doing the *Boogie*. She was…it suited her."

I raised an eyebrow.

"She's been great," Bryan continued. "With this whole car-jacking thing. Pretty brave. It hasn't gotten her down at all."

"Yes." I stared at the untamed adoration evident on his face. "She's an amazing woman."

"Yeah. Yeah, I know." He glanced down the hallway, toward the circle of rooms. "I guess I'll get back to her, in case she needs me."

"She's asleep."

Alarm lit his eyes. "Asleep?"

"The nurses know."

"Oh. Well, all right. But I still need to get back. Just in case."

And he was gone, without a backward glance.

◇◇◇

"So what, exactly, don't you like about him?" Nick's voice was clear, as if he were right in the room with me, rather than two hundred miles away.

"I don't know. He's just…weird."

"Weird. Sure. That explains it."

"Maybe it's the cowboy thing."

"What cowboy thing?"

"Pointy boots, hugeass belt buckle. I'm sure the five-gallon hat was in his car. Or hanging on some horse he tied to a post."

Nick laughed. "Well you know, you've got the *biker* thing."

I leaned back on the kitchen chair and rested my head against the wall, looking at the clock. It was late, and I was tired. "I know, I know. Forgive me for being *mean*."

"Nah. I think you're just ticked you didn't know about him earlier."

I considered it. "That could be. But it was like he was afraid of me when I walked into the room."

"Like I said. Biker thing."

"Whatever."

"So how's Carla doing?" Something rustled on his end of the phone.

"She seemed pretty upbeat, actually. Didn't act like she'd just been mugged."

Something clanked, and I heard Nick breathing.

"Although if you'd seen her face you'd think she'd been for a few too many rounds in the ring."

Different Paths 15

A door slammed.

"Nick, what are you *doing*?"

"The dishes. If that's okay with you."

"Of course, you numbskull. But how come your sisters and mom aren't there taking care of you?"

He laughed again. "'Cause I didn't tell them you went home. I want an evening—and a night's sleep—without them hovering."

"Don't blame you." I considered asking him how he was feeling, but decided against it. If there was something to tell, he'd tell it.

Things went quiet on his end, like he'd stopped moving. "I have to say, though, that I wish you hadn't had to leave."

"Me, too, especially since Carla's going to be fine." I thought back to the moments before Lucy's phone call that afternoon. "I at least wish Lucy could've waited a few more minutes to call."

"Only a few more?"

"Well," I said, "in a few more minutes I don't think you would've been answering the phone."

Chapter Four

I went directly to bed after hanging up with Nick and slept through to my five AM alarm. A glass of orange juice and a chocolate chunk granola bar later, I headed out to the barn. Queenie met me in the parlor, and I rubbed her as she stretched. "That's a good girl. That's a good one." She groaned happily and sniffed my face, her wet nose giving me chills.

A lot of the cows were already in the barn, enjoying the coolness of their stalls, and it didn't take Queenie and me long to herd the rest of them in. Skittish and wide-eyed, they sprinted madly to their places, as if they hadn't done it a zillion times before. Silly girls.

I turned the radio on to the Temple University station, where a soothing orchestral piece began to work its magic on the few crazies. Soon the herd was completely settled in, like the frenzied rush to the stalls had never happened.

I'd gotten the cows clipped in and was distributing grain when I heard footsteps. I didn't look up. "Mornin', Zach."

He grunted. Fifteen-year-olds usually don't like to get up at five-o'clock to milk cows, but Zach Granger was an exception. He thrived on the rural atmosphere, and from day one of his summer break he'd been a constant presence on my farm.

But that didn't mean he was talkative in the wee hours of the morning.

A lot of Zach's time was spent working for me, but a good portion of his days was also spent with Barnabas, his 4-H calf.

Just the summer before Zach had lost a calf, Gus, to the hands of a saboteur, and I wasn't sure he'd be ready for a new one this year. But he'd surprised us all with his resilience, as young people often do, and had taken on Barnabas with energy and care. If, perhaps, a little less all-out love and enthusiasm. Afraid of getting hurt again, I was sure.

I continued with feeding while Zach began the milking process, washing off the cows' udders and slipping on the milkers. He and I had a routine, and very rarely did we need to discuss anything about getting the job done.

I loved the barn. The cows. The feel of the warm, leathery udders under my fingers. My farm had been my home for almost thirty years, ever since I was born. Both of my parents had died there—my dad in a tractor accident, my mother from breast cancer—as well as my guardian and farmhand, Howie. I'd seen several generations of dogs, and more than that of the farm cats. The house had been through renovations, I'd lost a barn and built another, and the battle to keep the operation solvent had become an all-out war. The bills, the emergencies, the developers knocking on the door...

The music ended—Brahms, apparently—and the college-age announcer came on with snippets of news. The words didn't register until I heard Carla's name.

"Carla Beaumont, a veterinarian in Bucks County, was assaulted yesterday when her truck was stolen in the parking lot of the Roy-El diner in Sellersville. The truck is a white Ford F250, license plate DZ8453. If you have any information about the truck or the car-jacking itself, please call the police." He rattled off a phone number and was on to the next subject.

"You went to see her last night, right?" Zach asked from down the row.

"Carla? Yeah, I stopped in yesterday. You know much about what happened?"

"Nope."

I explained what I knew. He worked while I talked, and when I finished his response was, "Huh."

I went back to work.

I'd known Carla, and been friends with her, longer than I'd even been acquainted with most people. From the time she graduated from veterinary school and interned at her present practice, she was the one I'd call. Well, first Howie called her, and then I did. Almost sixteen years it was now. Other than the Grangers and some of my biker pals, I hadn't known anyone—or had a relationship with them, at least—anywhere near that long. She was part of my life. Part of my home. And the thought that I could've lost her the day before made my hands shake as I applied the milkers, and as I wrung soapy water out of my cleaning towel.

Almost an hour later, as Zach and I worked in compatible silence, the shrilling phone scared me out of my thoughts. I trotted to the office to answer.

"Stella?" It was Ma Granger, Zach's grandma and the matriarch of the large Granger clan.

I glanced at the clock. Six-twenty-five. "Awful early for you to be calling, isn't it, Ma?"

"Don't be ridiculous. Now, I'm having a supper tonight and I'd like you here since you came home from Virginia early. Will that work?"

No reason to look at the calendar. "Sure."

"Good. Come at five."

"Yes, ma'am."

And she hung up before I could ask how she knew I was home, or if I should bring anything. Not that she'd want anything from my kitchen.

I grabbed a piece of scrap paper and scribbled a note for Lucy, telling her I was taken care of for supper. When Lucy married my friend Lenny Spruce during the past spring, she and Tess had moved out of my house and into Lenny's Perkasie townhome. That meant my in-house cook was gone and I had to fend for myself.

But I really didn't have to very often.

Most days Lucy brought me some of what they'd had the night before, what they'd be having that night, or else the entire family of three would just eat supper at my house. I certainly wasn't complaining. As I had told Nick's family, I'm a terrible cook. If I were really left to my own devices I probably wouldn't eat much more than cereal, PB&Js, and apples.

Not a great diet to be sure, even if full of fiber and protein.

I went out to the parlor and pinned the note to a message board Lucy and I had taken to using since she'd moved out. After a few experiences of forgotten messages and miscommunication, we figured something needed to happen. The bulletin board was our solution. It had worked so far.

Queenie raced out of the parlor, barking, and I looked toward the drive to see a tanker truck pulling up to our milkhouse. I stepped outside in time to see Doug, the driver, jump down from his cab and snip off the cable tie that secured the tanker's hose door as he traveled from farm to farm. He disappeared into the milkhouse, pulling the hose with him, and I walked over to pick up the plastic tie and stick it in my pocket.

"Hey, Doug." I went in the doorway as he was attaching the hose to the tank.

He lifted his eyes. "Stella. Nice morning. Gonna be a hot one."

"Probably. Anything exciting going on these days?"

"Nah."

"How's your sister? Patty? The one who adopted the girl from China?"

"She's good. Busy." He grinned.

"Being a single mom's hard work."

"Aw, she can do it. Brings Iris into the office with her each day so she can still do our books and schedules and stuff. Don't know how much work anybody *else* gets done, they're so busy giving Iris the googly eyes, but Patty somehow manages to keep the place running."

"A good businesswoman."

He laughed. "Or a smart mom. She knows where to take Iris to get all that attention the kid craves."

"So Iris will be a good businesswoman, too."

He chuckled some more. "Already is."

I patted the milk tank. "You need anything?"

"Got it under control. You get back to your own girls."

Zach was a good way down the row when I returned to the parlor. He stood up from where he'd been crouching by Pocahontas. "You notice Wendy's missing?"

"Hadn't thought about it." I looked toward her usual spot at the end of the row. "I guess she is. I'll go find her. Maybe she's finally ready to have that calf." I turned to go, then stopped. "That was your grandma on the phone earlier. Invited me over for dinner."

"Yeah, us, too." He squatted back down by the cow, his voice sounding strained. "I guess there's some new minister in town and Ma wants us all to get introduced."

"Not for Sellersville Mennonite?" The Grangers' church.

"No. Kulpsville, I think." He flicked a finger at a fly on his neck, and looked at the ground. "But it's some family friend, so Grandma's doing the Welcome Wagon thing."

"Yeah, she would." Darn it. Like I wanted to sit around being careful what I said for a whole meal. I sighed. It wasn't like I could back out of it, now that Ma was planning on me.

As if I could've said no to begin with. When Ma called, people answered. That was just the way it worked.

I took another look at Zach before I left, wondering why the new minister would make him so nervous, and was startled by the paleness of his face as he sat staring at the back end of a cow. "Zach? You okay?"

"What?" He snapped his head toward me.

"You don't look so good."

"No. No, I'm fine." He stood and grabbed a rag from the bucket of soapy water. "You go on. Make sure Wendy's okay."

It wasn't until I was out the door that I remembered. Gus, Zach's dead calf, had been Wendy's previous off-spring.

I walked back into the barn. "Zach?"

He didn't look up.

"You want to check on her?"

He hesitated for just a moment before shaking his head and turning his face away.

I felt an urge to wrap my arms around him, but knew that was the last thing he'd want. Besides being a teen-age boy and not liking any big shows of affection, a hug could have the uncomfortable effect of making one of us cry. I left before either one of us embarrassed ourselves.

Chapter Five

I discovered Wendy where I expected to, in the far corner of the pasture, where soon-to-be mothers hung out. From the looks of her back end she'd be going into labor sometime in the next day or so. She acted calm and pain-free, chewing her cud in a regular rhythm, so I backed off and left her alone, the way cows like it. The less human involvement, the better, as far as they're concerned. As far as I'm concerned, too.

By the time Zach and I had finished mucking out the stalls Lucy was at the calf hutches, feeding bottles to a few new additions to the herd. I scratched one of the babies on the head and looked at the blue sky, wondering when we'd ever get some of that rain I'd seen in Harrisonburg that turned the Shenandoah Valley green and vibrant.

But I didn't want to think about the pleasures of Virginia.

"So you've got supper plans with Ma?" Lucy asked. "That's nice."

I wrinkled my nose. "Yeah."

"What's that attitude for? Ma makes great food."

"Well, sure, it's just—"

"—that you've got to meet the new minister?"

I looked at her. "How'd you know?"

She tapped a finger on the side of her nose.

I frowned. "What's that supposed to mean?"

She placed both hands on the bottle and planted her feet more firmly as the calf tried to yank its breakfast away from her.

White spots of milk dotted the calf's fuzzy nose. "You know, I'm not sure. Santa does it in *'Twas the Night Before Christmas.* I think it's just supposed to look mysterious."

"Well, it doesn't. So how'd you know about the minister?"

"Peter told me."

"Reinford?"

"Yes, Peter Reinford. How many Peters do you know?"

Peter Reinford was the minister at Sellersville Mennonite, where Lucy attended. She hadn't had many options in churches, since the Grangers pretty much dragged her to theirs, but she'd never regretted the choice. It was a friendly congregation, and Peter was a caring and competent minister. The few times I went to church during a regular year it was at Sellersville—Christmas Eve, Easter, Zach's youth group fundraisers, Lucy's wedding, whenever Ma insisted I go… I had many memories from my childhood, fidgeting in the pew, wearing the one dress I owned that Ma had made for me. As I grew older I attended less and less, but every time I went I got a warm welcome. And I had to say this for Peter—he never pressured me.

"How'd Peter know I was going to the Grangers for supper?" I asked. "And don't tap your nose."

"I guess Ma told him she was inviting you. I don't know. Maybe God told him."

"Yeah." I put my hands on my hips and rolled my neck. "I'm going to head over to the hospital now and see Carla. That all right?"

"Sure. Zach's around, isn't he? We might get started replacing the water cups that need fixing in the parlor. There are at least three. Okay with you?"

I waved as I walked away. "Whatever. I shouldn't be gone too long."

"Take your time."

Queenie met me in the drive and trotted along to the garage, where I pulled out my Harley. "Sorry, girl. No truck today. It's too nice to travel in a cage. You wouldn't be allowed in the hospital, anyway, no matter how unfair that sounds."

She looked disappointed, but I'm sure she understood.

I found a parking spot in the front row at the hospital, close to the Emergency entrance, and carried my helmet in under my arm. Pennsylvania is a no-helmet-law state, and I didn't want to take the chance I'd get lectured by some well-meaning but annoying ER nurse. I always rode with my head protected, but that didn't mean I was going to tell everyone else they had to.

The nurse at the ICU station was a different one from the day before, and she studied me, her eyes lingering on the points of the steer head tattoo that snaked around from the back of my neck to the front.

I shifted the helmet to the other arm. "I'm here to visit Carla Beaumont."

"Are you family?"

Yes. "No. A friend."

She considered this. "I'll check with her." She walked purposefully to Carla's door and went inside. A moment later she was back.

"Sorry. I can't let in just anybody, you know. You can go on back."

I met her eyes, trying to determine if she was this protective with all visitors, or if it was the "biker thing" Nick had been talking about. No telling. I let it go and went to Carla's room, swinging open the door to face a severe frown. I stopped at the foot of the bed, trying not to grin at Carla's toddler-like expression. "Mornin', Sunshine."

Carla narrowed her eyes. "I don't want to hear about your breakfast. Eggs and pancakes and sausage and a glass of that whole milk, straight from the cow. And don't even begin to tell me about waffles and ice cream or even that piece of buttered toast. I don't want to know."

I pulled up the visitor's chair and plopped into it. "How 'bout a stale granola bar and a glass of OJ at five this morning? Want to hear about that?"

Her lips pursed. "That's all?"

"Only a glass of warmish water since."

"Well, all right." Her face relaxed and she grinned. "So how's your hot boyfriend?"

"He's good. Sends his regards. Hopes you can get out of here soon."

"He coming up to visit? I'd love to see him." She grinned and waggled her eyebrows, and I remembered those days a year ago, when she would come around to the farm just to watch him paint my heifer barn or simply walk around, being gorgeous. Those were the days before he and I were anything official. Well, other than as employer and employee. Before I knew he was a developer. Before I knew he would be the love of my life, who would contract a serious disease. Who would have a home and family two hundred miles away.

I tried to smile. "I hope he can come up soon. We don't have definite plans." Of any sort, which Miranda loved to rub in.

Carla waited for more, but I didn't offer anything. She tried again. "Sorry about not asking after him yesterday. I forgot when you were here."

"Guess you had other things on your mind. Speaking of which, how's your head?"

She waggled her hand back and forth. "Feels okay, but then, I think I'm still doped up. The nurses and doctors seem happy."

"That's a good sign."

"I guess. I just wish they'd let me eat."

"Patience."

She growled. "They claim they have to wait twenty-four hours and then I can start on real food again. Just in case I have to have brain surgery."

I grimaced. "Aren't head injuries supposed to make you nauseous, anyway?"

"Not me."

"Yeah, right."

"Really."

"So is there anything I can do for you?"

She brightened.

"*Other* than smuggle in food?"

She dimmed. "No."

"I didn't think about asking after Concord yesterday. You need me to do anything with him? Take him home with me? Queenie would love to have him."

Carla had adopted a greyhound only a month or so earlier, his name a testament to the purple tint of his smooth hair as well as to the speed at which he ran. Like a jet plane. He used to run that fast, anyway, before he aged and was deemed of no use at the racetrack. I was sure Carla wouldn't want him home alone.

"Bryan's taking care of him. He took him to his place so he can walk him and keep him company. Said he's adjusted pretty well. Poor guy's lived too many places and been treated too badly."

"Bryan?"

"Ha, ha."

"And where is your knight in NASCAR armor today? I'm surprised he's not glued to your bedside gazing at you with awe and wonder."

"Will you stop? He's at the Home Depot. The new one there at the corner of 113 and Old Bethlehem Pike. He works in the lumber department."

"I've never seen him there."

"So?"

She was right. "He really does seem to adore you."

"Yeah. It's something, isn't it? This flabby body and all."

"You're not…" Well, she was. Kinda. "You're *curvy*."

A giggle. "That's what Bryan says."

"I'm sure he does."

"But I am a little embarrassed…"

Uh-oh. "About what?"

She glanced down at her belly and pressed on it with her palms. "Those EMTs yesterday. They got a full view of me without my shirt on. You know, since it got ripped off by the truck door. I didn't think about it at the time, but now…"

"Carla, you're beautiful. It doesn't matter that you're…fluffy. I'm sure the EMTs didn't think anything about it."

She sighed. "Maybe you're right. But I'm still going to do something about it when they let me out of here."

I stared at her. "You're *not* going on a *diet*?"

"Are you nuts? No, I'm going to start working out at the gym."

"The gym."

"Sure. A new client gave me a free two-week pass as a gift for taking care of his dog. I'll try it out, see how it goes."

"What gym?"

"That one there in Souderton. Club Atlas. It's a fitness center for anybody, but lots of serious weight lifters go there, too. Another one of my clients actually runs the place, but *she's* never given me a free pass." She pouted, then smiled brightly. "So I could get a workout, plus see those hunky weightlifters at the same time. Two-for-one."

"Bonus. Just don't tell Bryan that's why you're going."

"I would never." She sat up. "Why don't you come with me? You could get in shape, too."

"Carla, I am in shape."

"Oh, come on. When's the last time you exercised?"

"I exercise every day."

"Work doesn't count. When have you actually gone for a run, or lifted weights, or been to an aerobics class? Something to purposefully boost your heart rate and burn calories?"

I stared at her. "Carla, think about it. Can you picture me at an aerobics class?"

"You wouldn't have to wear a fancy outfit. A Harley T-shirt and shorts would be fine."

"Carla…"

"Well, okay, maybe not, but lifting? Sure."

"I'm not going. I can't afford it."

"Sure you can."

"I can't."

Her smile took on an impish tilt. "You know that pass I told you about? It also says I can take a *guest*."

Chapter Six

The police department was on the way home, so I glided into a parking space and locked the bike. Regardless of what Carla thought, I wasn't so out of shape I couldn't handle the big machine. I gave it an extra waggle from side to side, feeling its weight, just to prove I could.

The receptionist, Gladys, greeted me with a smile. "Good morning, Stella. Can I help you with something?"

I set my helmet on the counter and leaned on it. "Willard in? I wanted to talk to him about my friend Carla."

Her forehead furrowed, then relaxed. "You mean Carla Beaumont, the one who got car-jacked yesterday? How is she?"

"She's fine, I think. I'm just coming from the hospital. She's there for observation, and I have a feeling she'll annoy them enough about getting food they'll be glad to see her go."

Gladys laughed. "I guess that's a good sign, if she's hungry."

"I guess. But then, she's always hungry."

Gladys pushed a button and the dividing door clicked. "Go on back. The detective's doing some paperwork on the truck theft and will probably be happy for the interruption."

I made my way to Willard's office and stuck my head in the door. Paperwork lay stacked on his desk, but he wasn't working on it. Instead, he sat back in his chair, looking out the window and bouncing a pencil in his hand.

"I don't know," I said. "My taxes shouldn't be paying for daydreaming."

He swiveled around in his chair. "Who's daydreaming? That was some focused theorizing you were watching."

I snorted.

"Have a seat." He waited until I did, then leaned forward on his desk. "What can I do for you? You're not having problems at the farm again?"

He was right to be concerned. In the almost-year we'd known each other he'd been out at the farm to deal with criminals way too many times. We'd seen arson, vandalism, animal cruelty, and, of course, Howie's murder. I pushed the thoughts from my mind.

"No problems at the farm, knock on wood." I reached out and tapped his desk, which was made of fiberboard, so I hoped it counted. "I wanted to find out what's going on with Carla's truck and the investigation."

His face changed. "You mean Dr. Beaumont? You know her?"

"Sure. We're good friends. Plus, she's my vet."

He shook his head. "Should've figured it. I just hadn't made the connection. Have you been to see her?"

"Yup, just now." I filled him in on her health, then said, "So I was wondering what you could tell me about what happened yesterday? Stuff I wouldn't have seen on the news."

"Not too much, except for the newest development. I just got off the phone with the Green Lane police. We put out an alert on the truck yesterday as soon as we were notified of the theft, and Green Lane received it and found Dr. Beaumont's truck abandoned down there."

"You tell her yet?"

He winced. "No. I didn't want to bother her until I knew the full extent of the damage. But…it doesn't look good."

"How come?"

"Well, from what the Green Lane cop told me it's pretty much a lost cause. Everything that wasn't stolen was destroyed, and the truck's most likely totaled. We won't know for sure until we examine it, but that's how it's looking."

Poor Carla. She loved that truck. "The Port-a-Vet, too?"

He nodded.

Damn. "Where is it?"

"Jerry's Auto Body, out on Bethlehem Pike. Where we always have things towed and stored until we can process them."

"What do you hope to find?"

He leaned back in his chair. "You never know. Hopefully something to identify the attacker. Criminals are amazingly stupid. They'll do things like take the stolen vehicle through a drive-through and toss the trash in the back seat. That greasy paper is prime for fingerprints. Or the receipt will be in the bag with a time stamp, placing them in the vicinity at the time of the attack. Dumb stuff like that."

"What about fingerprints on the car?"

"They wipe all the obvious places. Steering wheel. Door handle. But they forget a couple of prime areas, where we almost always hit pay dirt. The rear view mirror and the visor. They don't think about it, that they touched those spots, and we'll snag 'em."

"They really are dumb."

"Well, they're criminals, after all. Not the smartest occupation to enter, no matter what the movies like to show." He flipped his pencil onto the desk. "Our crime scene guy is over at Jerry's now, checking out the truck. I was just about ready to head over."

Cool. "Can I come?"

"Why not?" He gestured at my helmet. "You want to ride with me or take your bike?"

"You driving a cop car?"

"Sorry. Not today. No flashing lights for driving around town."

"Darn. Guess I'll follow you on the bike."

"Your choice."

He grabbed his keys off of his file cabinet and stood up, moving toward the door.

"Willard."

He stopped.

"Did you hear about the police department that was burglarized and all its toilets were stolen?"

He blinked slowly. "No."

"It was a shame. They couldn't figure out who did it because they had nothing to go on."

He kept looking at me, blinking.

"Sorry. Zach Granger's fault."

"And you had to repeat it?"

I shrugged. "It seemed right at the time."

He walked out of the office and I stood up to follow.

Spoil sport.

◇◇◇

The ride to Jerry's Auto Body was a short one, and I drove after Willard through the gate into the tow yard. He waited for me as I parked the bike and set my helmet on the ground, then led me toward the far side of the fenced-in area. I stopped suddenly when I recognized the officer who was processing the scene, and grabbed at Willard's elbow.

"Is that Officer *Meadows*?"

He grinned. "It is. Want to tell him your joke?"

"No. But I'd like to stick his head in one of those toilets."

"My, my. You are regressing today, aren't you?"

An image of Miranda flashed through my mind and I felt myself redden. "Sorry. But what is he doing with an important job like this?"

Willard pulled his elbow from my grasp. "I know you've had your run-ins with Officer Meadows, but he's grown up in the last year."

I lifted an eyebrow.

"Really, he has."

I wasn't going to believe that without seeing it. When my farm had been sabotaged the past summer Meadows had been the first to respond. The first to respond but the last to actually believe anything had really happened. He was rude, nasty, and unprofessional. And that was just to start with.

Willard resumed walking toward Carla's truck, and I followed grumpily. My thoughts of Meadows were soon tempered by the sight of my friend's beloved Ford. The Port-a-Vet had been ripped open, with everything in it either gone or damaged. The tires were slashed, and the paint on the side had been keyed, or some such thing. The hood was smashed and crumpled, like the way Volvo advertises the "accordion" look.

I studied the car. "The guy didn't run into any other vehicles?"

"Not that's been reported. We're thinking it was probably a building or some other stationary object he hit, and after he abandoned it someone else came along to finish the job. We haven't been able to figure it all out yet."

We reached the truck and Officer Meadows pulled his head out of the car's interior. He stopped short at the sight of me. "This isn't *her* truck?"

Willard shook his head.

"Then what's she doing here?"

"Officer. What have you found?"

"But she—"

"*Meadows.*"

The dipwad got control of himself and turned so he was addressing only Willard. "There's no trash. No food wrappers, receipts, tissues, nothing. And the steering wheel and door handle have been wiped clean. From everything I can find on the truck bed he must've been wearing gloves when he trashed it. Probably a pair of the victim's latex ones, from the box in the back. But…" He straightened, his eyes sparkling. "We got a hit on the rear view mirror. Several clear, whole prints. He mustn't have put the gloves on until he was ready to trash the vehicle."

"You're sure they're not Dr. Beaumont's?"

"Well, I can't be sure, of course, until I run them through the computer, but there are a lot there. I'm making cards of them now."

"Great." Willard turned to me. "Told you those rear view mirrors come in handy."

I waved a hand toward the ruined Port-a-Vet. "What about all her stuff? Aren't there drugs or scalpels or something to be concerned about?"

Willard's face went serious. "Just one narcotic that I'm aware of. I asked her about medications and she said she was carrying some Ketamine in the back because she always takes some during on-call days, in case she needs to work on a horse."

"What's Ketamine?"

"An anesthetic. But it's also used as a date rape drug they call Special K."

"So what do you do?"

"Follow it up. Check out the drug angle however we can. When we put out the alert on the truck yesterday we attached a special note about the Ketamine. Most likely it was just a coincidence that the drug was on board, but you never know. Only a few people were aware she'd been called out to a horse farm, but some criminals probably think vets always carry narcotics. Remember, they're dumb, so they wouldn't exactly do research."

"You think you'll get him from the fingerprints?"

"We might, assuming the prints aren't all Dr. Beaumont's. But we're also looking for witnesses, getting descriptions of anyone seen in the parking lot or driving a truck like this. It's an unusual vehicle, so people have a better chance of remembering it."

Meadows pointed his chin at me. "We'll get him."

"Good." I could've pointed my chin back at him, but that would've been childish. I looked at Willard. "Any chance I could take Carla's personal things along?"

Meadows crossed his arms over his chest. "No."

"I wasn't talking to you." *Dumbass.*

"But I can answer the question."

Willard glared at his subordinate and turned to me. "After Officer Meadows is done processing the vehicle he'll bag up anything that can come with him and isn't needed for evidence. Dr. Beaumont will get it all back."

I looked steadily at Meadows. "Everything."

He didn't respond.

Willard sighed. Loudly. "Anything else I need to know, Officer?"

Meadows angled his pointed chin toward the detective. "Not yet."

"Okay, then. I guess we'll be going."

I stepped back, ready to get away from Mister Annoying.

"Unless," Willard said, "Ms. Crown wants to tell you a joke."

If he hadn't been a policeman, I'd have slugged him.

Chapter Seven

Nick's phone rang only once before it was picked up. But it wasn't Nick's voice I heard. I suppressed a groan. "Miranda?"

A quick breath. "Oh, it's *you*."

"Where's Nick?"

"Out."

"Out where?"

"Look, what do you want?"

I stifled a swear word. "What do you think I want? I want to talk to Nick."

"Well, you can't. He's not here."

I didn't feel guilty any longer about wanting to smack her on the head. "When's he getting home?"

"Don't know. He's pretty busy today."

"Okay. Fine. Will you at least leave him a message to call me?"

"I'll leave a message."

Spoken like I'd asked for the world.

"Thank you," I said. "So much." I don't think I was successful keeping the sarcasm out of my voice. I slammed down my phone.

"Who was that?"

I looked up and leaned back in my office chair to stretch, my feet still resting on the desk. I was pooped from an afternoon of chores: finishing up the water cups, checking fences, cleaning the heifer barn… I'd checked on Wendy several times, but she still hadn't produced much more than that cud she kept recycling.

"It was Nick's annoying sister."

Lucy grinned. "The younger one. Miranda."

"Yeah. The older one's fine."

"Liz, right?"

I grunted a yes. I didn't want to talk about Nick's sisters, who knew his schedule better than I did. Knew what he was busy doing, and would be seeing him yet that day.

I pulled my feet off my desk. "Lucy?"

She was flipping through folders in the filing cabinet, pausing now and then to check a tab before moving on. "Yeah?"

"How long do you think you're going to work for me?"

She looked up, her fingers stuck in the drawer, holding her spot. "What?"

"You think you'll want to work for me for a while?"

She frowned. "Well, sure. Why would I stop?"

I looked down at my desk, then back at her. "Just wondering."

"Stella—"

"Never mind. I'm just…trying to plan."

She pulled her hand out of the drawer and turned toward me, crossing her arms over her chest. "Stella, what's going on?"

"Nothing."

"But—"

"You heading out for supper soon?"

She stood there, eyes narrowed.

I stared back.

She finally gave a little shake of her head. "I thought I would go home for supper, since you're taken care of for food."

"You can always go home, even if I'm not having supper made for me."

She breathed a laugh through her nose. "Like I'm going to leave you to your toast and apple butter every night."

"Apple butter? Who gets that gourmet?"

Now she laughed out loud. "Have fun at Ma's. I'll be back to do the milking, as usual."

"Zach still here?"

"Nope. He just took off with Randy to go check on Randy's calf. Zach's supposed to be at Ma's house for supper, too, so you'll see him there."

"Randy can drive?"

"Got his license two days ago."

I shivered at the thought of Zach in a car with a sixteen-year-old driver, even if that driver was Zach's responsible and good-natured friend Randy. They attended 4-H meetings together and Randy had bought one of my calves that winter to be his project. He and Zach made a good team. But that didn't mean I was comfortable with my "nephew" in the hands of a teen-age driver. And a boy driver at that.

"What's he driving? Don't tell me some suped-up Trans Am or something."

Lucy smiled. "Nope. An old Caddy. One of those huge ones. If he gets in a wreck it'll be the other car that suffers."

"Unless it's an SUV."

She sobered. "We'll just keep our thoughts positive, won't we? And pray for safety on the roads."

"I'll leave that up to you. You're better at it."

"Praying or positive thinking?"

"Both."

She sighed. "Oh, Stella. I wish you'd—"

"What?"

"Nothing. Never mind. Don't know if I'll see you tonight or not. Depends how late you're out partying with the Grangers."

"I'm gonna eat and run."

"Really?"

"That's my plan."

"Yeah?" Lucy smiled. "Well, good luck with that."

I set my helmet on the ground by my bike because there was no point in taking it into Ma's house. She knew I always wore it, and nobody else would dare say anything. Besides, no one would swipe it from under my bike in her neighborhood.

The small front porch was crammed with people, and I took a deep breath before heading up the sidewalk. I responded to the greetings as nicely as I could, but was glad to escape the crush, especially since there were several faces I didn't recognize. I let myself in the front door as quickly as I could, only to find more people in the living room. I waved at Jethro and Belle, Zach's parents, but continued past them. Ma was in the kitchen, taking the Saran wrap off the top of some almond spinach salad, and I leaned against the counter as she crumpled up the plastic and threw it away.

Mallory, Zach's older sister, sat at the table with her boyfriend, Brady Willard, Detective Willard's son, who had met the Grangers—and therefore Mallory—through trouble at my farm. Now they were scooping homemade strawberry jam into a couple of cut-glass bowls, trying to keep the sticky mess from getting on their fingers.

Ma glanced up at me, then at her watch. "Glad you could make it."

"I'm not late."

"Didn't say you were. But come on now, it's time to eat."

Mallory and Brady led the way with the jam while I followed Ma into the dining room and listened as she called the rest of the folks to the table. Two couples I didn't know—who'd been on the front porch—filed into the room, and Ma grabbed my arm and dragged me toward them.

"Katherine and Alan Hershberger," she said. "This is Stella Crown, my all-but-formally-adopted daughter."

"Pleased to meet you." The man, Alan, held out a hand, and I shook it.

"So you're here to take over one of the churches, huh?" I said. "Kulpsville, is it?"

He smiled crookedly and looked at his wife, dropping my hand.

Katherine laughed. "Actually, I'm the one stepping into the pulpit. But don't worry, you're not the first to make that mistake."

Whoops. "Sorry. I shouldn't have assumed…"

She glanced at Alan and slid a hand around his elbow. "Really, it's all right. It's perfectly natural for you to expect a male minister. My feelings don't get hurt that easily. Oh." She gestured to the couple beside her. "This is my sister, Tricia, and her husband, David Stoltzfus."

David grinned and nodded. Tricia gave me a tight-lipped smile and stood close to David, her arms flat against her sides. Looked like she enjoyed large get-togethers about as much as I did. She was a tallish woman, her head about even with mine, but standing next to her husband she looked small. David was huge. Not a lot of height, but built like a brick chicken house, as my high school phys ed teacher would've said.

Beside Tricia stood a young woman who was practically a carbon copy of her. Although this copy was young, fresh, and holding out her hand. "I'm Sarah. Their daughter." She tilted her head toward Tricia and the Schwarzenegger look-alike while she gripped my hand so hard I winced.

Katherine looked around the room. "Our son, Trevor, is here somewhere…"

Ma clapped her hands. "Have a seat, everyone. Wherever you fit is fine. No need to be formal."

I found a chair next to Zach and he smirked at me from under his bangs. "Smooth move with the lady pastor."

"Oh, shut up."

Randy, who was a member of Katherine's new church, had followed Zach to supper, and sat on Zach's other side. He grinned, too, and I gave him a glare for good measure.

Ma stood at the head of the table. "Katherine has agreed to offer the blessing, so if you'll take the hands of the people next to you…"

Zach offered his hand on my left and Katherine's sister, Tricia, who had slid into the chair next to me, took my right.

When everyone had settled in Katherine smiled. "Let's pray together." She closed her eyes and began speaking. "Our loving God, we gather together today as old friends and new, looking forward to a renewal of relationship and the celebration of relationship to come. We thank you for the people gathered around this table and for the food we are about to eat. Please bless it to our bodies and bless the hands that prepared it. Bless also our conversation and our fellowship so that it may all be pleasing in your sight. In the name of our risen Lord, Amen."

Murmurs of "Amen" echoed around the table, and I dropped my neighbors' hands. The prayer had been a good one, but what had interested me even more was the fact that neither Alan nor the Hershbergers' son, Trevor—who had showed up to the table just in time—had closed their eyes during the prayer, instead choosing to stare either at the tablecloth or the ceiling. I wondered if Katherine was aware of this, or if it was just a one-time thing. It would be kind of embarrassing, I thought, for a minister's family not to pay proper respect during a prayer.

But then, I wasn't about to tell her. Besides it being none of my business, the fact that I saw them with their eyes open meant mine hadn't been shut, either.

"So where is Tori these days?" Jethro boomed out. "Some fancy new job?"

Alan shook his head. "Actually, she's on a mission trip to Honduras. She graduated this spring with a B.A. in International Relations and headed right down south to put that diploma to work."

"Good for her," Ma said. "She'll do a bang-up job."

"You know her well, then," the brother-in-law, David, said, smiling.

Ma shook her head. "Not well. I've met her a time or two. But I know her mother here, and if Tori's anything like Katherine was at that age, she'll be setting the world on fire before we know it."

Alan laughed. "You've got that right. Like mother, like daughter."

"Sarah decided to step out on her own, too." David put his arm around the back of his daughter's chair. "Was accepted into Temple Law School last week. Tricia and I are proud as peacocks." He looked toward his wife, his face alight with excitement.

Tricia, beside me, scraped her food around on her plate with her fork before offering another tight smile. I guessed she was following through with the whole peacock idea, letting her husband strut his stuff.

"We're proud of Sarah, too," Katherine said. "She's worked hard through college, and it's paid off."

"Of course it did," Ma said. "From everything I've seen so far, Sarah's a smart girl."

Sarah laughed. "I try. I just can't wait to get started this fall. Being a lawyer will just be, you know, so exciting."

She was just so, you know, *young*.

I saw Katherine sneak a smile at Ma and tried to figure out the connection between these two families. "So you've known the Grangers a while?" I looked at Katherine, remembering the mention of "old friends" in her prayer.

"Oh, boy." She caught Ma's eye. "How many years would it be?"

Ma's forehead crinkled even more than usual. "How old are you?"

"Forty-three."

"Then I've known you forty-three years. And Tricia for forty-one?"

Tricia nodded.

I frowned. "How come I've never met you folks?"

Katherine took the plate of mashed potatoes Alan handed her and plunked a spoonful onto her plate. "Our family moved away when I was twelve and Tricia was ten. Went up to New York State to plant a church. I met Alan and stayed up there. Most of my communication with the Grangers these past…thirty years?…has been through my parents and then through letters. And now e-mail. I've been back a time or two, but nothing recently."

"And you?" I turned to Tricia.

She looked over at me briefly, then back down to the roll she was holding. "I met David at a Mennonite youth convention during high school, and after we got married I moved down to Lancaster to be with him. I haven't been back here since I was a kid. Didn't keep in touch like Katherine has, either."

Well, that explained it, then. I hadn't "joined" the Granger family until I was eleven and had saved the youngest Granger son, Abe, from drowning. After that I'd been welcomed into the Granger fold, which was good since I lost my mother five years later. My dad had already been gone a good dozen years before that. Other than Howie, who'd served as my guardian and farmhand, I'd have been alone in the world if it hadn't been for this loving and blessedly large family.

"And Trevor," Ma said, passing him the bread, "you've certainly grown up since I saw you last."

He peered at her. "When was that?"

"He would've been...what?" She looked at Katherine. "When was the last time you were here?"

"Ten years ago, maybe. He was only seven."

"So that means..." I looked at Mallory. "He's your age?"

She made a face that said she didn't know, and Brady shrugged.

"He'll be a senior at Christopher Dock this year," Alan said. The Mennonite high school where Mallory and Zach both attended. So Mallory *would* be in his class that fall.

"A tough year to move," I said.

Trevor finally looked up, right at me, but didn't say anything. The expression on his face was enough to tell me what he thought. It hadn't been *his* choice to move before his last year of high school.

"We considered that, of course," Katherine said. "It was a hard decision for all of us."

I didn't look away from Trevor, and he ducked his head toward his plate. I wondered how much say he'd actually had in the matter.

But then, like the eyes-open-during-the-prayer thing, their family business was certainly not mine.

Ma set down her fork. "I was so sorry not to get to your mother's funeral this spring."

Tricia made a choking sound beside me, and I looked to make sure she was all right.

"We did miss you," Katherine said, "but we understood. You were going through some rough times here, too."

I looked at Ma, who met my eyes with her sad ones. Just this spring her son Jordan's fiancée had been killed, and he'd been a mess. It must have been during that time that Katherine and Tricia's mother had died, and Ma felt she couldn't leave Jordan alone. Or expect him to attend another funeral.

An uncomfortable silence stretched until Jethro broke it. "So, David and Tricia—and Sarah—how long will you be in town to help out with the move?"

David made a circle in the air with his fork while he finished chewing. "For a few days. There are some rooms that need painting, some bigger things that need unpacking. That sort of thing."

Alan pointed at his brother-in-law's bulging arms. "Those muscles really come in handy."

"I'm glad to help out."

"And Tricia's great with decorating," Katherine said. "I've never had an eye for that sort of thing, so she's invaluable."

Tricia squirmed in her seat beside me. "Thanks, Kathy. You know I enjoy it." She glanced at David. "But we can't stay too long. Our daughter Elena is at home and we need to get back to her. She's sixteen and has a summer baby-sitting job she couldn't leave."

"Ugh," Sarah said. "I remember those days. Taking care of kids all day long. What an awful way to spend a summer."

Tricia's fork stilled. "It's a good job."

"Sure. I'm just glad I'm past all that so I can get to something better. Much more interesting, you know."

Ma stood up to refill water glasses. "Have you moved into the church office yet, Katherine?"

Katherine had just taken a bite, so she nodded while she chewed and swallowed. "We've lugged most of my stuff over there. Boxes and boxes of books—again David's been a big help—the artwork I've collected through the years, that sort of thing. I'm looking forward to getting the place organized."

Belle, Zach's mom, leaned across the other side of Randy to better see Katherine. "And have you met any of your congregants?"

"Well, we got to know a lot of them when I was candidating and coming down for search committee meetings during the past year. And we were able to be at the service this past Sunday morning—"

Sarah waved her hand at her shoulder. "Me, too."

Katherine smiled. "Yes, Sarah joined us." She flicked amused eyes toward Tricia, who didn't respond. And who I guessed hadn't gone to church. "We thought we would go even though I'm not officially on duty until this weekend. Since we'd arrived on Saturday we figured we might as well attend."

"And your reception?" Belle's expression was serious.

"Very warm. Very friendly. It was a relief, which was silly, since they *did* ask me to take the job."

Sarah nodded. "They were really happy to see her."

I looked at Katherine. "You were worried how they'd treat you?"

"Sure. There are always some people, no matter where you go, who don't think women should be preaching. Franconia Conference, where we are here, is progressing—there have been a few churches with women pastors, like Zion and Perkasie—but there are still some areas that won't even entertain the idea. I've had my share of nasty letters and phone calls. But a lot of support, too. I really can't complain."

"Well, you should." Ma set her water glass down so hard it almost spilled. "Nasty letters aren't Christian. Especially if they aren't signed. And those weren't, were they?"

Katherine grinned and her eyes held a mischievous sparkle. "A *few* of them might have been."

Alan put his arm around the back of his wife's chair. "Katherine will be okay. She's dealt with crazies in the past, she can do it again."

They smiled at each other.

"Not all people against women in ministry are crazies."

We turned as one to look at David.

He glanced around at our faces, his words faltering. But he continued. "Remember that couple up in New York? They liked you as a person, Katherine, but with the way they interpreted the Scriptures they just couldn't accept you. And those men that wrote to you from Lancaster when you were testing the waters out there, wanting to move closer to us. They weren't crazy. Just conservative."

Jethro snorted. "Seems to me those things often go together."

"Just like with liberals," Ma snapped. "There are some in every group."

Jethro stopped his sniggering and was almost able to look meek.

"Please continue, David." Ma returned her attention to her guest.

"I don't really have anything else to say."

"We try not to get too worked up about the letters," Katherine said. "Like David told you, a lot of them are people just trying to express their beliefs."

"Have you had any mean letters from this area?" I asked.

Ma clicked her tongue. "Not already, surely."

"Nothing yet," Katherine said. "I hope that's a good sign."

Alan pushed a few final kernels of corn onto his fork. "As we said earlier, at least she's not the first woman to grace the pulpit in the conference. A few others have paved the way."

"And this is the time for women," Sarah said. "I mean, women can run for president now. And be important things like lawyers and ministers. Make a difference."

Jethro pointed his knife at Trevor. "You're probably used to the controversy by now. What do you think?"

Trevor sat slouched in his chair, his plate empty. He looked up at Jethro. "What do *I* think? Who cares? It's not like it's mattered before." His face turned red, and he looked down toward his lap, where he messed with the buttons on his watch.

The rest of us looked anywhere but at his parents, so I'm not sure what they were doing.

But Trevor's comments pretty much changed the subject for good.

Chapter Eight

"It was awful," I said.

Lucy shook her head slowly, her elbow resting on the door of her Civic. "Poor boy. And poor parents. I'm sure it wasn't an easy decision to make, coming down here for his senior year."

"They're lucky he came along. I would've just found someone else to live with for the year."

Lucy barked a laugh. "You think anyone would've had you?"

"Hey, now."

Lucy got in her car and shut the door.

I leaned toward her open window, my hand on the top of her car. "But Katherine and her husband seem like nice folks. You might want to get to know them once her sister and brother-in-law leave town. Have them over for some of your famous chili."

"Yeah, we'll see. Right now I have to get home and make sure my own family ate some decent supper."

"I thought you did that earlier."

"I did, but they weren't hungry. Seems they'd just eaten a whole batch of popcorn before I got home."

I laughed.

"Yeah, go ahead and laugh. Sometimes those two get so caught up in doing the new father-daughter thing they forget to eat properly. Or supper consists of going to Mom's Ice Cream Shop."

"Could be worse."

"I guess. They could forget to eat at all." She smiled brightly. "See you tomorrow."

I tapped the roof of the car and tried to step back, but Queenie stood so close I almost tripped. I led her away and watched as Lucy pulled out the drive. I stood there for a few more moments, looking at my quiet, empty house.

"So, Queenie."

Her eyebrows twitched as she watched my face.

"Let's go check on Wendy."

There was still enough light for us to walk out to the back corner of the pasture, where Wendy stood.

"Oh, good. Look, Queenie. Her hind end's looking a bit more engorged, wouldn't you say? I wouldn't be surprised if we had a baby by morning."

Queenie's nose twitched, and she sneezed.

"All right. So you don't really care."

I gave Wendy a few encouraging words and we left her on her own. Soon we were back at the sidewalk that led up to the house. Twilight had now come, and along with the silencing of the birds came the darkness of my windows. I reached down to scratch Queenie's head. "Want to come in for a while?"

She did, and she followed me into the kitchen, toenails clicking on the Linoleum. I went to the phone, looked up the number of the hospital, and called Carla. After making my way past the receptionist and the guard nurse—sorry, *duty* nurse—I heard the phone in Carla's room pick up. But, as earlier when I called Nick, I didn't hear the voice I wanted.

"Bryan?"

"Yes, this is he."

Oh, so grammatically *correct*. "Stella here. Can I talk to Carla?"

"I'm sorry, but she's having her vitals taken right now."

I heard Carla's voice in the background, and that static sound you get when someone holds his hand over the mouthpiece of a phone.

Bryan was back. "She says to tell you she's fine. There's nothing new."

Actually, there were a lot of new things. The discovery of her truck, for instance. And I had questions, like whether or not they'd let her eat, if she was still on pain meds, whether or not Willard had told her about her truck, and, most importantly, how the injury in her head was faring.

But I didn't want to talk to Bryan about any of it.

"All right. Tell her I'll see her tomorrow."

"I will. Thank you for calling."

I hung up. "*Thank you for calling.*"

Queenie looked up from her spot on the floor.

"Sorry, girl. I wasn't talking to you."

Hoping my bad luck wasn't going to hold, I picked up the phone again and dialed Nick's number. It's hard to dial when your fingers are crossed.

"Hey, Stella."

"Oh, thank God."

He laughed. "What? Why?"

"I was afraid I was going to get Miss Crabby Pants again."

"Miss Crabby Pants?"

"Your beloved little sister. Miranda. The one who hates my guts."

"She doesn't hate you. But why would you get her by calling my phone?"

I took a breath and shared a look with Queenie. "She didn't tell you."

"Didn't tell me what?"

"That I called earlier today. And that she answered your phone."

"She did?" He went quiet for a few seconds. "I went out for lunch with Robbie. Liz's boyfriend. I left the phone here to charge."

"Well, it wasn't charging all that time, because little Miss… Miranda…answered it."

Silence again. I was sure Nick was wondering just what his sister had been doing with his phone.

"So," he said. "What's going on with Carla?"

I opened my mouth to say something more about Miranda, but decided to let it go. Instead, I told him all about my visit with Willard.

"So at least they have her truck."

"Lots of good that'll do," I said. "Thing's totaled."

"But the fingerprints…"

"Yeah. We'll see if that pans out."

"Does Carla know about it?"

"I don't know. I tried to call her just now, but got the weird boyfriend, instead."

"Stella…"

"The man's only known her three weeks, and he's screening her calls?"

"Why didn't she answer?"

"He said she was having her vitals taken."

"So it sounds like she *couldn't* have answered the phone herself just then."

"Well, no, but…"

"You want to go sit by her bedside all day? I don't think so."

I bristled. "I would if she needed me to."

"So maybe that's why he's there. He thinks she *does* need him to. Maybe—and don't yell at me here—she likes it."

"Yeah. Maybe." I hesitated. "*You* don't like it."

"What?"

"People hanging around all day, taking care of you."

"But that's my mom. My sisters. If it were *you*, it would be a lot easier to take. In fact, I think I'd like it a lot."

"Really?"

"Really. Because, you know, I do love you. And not just because you're hot."

I laughed, startling Queenie from her half-slumber at my feet. "I know. It's because I'm so sweet and submissive and will do anything you say."

Now he laughed. "Right. In fact, it's too bad you're not here right now or I'd really give you something to do."

"Oh, yeah? And what would that be?"

He told me.

I turned away from Queenie so she wouldn't see me blush.

Chapter Nine

"You hear that?"

I came out from the feed room, pushing the grain cart. "What?"

Zach hitched up his jeans. "On the radio. They're asking anyone with information about Carla's truck to call the police."

"Still? Interesting." But also disturbing. A second plea for calls must mean those fingerprints hadn't worked out. Although Willard did say they were hoping for witnesses, or people who had seen the truck. I wondered if the cops had anything at all to go on. And I didn't mean their toilets.

Zach was still standing beside Briar Rose. "Think they'll get any tips?"

I dumped grain into a feed bowl, making a clatter. "Don't know. Probably lots of people who *think* they know something, but really don't. Or people who just want to feel important by calling the police."

He grunted, and that was the end of the conversation.

Twenty minutes into some concerto or other on the radio, the phone rang.

I looked at the clock, and Zach looked at me. "Who'd be calling before six?"

I shook my head. "Can't imagine." Ma wouldn't ask me to supper again that night, would she?

It rang again, and I jogged to the office and yanked up the receiver. "Yeah?"

"Stella, it's Lucy."

"What's wrong?" Because something had to be wrong for her to call that early. Maybe Tess was sick and Lucy was going to be late.

"The church was vandalized."

"Oh, no. Peter's okay, isn't he?" I pictured their kind minister, and the beautiful clean lines of the brick church and newly-painted sanctuary.

"Not our church. Kulpsville. Katherine's church."

"Katherine's?"

"The woman who you met last night. The new minister."

"I know who you mean, it's just… What happened? Is she all right?"

"I guess so. I don't know much else. Lenny went to The Towne for breakfast and one of the guys mentioned seeing a bunch of cop cars at the church, and heard something about a break-in, but he didn't have details. I thought you might know something."

"Nope. But I can think of someone who will have all the facts."

"Ma?"

"You got it. I'll call you back."

I punched the flash button and dialed Ma's number. She answered on the first ring.

"Ma? What happened at Katherine's church? Is she okay?"

"You heard already?"

I explained Lenny's early breakfast.

She harrumphed. "News sure does travel. Katherine's fine. She wasn't there since it happened in the middle of the night."

I glanced at the clock again, even though I knew what time it was. "Then how did she find out already?" How did *everybody* find out?

"Her brother-in-law, David. He goes for a run each morning, real early. On his way back he went past the church and thought something looked off, so he jogged up to the door and saw it was open. He went right back to Katherine's house to get Alan, and they went into the church together and found a mess."

"What did the vandals do?" I hadn't been inside that church for years, if ever, so I couldn't picture their sanctuary or even any of their lay-out.

"The damage is mostly in Katherine's office. The Pastor's Study. She'd hardly unpacked anything yet, but the boxes were torn open. Her books were destroyed, all of her family pictures and artwork. It's awful." Her voice was steely. "And they broke into the computer and the filing cabinet. Who knows what personal things were in there. Notes the interim pastor left, information about people in the congregation. The members are not going to be happy."

I closed my eyes. Not a good way for Katherine to get started. Even if it wasn't her fault. "I hear they called the police."

"Of course they did. They're over there now."

It wouldn't be Willard. Kulpsville was out of his jurisdiction. "Will you let me know what they find out?"

"Yes. But I haven't told you the worst of it."

"What? I thought you said Katherine was okay. "

"She is. Physically. But she's pretty shaken up. She was doing all right until she saw what they'd spray-painted on the wall of her office. Alan wanted to hide it from her, but there was no getting around it."

Oh, crap. "What did it say?"

Ma's breath went loudly in and out. "It took up almost the entire wall. In bright red. It said, 'GO HOME SINNER.'"

"Poor Katherine." Lucy stood beside me, leaning on her pitchfork. She'd shooed Zach off to check on his calf, and taken over his cleaning responsibilities. "And you know why they did it."

I grunted and threw a load of wet shredded newspaper onto the manure conveyor.

Lucy continued. "It's because she's a woman. You know it is. I can't imagine they have anything else in her life to complain about. And I certainly haven't heard of any *other* new pastors getting that kind of a welcome. But, oh gee, they just all happen to be *men*."

I peered at Lucy over my shoulder.

She picked up her pitchfork and jabbed it into the bedding of the stall next to mine. "I know, I know. I need to chill."

"I didn't say that. It's just interesting to see you all het up about something."

She raised her eyebrows. "Oh, don't get me started on this topic." She threw her load out of the stall. "I'll just focus my anger adrenaline into my work."

I stood up and stretched my back. "So I can leave this all to you?"

She looked down the row. "Sure. There aren't that many left, anyway."

"Great." I leaned my pitchfork against the wall. "I'm going to check on Wendy. Zach went out earlier and reported no new calf, but I'm going to go see for myself, to make sure we don't need a vet." When Gus, Zach's first calf, had been born the summer before, Wendy had needed a C-section. I was keeping my fingers crossed she wouldn't need one this time. Especially since Carla wouldn't be making house calls anytime soon.

Lucy flung another load out of the stall and I got out of the way. Real quick.

Wendy had moved to another corner of the pasture, and it didn't take an expert to know that birthing was imminent. A circle of wet splotched the ground behind her, and her back end, while not showing any little hooves, looked about ready to burst open. I stepped a little closer to pat her haunch, and she scuttled sideways, crunching my foot under her hoof.

I smothered the shout that rose up my throat and channeled the energy into shoving Wendy off my foot. When she finally shifted I hopped away, cursing. An attempt to step on my left foot sent sparks of pain up my ankle and leg, and I swore some more.

"Thanks a whole helluva lot." I glared at Wendy. She gazed at me with her wide gentle eyes. She thought it was my own damn fault. She was probably right.

I hobbled back up the hill to the barn and limped into the parlor.

Lucy dropped the clean bedding from her arms and trotted over to me. "What happened? Is it Wendy?" She grabbed my arm. "Are you going to faint?"

"I am *not* going to faint. But I need to sit down."

She guided me to a bale of straw and lowered me onto it. "What's wrong?"

"Wendy—"

"The calf?"

"No. My foot. She stepped on it."

"Oh, no." Lucy looked down at my boot. "Can you walk?"

"Sort of."

She gave me a flat look.

"Just go finish the stalls. I'll sit here. It'll be fine."

"You need to go to the doctor."

"No. I need to sit. Go away."

She looked at me some more, then shook her head. "You're worse than Tess."

"So?"

She made a growling sound and spun around, going back to work.

I leaned against the wall, hoping the dizziness in my head would soon go away.

It didn't.

A half hour later, Lucy was back. "Stand up."

"What?"

"Stand up. If you can walk without wincing, I'll leave you alone."

I glared at her. "Are you my mother?"

She tapped her foot.

I stood up. But not without wincing.

She pushed me back onto the straw. "I'm going to tell Zach where we'll be. Don't go anywhere."

As if.

Chapter Ten

I popped some ibuprofen and Lucy situated me in the passenger seat of the Civic. The seat went back almost far enough I didn't have to scrunch my foot under the dash.

Lucy started the car. "Maybe I can visit Carla while you're in the ER."

"We're not going to the ER."

Lucy squinted at me. "Yes, we are."

"No, we're not. We're going to my doctor."

"She can't help with this."

"Sure she can. She can take a look and tell us it's not broken."

Lucy shook her head and took off down the lane. "You're impossible, you know."

"Yeah. I know."

Dr. Rachel Peterson had been my doctor for only a year. She'd treated me following my motorcycle accident the summer before, and I'd stuck with her. Before that, the last doctor I'd seen regularly had been my pediatrician. Dr. Peterson convinced me it was good to see a physician for more than just an emergency every ten years.

Not that I'd been in that often.

The waiting room held several people, but after a slight amount of Lucy's badgering, the receptionist said Dr. Rachel would be able to squeeze us in. The receptionist wasn't very *happy* about it, but what could she do? Lucy wasn't going away.

We'd been waiting about fifteen minutes, alternately trying to avoid being sneezed on by sick people and reading pamphlets on nutrition for the pregnant woman, when the outside door opened and a man came in. He strode up to the reception desk, his comb-over flying high as he walked. "Dr. Peterson said I should stop by sometime to talk about my prescription." He took a pill bottle out of his pocket and set it on the desk.

The receptionist smiled. "All right. I'll let her know you're here. And your name is…?"

The man went red. "Not *her*. It's Dr. *James* Peterson I want."

"Oh, I'm sorry. Dr. James isn't in today. But Dr. Rachel would be happy to—"

"I don't *want* her. I want *him*. When will he be in?"

The smile on the receptionist's face faltered. "Today is Wednesday. He won't be in again until Saturday morning."

"Satur— But my prescription runs out tomorrow!"

"I'm sorry, sir. But, like I said, Dr. Rachel will be glad—"

"Forget it. Just forget it. And tell Dr. James he can forget me, too. This is the last time I'll be put off by him. I'll have my *new* doctor send for my records. *Today*."

He spun on his heel, strode toward the door, and shoved it open. He disappeared outside, but was soon back, stomping toward the reception desk. My muscles went tight, and I wondered how quickly my foot would allow me to get to the desk if he got violent. His hand shot out from his side, and he swiped his prescription bottle from the desk, knocking over a pen holder and scattering its contents onto the floor.

I hoped the door would smack his ass as he left.

"Well." Lucy slipped from her chair and picked the array of pens and pencils off of the tile floor. She righted the holder and placed the pens back into it, setting it gently in front of the receptionist. "I guess *that's* not something you see every day."

The receptionist's fingers fluttered toward her hair, then to the arm of her glasses. "Not every day, no, but far too often for my taste."

"I'm sorry."

Lucy sat back down and I watched the bright color on the receptionist's face slowly fade. When the phone rang a few minutes later she jumped, but her voice sounded steady as she spoke.

A nurse soon called my name and I pushed myself from my chair. Lucy rose to come with me, but I waved her back. "I don't want my mommy."

She frowned. "What if you need me?"

"I promise to have the nurse get you if I think I'm going to cry."

She rolled her eyes, and sat back down.

"Besides," I said, "shouldn't you be reading that brochure about quitting your smoking habit?"

A young mother close by glanced at Lucy, and I grinned at the fire I could imagine coming out of Lucy's eyes.

The nurse did the usual—temperature, blood pressure, embarrassing questions—and left me alone in the examining room. She didn't attempt to take off my shoe, and I didn't get into a gown.

Dr. Peterson came in just about the time I'd decided it was too cold in the room and was standing on my good foot, rooting around below the sink for something to drape over my shoulders.

"Help you with something?"

I pulled my head out of the cabinet. "Blankets?"

"Ha, ha." She pointed at the examining table. "Sit."

I hopped up, and she stood in front of me, arms crossed. "So. You got stepped on?"

"Huge pregnant cow."

"Ouch. I guess we'd better take a look."

She gently untied my boot and slid it off my foot. It hurt, but there were no tears. Lucy could stay in the waiting room.

Dr. Peterson peeled off my sock and together we stared at the swollen black and blue mass that used to be my foot. She pushed on a few spots with her fingers while I clenched my teeth.

"Well." She stood up. "It's x-ray time for you."

"Damn."

"Yup." She rolled a stool over and began filling out a prescription for the procedure. "You can go right next door to the hospital. No need to even drive anywhere."

"Great."

She laughed. "You don't sound too pleased."

"Why should I be? This will set me back a day of work."

She stopped laughing, but kept grinning, shaking her head. "It's going to set you back more than that."

I closed my eyes. Of course she was right.

"You'd better get Lucy," I said. "I think I'm going to cry."

Chapter Eleven

Dr. Peterson did get Lucy, but it was because she wanted her to wheel me over to the hospital. I looked down at the wheelchair, then up at the doctor. "You've got to be kidding."

She wasn't. She pointed at the chair, and I sat in it. Lucy began pushing me toward the door, but Dr. Peterson stepped in front of us, searing me with a schoolteacher stare. "Now I don't want to hear any reports that you've been a difficult patient. You go in and do what you're told."

"Yes, ma'am."

And I did. It wasn't hard setting my foot on the table and holding it still. Even I could manage that. Fifteen minutes later I was out of the room and headed back to the doctors' office. We were part way to the door when I grabbed the wheel. The chair lurched to a stop and Lucy banged into the back of it.

"Let's go see Carla while we're here."

"We really ought to get you back to—"

"It'll take a couple of minutes for Dr. Peterson to get the x-rays and read them. Come on. She's just over here." I gestured toward the ICU.

Lucy sighed. "Fine. I'd like to see her, anyway." She started to push, but the chair refused to move. "Stella, hands off."

"Sorry." I let go of the wheel, and we were soon in front of the ICU nurses' station.

The nurse, a familiar face from yesterday, looked at Lucy, and then at me. "Weren't you standing up yesterday?"

"Yup. Carla in?"

She waved her hand. "Go ahead. Boyfriend's in there, though."

"Oh, great."

Lucy grinned. "Good. I want to meet this guy."

Bryan jumped to his feet when we opened the door, but still kept a hold of Carla's hand. Tightly, if the grimace on her face meant anything. She pulled her fingers out of his and flexed them.

Carla's forehead furrowed as she stared at my wheelchair. "What in the world?"

I pointed at my foot. "Cow stepped on me. That real pregnant one."

"Wendy?"

"That's the one."

"She still hasn't had that calf?"

"'Fraid not."

She thought for a moment, probably remembering the C-section last summer, then shook her head. "You'll have to have Bruce or Tim come out if there's a problem again. Don't think I'll be delivering calves any time soon."

"She'll be fine. It's my foot that won't."

"Broken?"

"Guess we'll see. I was just getting an x-ray."

Carla brightened. "Those folks are nice down there, aren't they? Did you have Nancy as your technician?"

I looked at her and tried not to laugh. "Sorry. Didn't make it a point to get to know her."

"Well, it's your own fault."

Lucy put her hand out toward Bryan. "Lucy Spruce. Friend of Carla's."

Spruce. It still took me a moment to think who she was talking about, without the old "Lapp" after her name.

Bryan cleared his throat, looking briefly at Lucy's face before ending up gazing somewhere past her shoulder. "Bryan Walker. Um. Friend of Carla's." He shook Lucy's hand. "I think…uh…

I'll go get some coffee. Or lunch. Or…something." He swiveled his eyes toward Carla, his face pleading.

"You do that, sweetie. These ladies will keep me company for a bit."

He tried to grab Carla's hand again, but she avoided the clutch and patted his arm. "Go ahead."

He scurried toward the door, not looking back.

I raised my eyebrows. "What's up with him?"

"You are."

"What?"

"You make him nervous. He thinks you don't like him."

"Oh. Well…"

"I told him that was ridiculous. What's not to like?" She pierced me with a steady gaze.

Lucy giggled. "I think he's adorable."

I looked up at her so quickly I got a crick in my neck. "You do?"

"Absolutely."

"And why shouldn't she?" Carla said. "He *is* adorable."

My mouth opened, but I shut it before any sound came out. I leaned my head down and rubbed the back of my neck.

Carla and Lucy rehashed how the two new lovers had met, from the dance, to what Carla was wearing, to exactly how long it took him to kiss her (three dates). Carla explained what all she knew about him (not much beyond his job and what kind of music he liked) and how sweet he was with her dog, Concord. I was about to scream when Lucy finally said, "So, how are you today? How's your head?"

Carla wrinkled her nose. "Yesterday they said they'd let me eat."

"And?"

"Jello and chicken broth."

I laughed, the pain in my neck forgotten.

Lucy gave me a stern look. "Better than nothing, right?"

I snorted. "Not for this woman. But look up, Carla, by tomorrow you'll be able to have pureed carrots."

She groaned. "At least they're considering letting me go home today."

I blinked. "Already?"

"They say my vessel tear isn't expanding. The blood's being reabsorbed into my body, and apparently that's a good thing."

"It is." Lucy's voice was flat. From the look on her face, she'd had personal experience with Carla's type of situation. Probably when Lucy's first husband, Brad, took the fall down the stairs that first paralyzed, and finally killed him.

Carla looked down at herself. "I just want to take a shower—I feel so disgusting. And wear my own clothes. And raid my own refrigerator…" Her voice took on a dreamy quality.

Lucy smiled. "When will you know?"

"When the doc makes his afternoon rounds. He has to okay it."

"You won't be able to go back to work right away, will you?" I thought of Wendy, and of the other guys in Carla's practice whom I liked, but not as well as Carla.

"Nope. Lots of restrictions. No heavy lifting, no driving, no aerobic activities."

"You need me to come stay with you tonight?"

Carla looked at me, and then at my foot. "Lotta help you'd be. But thanks, anyway. Bryan said he'll stay. He'll bring Concord back over and take care of both of us."

I didn't like that. "Carla—"

"I don't know," Lucy said. "I thought the doctor said no aerobic activities."

Carla looked confused for a moment, then laughed when she saw the corners of Lucy's mouth twitching upward. "Don't worry. Bryan will be sleeping on the couch. Besides, he's a *gentleman*."

I snorted again.

"You have a problem?" Carla scowled at me.

"No. No problem." Unless you count her brand new boyfriend that I didn't trust farther than I could throw a lasso.

Lucy kicked my wheelchair, then said, "Any word from the detective today?"

Carla turned her frown toward Lucy. "Nope. Last I heard was yesterday. My truck's totaled."

I thought of my visit with Willard. "So no information about the guy who did it?"

"Nope. They don't seem to know anything about him at all."

"Except," said Lucy, "that *he* is definitely *not* a gentleman."

Neither Carla nor I argued with that.

Chapter Twelve

There were no irate men in Dr. Peterson's waiting room this time, and we were immediately sent back to her office. Lucy wheeled me in, and stayed. I guess she was afraid I'd cry when I heard the results of the x-ray.

Dr. Peterson swiveled her computer monitor around so we could see it. "Straight metatarsal fracture."

I looked at her, then back at the x-ray. "Huh?"

She smiled. "That's good news. It's a non-displaced break. Nothing is out of alignment. Just fractured. Which means it should heal easily and I can do a walking cast right here in the office."

A cast. I must've looked upset, because she added, "You'll be able to get back to work in a day or two. With some restrictions, of course."

I didn't say anything, because whatever came out wouldn't be nice.

"So," Dr. Peterson said to Lucy, "if you could please wheel her out and into exam room three. I think I have an old pair of sweats in my trunk she can use."

She did, and I was soon wearing them, my jeans folded into a Landis' Supermarket bag.

After I was situated on the exam table, Lucy looking anxious, like she might need to hold my hand, Dr. Peterson got to work rolling an elastic stocking type thing onto my foot, and then wrapping it in batting.

"I didn't know you were a quilter," I said. "With the batting and all. Can I pick the colors?"

It was supposed to be funny, but Dr. Peterson—now in full doctor mode—didn't laugh. I watched as she finished up with the padding, then filled a bag of something with warm water. She mushed it around a bit, then emptied out some of the water before pulling out a roll of sticky material.

"This is the cast," she said. "So hold still while I wrap it around."

I wasn't about to disobey. She was scary when she became "The Doctor."

I watched the top of her head as she worked. "So what's up with the angry patients in the waiting room?"

There was a hitch in her movements, but she didn't look up. "What do you mean?"

I glanced at Lucy, and she gave a brief shake of her head. I chose to ignore it. "While we were waiting some guy came in. Threw a hissy fit because your dad's not working today. Your receptionist said it wasn't the first time."

Dr. Peterson finished up the roll of material and added water to another bag. She squished it around, let out the water, and pulled out a new roll. "My dad's retiring. He figures he's put a good forty-five years into this practice, he deserves some time off. So he's been weaning the patients off of him. He hardly has office hours anymore. Saturday mornings. Some Mondays, to help when it's really busy."

"And the patients?"

"Aren't taking it well." She bent back over my leg and began wrapping. "The men I guess I can understand. It's embarrassing for them to come to me. They're men, after all, and I'm a young woman." She gave me a quick grin. "Relatively young, anyway. They feel strange talking to me about their physical problems. The women…I thought they'd be glad. You know, to have a female as their doctor. The younger women are fine. No problems with them. But the older ones? They're almost as bad as the men. If not worse. They act like I'm a little girl and there's no way I can know as much as my father." She smacked the end of the roll onto my calf.

I jumped. "Hey!"

"Sorry. It gets to me."

Lucy clicked her tongue. "I can see why."

I held out a hand, palm out. "Just don't take it out on me."

"I said I was sorry."

The cast material was already beginning to harden. Dr. Peterson got some hand soap from the sink and rinsed down my leg, wiping the cast. When she was done she took a few inches of the padding and stocking thing that were still sticking out of the top of the cast and rolled them over the highest part of the cast, which ended right below my knee.

I frowned at my toes, bare and sticking out of the cast. "If it's my foot that's broken, why's the cast so huge?"

"To protect you. Keeps your leg from moving your ankle and foot around."

"But how am I supposed to—"

"You can walk on it. Look." She pulled a shoe-type thing out of a bag. "This will go over your foot. You strap the Velcro over the top. After a day or two you can use this to work again. Make sure you put a bag over the cast when you do get back to the barn—and tape it to your skin at the top so stuff doesn't get in. You can wear an extra large boot over it if you want."

"But I can't walk on it today?"

"You like pain?"

I frowned at her.

"Give it a couple of days to heal, Stella. Take it easy. Pop some Tylenol and let other people do stuff for you."

"She won't let me, you know." Lucy looked almost irritated.

"Well, then, I guess that's her problem. If she wants to heal, she'll take my advice."

"She's not always so good at that."

"Hey," I said. "Right here. Haven't left the room."

Dr. Peterson kept looking at Lucy. "Maybe you'll need to take some Tylenol, too."

Lucy nodded. "I just might."

I wriggled off the table. "Will you two shut up?"

Dr. Peterson grabbed my elbow. "Fine. Now stay there for a minute." She left, but was back moments later with a battered pair of crutches. "Use these. I'll give you a prescription to get a better pair at the medical supply store, but these will do you till then."

"A prescription?" I watched as she scribbled on her pad. "For crutches?"

"Insurance won't let us sell them to you. They want to pay much less than they think we'd charge. So some patients kindly give us their old pair and we can loan them out. Just try to bring them back when you're done with them."

"Sure."

Dr. Peterson stuck the crutches under my arms and adjusted them for my height. "These will do you fine until you get your new ones. Come here." She opened the door and gestured to the hallway. "Try them out. Let me make sure you can manage."

I must've done fine, because she said good-bye and good luck and headed for another exam room.

"Dr. Peterson," I said.

She looked back.

"Thanks."

"You're welcome."

I grinned. "You did pretty good for a woman doctor."

I almost fell over when I ducked the prescription pad she aimed at my head.

Chapter Thirteen

"One more stop," I said.

Lucy slowed at the corner of Bethlehem Pike and Reliance Road and made a right. "Where? Grocery store?"

"Police station."

She glanced at me. "What for?"

"I want to see if Willard got any answers yesterday when they finished with Carla's truck. From the sound of the news this morning they still don't have a suspect, and I want to know what's going on."

"Carla hadn't heard anything."

"Yeah, but maybe Willard didn't want to bother her in the hospital."

She considered that. "Okay. Your wish is my command."

Right.

Lucy parked across the street from the station and helped me out of the passenger seat.

I took a deep breath. "I'm okay from here."

"You sure?"

"Positive."

She glanced across the tracks in the direction of Landis' Supermarket. "Then I'm gonna run to the grocery store. Putting your jeans in that bag reminded me of some things I need."

"Bring a donut back for me? Please?"

She smiled. "Just don't tell Lenny, or he'll feel left out."

I zipped my lips with my fingers and almost fell over. Lucy got a good laugh.

My entrance into the police station was just as clumsy, and Gladys, the receptionist, regarded me with wide eyes. "What happened to you?"

I yanked my crutch from where it was stuck in the outside door and rested on it. "Short version? Big cow, broken foot."

"Ouch. Gonna lay you up a while?"

"Not if I can help it."

"But no more motorcycle."

"Not for now." I used a crutch to point toward the back. "Willard in?"

"Sure. Let me help you." She buzzed the door, then got up to hold it open while I stumbled through. I managed to club her both in the ribs and the shin.

"Sorry."

She held a hand to her side. "S'alright. I'll survive. Just remember Willard does have a gun. And he's not afraid to use it."

I could hear Willard's voice as I clumped down the hallway, and I stopped outside his office. When the receiver hit the cradle I poked my head in. "Busy?"

He looked up and froze, expressionless, at the sight of my crutches.

"Big cow, broken foot," I said.

"Ah. Want to have a seat?"

"I thought you'd never ask." I somehow got myself into the chair without knocking anything over, and set the crutches across the arms of the chair. Willard and I both breathed a sigh of relief.

"Today?" Willard asked.

"Just now."

"Bummer."

"You could say that. So'd you hear anything from the requests on the radio the past two mornings?"

"You caught that, huh?" He drummed his pencil on the desk. "Nothing new. Got a couple of calls from people who think they saw the truck, but nothing concrete, and no further description of the driver."

"What about the fingerprints from the rear view mirror? Anything from them?"

He sighed. "Got some pretty prints. Clear as day, no question. Ran the ones that didn't match Dr. Beaumont through the Automated Fingerprint Identification System. Not one match. Whoever left those prints has never been in the computer."

My turn to say, "Bummer."

"It is. Makes it even more unlikely that he was after the drugs, because most druggies and dealers have been caught multiple times and would certainly be in the database." He tossed the pencil in the air and caught it. "But I guess there's always a first time."

"So you're still checking the drug angle?"

"Have to. It's the only thing we have going for us at this point. Whoever it was didn't get seen by anyone who can help us. Or anyone who knows it, anyway."

I leaned my elbows on the crutches, and put my chin in my hands. "So you really didn't have anything to tell Carla."

He looked puzzled. "No. Why?"

"I thought maybe you were just saving her feelings."

"Nope. But it's nice you think I'm one of those sensitive guys."

"Yeah, right. Hey, did you hear about Kulpsville Mennonite?"

"The church? What about it?"

"It was vandalized last night. Somebody destroyed a bunch of the new minister's personal property and painted graffiti in the building."

"They must still be checking it out, or I'd have heard by now."

"Will you let me know if you find out anything interesting about it?"

He bounced his pencil on its eraser. "Why? You have connections?"

"The new minister is a friend of the Grangers. I met her the other night."

"Her?"

"Yup. It's a woman."

He nodded, curiosity lighting his face. "I guess those Mennonites might join the twenty-first century, after all."

I thought about the discussion around Ma's dinner table the other night, and the message painted on Katherine's office wall. "I don't know," I told Willard. "But I wouldn't bet the farm on it."

Chapter Fourteen

Queenie ran circles around the Civic when we pulled into the drive, and Lucy honked the horn at her, laughing. "What's gotten into her?"

"Dunno."

Zach loped out of the barn, followed by his friend Randy, and reached me as I clambered out of the car.

Randy stared at my cast. "What happened to you?"

"Stupid Wendy."

His eyes widened, like he was trying to look concerned while keeping himself from laughing.

Zach *did* laugh.

I scowled at him. "What?"

"Stupid Wendy had a beautiful calf."

I waited expectantly for the gender.

He grinned. "Heifer."

I let out a breath of disbelief. At least the dumb cow had had the sense to produce a girl this time. I have nothing against boys in general, of course, Zach being one of my favorite people—not to mention Nick—but in the dairy business boys aren't really a whole lot of help. Girls I can keep and add to my milking herd. Boys I sell to another farmer who raises beef, or to kids like Randy, who need a 4-H project.

"You have to do anything for her?" I asked.

"Nah. She pretty much took care of it."

"It's about time." I slammed the car door and hitched the crutch under my arm. The boys backed out of the way as I lurched past them. They stood there, staring, as I made my way toward the barn. I turned on them. "Don't you have something you should be doing?"

Zach opened his mouth, then shut it, his face a blank. "Sure. Sure we do."

"Then go do it."

He and Randy glanced at each other, then scootched past me toward the barn, skirting widely around, out of range of my crutches.

I looked at Lucy, whose eyes crinkled as she regarded me, her mouth twitching. She looked at the ground, then back at me, her expression under control. "Um, what are you planning to do for the rest of the day?"

"I'm going to my office. You have a problem with that?"

"Nope. No problem. You going to go see the new calf?"

"Maybe someday. When I don't feel like sending her mother to the meat packer." I turned to clump away as gracefully as I could.

Lucy's voice followed me. "Let me know if you need anything."

I didn't bother to respond.

Between my computer and a few doses of ibuprofen I made it through the afternoon. Lucy brought me a sandwich at one point, but other than that she pretty much left me alone, which was surprising. I expected her to be checking in every five minutes to make sure I wasn't overdoing myself. Queenie hadn't even stayed to give me company, preferring the activity of the farm.

Zach stuck around, helping Lucy with the work I should've been doing. Randy stayed, too, alternately helping and watching, seeing how he wasn't being paid. When Mallory drove up to the house a little before five, I pushed myself up from the desk to go say hello. My muscles were stiff, and it took me a while to make it all the way outside.

Mallory and Brady Willard stood beside the car, staring at me.

"Cow stepped on me." I was getting tired of saying it.

Mallory nodded, but Brady looked confused. "What?"

"Ever drop five hundred pounds on your foot?" I asked.

He shook his head, clearly impressed.

I looked at Mallory. "You here for Zach?"

"Yeah. He said he could take the night off."

"Oh, really?"

She looked surprised. "He can't?"

I glanced around and saw him coming from the barn with Randy. "I gave you the night off?"

He stopped beside me. "I asked last week. You said yes."

"Oh. All right."

"Didn't know that broken foot would cause memory loss."

I swung a crutch at him and lost my balance, falling onto Mallory, who staggered, but kept us both upright.

I righted myself. "Like I'm going to keep you here twenty-four seven. Where you off to tonight?"

"MYF," Mallory said, meaning Mennonite Youth Fellowship, the church youth group. "We're having a joint meeting with Kulpsville, to meet the new minister."

"Are you going there?" I couldn't imagine the church hosting an event when it had just been vandalized. But then, the MYF wouldn't be partying in Katherine's office.

"Yeah. They've got a pretty nice fellowship hall. And it's air-conditioned."

I pointed a crutch at Randy. "You going?"

He nodded. "Everyone from our MYF is supposed to go, since she's our new pastor."

Mallory continued. "Other groups are coming, too. Blooming Glen, I think. And Perkasie."

"Katherine's son going to be there?"

Mallory wrinkled her nose. "Trevor? I suppose."

Zach shook his head and looked at Randy.

I caught the look. "What?"

"Nothing. He's just…weird."

"Zach." Mallory frowned.

"Well, he is."

"Yeah," Randy said. "Super weird. You should've seen what he wore to church last Sunday. My mom wouldn't let me come to the *farm* in those jeans."

Mallory turned her frown on him. "You'd be upset, too, if your parents dragged you across a couple of states before your senior year. And how was he supposed to know what kids wear to church around here?"

Brady looked at Mallory with surprise. "How come you're defending him?"

"Because he's not weird."

Zach and Randy made disbelieving sounds.

"Okay, fine," Mallory said. "He might be weird, but that's no reason to be nasty. It can't be easy being a PK, especially when the P in question is a woman." She held up her keys. "Now are you guys coming, or not?"

Randy hooked his thumb over his shoulder. "I drove over. I thought Zach was coming with me."

"We can drop you off here afterward, for your car."

"But I want to drive."

Mallory bit her lip. "Um, okay, but Mom wants me to drive Zach."

Randy nodded. "Sure. I get it. She doesn't trust me."

"It's not that…"

"No, never mind." He lifted his chin at Zach. "See you there. *If I make it in one piece.*"

So sarcasm wasn't reserved solely for adults.

We watched him drive ever so slowly out the drive in his big old Caddy, the car making a little whining noise I didn't like. He didn't spit out so much as one piece of gravel.

"Way to go, Mal," Zach said.

Mallory rubbed her forehead, keys clanking. "I was hoping he wouldn't say anything, and just come with us."

Zach gave my crutches one last look and slumped into the back seat of Mallory's car. She threw me a sick look before sliding into the driver's seat, Brady sitting shotgun. I waved with my elbow, and they were gone.

I was trying to balance in front of my refrigerator, looking for something easy to eat, when the window above my kitchen sink began vibrating. I hobbled over and saw Lenny and Tess astride his hog, parking to the side of the driveway. I couldn't help but smile at the sight—Lenny with his big bike, big beard, and big body, completely overwhelming the small girl behind him. He stepped off the bike, then gently lifted Tess down, keeping her far from the hot pipes. Together they pulled the helmet off of her head and set it on the ground. He ruffled her hair, and I had a hard time believing anyone could be a better dad for Lucy's daughter.

Queenie ran around them as they made their way toward my door, and Tess fell over her, laughing. Queenie made sure there weren't any spots left on Tess' face that weren't licked clean.

By the time I made it out of the kitchen, Tess was barging in the front door. "Mom said you broke your foot! Let me see! Does it hurt? Those crutches are so cool! Can I try them?"

Lenny, who followed her in, gave a guffaw. "Take a breath, honeypie. Don't want you keeling over. Stella here can't catch you."

"Gee, thanks." I tried to frown, but couldn't with the sight of Lenny's grin.

"Big ol' cow got ya, huh?"

"Yup."

"Too bad. Lucy called and said we should come on over for supper and she'd feed us all here. 'Cause you know, you might starve otherwise." He smiled bigger, exposing the gap between his front teeth.

"I just might."

"Where is Mom?" Tess skipped to the sink and hoisted herself up so she could see out the window.

"I don't know. Figured she was here somewhere."

Lenny pointed outside with his thumb. "Car's not here."

"It's not? Huh."

Lenny snorted. "Such an observant boss."

"Hey. I trust my employees, that's all."

"Uh-huh. Taken much painkiller today?"

"Oh, shut up."

"Something," Lenny said to Tess, "that we should never say to people."

I glared at him, and he gave me his innocent look.

"There's a new calf," I told Tess. "If you want to see it."

"Really?" She jumped up and down, grabbing Lenny's arm. "Can we? Can we?"

"Sure, sugar. Let's go." He stopped Tess' forward progress for a moment as he looked back at me. "You coming?"

I hadn't seen the new calf yet, so I agreed. Tess ran ahead and was already oohing and aahing over the new heifer by the time I got there. The calf was a pretty little girl, with black circles over each eye, and white stocking feet.

"Does she have a name?" Tess asked.

"Not yet." I looked at Tess' eager face. "Want to name her?"

She let out a little shriek. "Yes! Yes, yes, yes!"

Lenny winked at me. "I think she wants to."

I laughed. "So what's it gonna be?"

She bit her lip and hopped from one foot to the other as she considered. "Can I think about it?"

"Sure. No rush. You can—"

Lucy's car pulled into the drive and Tess whipped around. "Mom!" The girl jumped up and ran across the yard to her mother, hugging Lucy's waist as she held up two bags of groceries. We could hear Tess' excited yammering from where we stood by the hutches. "Stella's gonna let me name the new calf, but I don't know what yet. What're we having? I'm starved!"

Lucy laughed, catching Lenny's eye as we walked up. "That's great about the calf, honey. And we're having tacos for everybody. I even got a couple of avocados to make that guacamole Stella likes."

My stomach rumbled, and I wondered how fast supper could be ready.

It was on the table in record time, with everyone helping. Lenny and Tess set out the plates and glasses, and I was put to work chopping tomatoes. When I reminded Lucy of my lack of cooking skills, she assured me that no one had ever died from a badly sliced vegetable.

"So," I said once the food was ready, grace had been given, and Lucy's taco was poised underneath her open mouth. "You really thought Bryan was cute?"

Lenny looked at his wife, eyebrows raised. "Don't like the sound of that."

She set down her taco and patted his hand. "Don't worry, darling, he's not my type." To me, she said, "Yes, I did. He seemed very sweet, and obviously adores Carla."

"Oh," Lenny said. "Carla's new man?"

Tess clapped. "Carla has a boyfriend?" She thought about this a bit more and stopped clapping, a furrow on her forehead.

"He's weird," I said.

Lucy picked up her taco again. "No, he's not. He's nice."

"And you can tell that how? By the way his belt buckle takes up half the room?"

She frowned at me. "He likes Carla, and she likes him. That should be enough for you. No matter what the size of his accessories."

"But we don't know anything about him. He could be anybody."

"And so what? There's lot of nice 'anybodys' out there." She lifted up her taco, but stopped before taking a bite. "He works at the Home Depot, right? You know that."

"So he has a job," Lenny said. "That's good."

Lucy nodded. "And he's taking care of her dog. So he likes animals."

"Then he *must* be nice," Tess said.

Lucy smiled. "Try to swallow before you talk, honey."

I fiddled with my napkin. "I still don't like it."

"I know you don't." Lucy's voice was kind. "But *Carla* really likes *him*."

Tess held up a chunk of tomato. "How come these are in such big pieces?"

Lucy looked to me for an answer, and Bryan was forgotten.

By the time supper was over I was ready to help with the evening milking. I stood up at the end of the meal and made to follow Lucy out the door while Lenny and Tess cleaned up.

Lucy stopped, one hand on her hip. "And where do you think you're going?"

"To help milk."

"Uh-huh."

"Doctor said I could."

"Uh-huh."

We stood there for several seconds before Lucy shook her head, rolled her eyes, and continued out the door. The door slammed shut on my crutch, but Lucy didn't turn around to hold it for me. By the time I got it open and made my way down the side steps she was already in the barn. Stubborn woman.

I finally got into the parlor, where Lucy ignored me. She didn't say a word, but I soon learned one very important thing: crutches and cow crap don't work well together.

The third time I fell—also the third time Lucy pretended it hadn't happened—was enough. I gathered together what was left of my pride and stumbled to my office. Queenie stayed in the parlor, most likely afraid of getting a crutch in her eye or me falling on her head. Can't say I blamed her.

When I made it to my chair and had gotten my breath back, I called Carla's house. I wanted to know how it went, moving back home from the hospital.

There was no answer, so I called Grand View. Carla was still in her room.

"How come you're still there?"

Her frustration was almost visible at my end of the phone. "The doctor didn't get here till late this afternoon. Said he wanted to keep me overnight yet. Guess he needs to make one more payment on his yacht. Or his villa in Guadalupe."

"Carla—"

"I know, I know. It's for my own good."

"I wasn't going to say that. I was going to say that if he's anybody his villa is in Cancun."

She laughed harshly. "Yeah. Whatever. He said I can go home in the morning, as long as nothing happens overnight."

"You feeling okay?"

"I'm fine. How's your foot?"

"Peachy."

"Sure. Lucy kick you out of the barn yet?"

"Not exactly."

"Uh-huh."

"Bryan there?"

"Not right now. Went home to check on Concord. Poor dog's feeling neglected."

"Oh. Well. That's nice of him."

"Sure is. But then, he's a nice guy."

She wanted me to say something. I could feel it. So I did. "Give me a call in the morning if you need a ride home. I'll be glad to come get you."

She grunted. "Or have Lucy come get me, more like. Forget it. Bryan will take me home."

"But if I—"

"Goodnight, Stella." And she hung up.

Shit.

I put the phone back in its cradle and stood up. Blood rushed to my head, and I quickly sank back into the chair. The fuzziness in my head was soon replaced by the throbbing of my temples, and I opened a desk drawer to get some ibuprofen.

The bottle was empty.

I looked at the ceiling. Looked out the window. Blew my bangs off my forehead. And pushed myself back up to make the trek to the house.

Lucy was standing in the middle of a row of cows, her rag dripping soapy water back into the bucket as she watched me lumber through. Neither of us said anything.

Outside, Lenny and Tess were climbing onto his bike, helmets on. I hoped he'd wait to start it until my pounding head and I were behind the closed door of my house.

"You look like crap," Lenny said.

"Gee, thanks."

"Didn't mean it bad. Need some help?"

I shook my head, then regretted it. "I'll be fine. Thanks for coming over here for supper."

"No problem. We always enjoy seeing you."

Tess didn't look so sure, but that could've been because I was wincing with each step.

I passed the bike and began the trek up the sidewalk. "I'll see you guys soon."

"Sure." And he started the bike.

I went as fast as I could up the steps, but by the time I made it to the door he was already out the lane. I pushed my way inside and into the bathroom, where I found a partially filled bottle of painkillers. I downed the recommended dose and sank onto the sofa.

The sound of the door woke me, and I peered up at Lucy.

"Come on," she said.

She half-lifted me off the sofa and helped me up the stairs, where she peeled Dr. Peterson's sweatpants off of me, made sure I didn't pass out in the bathroom, and tucked me into bed.

"Need anything else?"

I glanced at my nightstand to make sure the phone was on its cradle, and lay back on the pillow. "Nothing else."

"All right. Call anytime. And don't get up for milking in the morning. Zach and I will take care of it."

I thought for a second she was going to kiss me goodnight, but better sense prevailed and she walked toward the door.

"Luce?"

She stopped.

"Thanks."

She smiled, and was gone. Her footsteps were quiet on the stairs.

I closed my eyes, took a deep breath, and prepared to fall asleep.

But of course I couldn't.

I counted sheep. I counted calves. I counted rows and rows of cornstalks, tassels blowing in the wind.

None of it worked.

I reached over, finally, and got the phone. I heard Nick pick up on the first ring, and started in before he could even say hello. "You're never going to believe my day."

So I told him. I told him about Carla being stuck in the hospital, I told him about Katherine's office getting vandalized, I told him about Lucy's defense of the still-unproven Bryan, and I told him about my broken foot. When I stopped to take a breath, he waited.

"I'm done," I said.

I could almost feel his sigh of relief. "Sounds like it's dangerous to be a woman up there these days. Maybe you'd be better off staying down here."

My throat went dry, and the ibuprofen that had been working suddenly stopped. "Yeah," I said. "Yeah, maybe so."

He laughed quietly. "Just joking, Stella. You know that. It was just a joke."

But jokes aren't supposed to make your stomach hurt.

Chapter Fifteen

When I woke up I felt sort of like a new person. My clock said six forty-five and I struggled to remember the last time I'd slept in that late. Maybe Saturdays in junior high, when my mother was still alive and Howie took care of the milking. But thinking about Howie, whose death the previous summer had almost destroyed me, threatened to get my head back to hurting, so I pushed all thoughts of him from my mind.

I sat up carefully and eased my legs over the side of the bed. The worst throbbing was gone, but a dull ache had settled into my leg, and it seemed to weigh twice its familiar heft. My morning trip to the bathroom took more than its usual time, and I washed the best I could, since I didn't feel up to waterproofing my cast yet. By the time I made it down to the kitchen for a bowl of Cheerios it was almost seven-thirty.

I hobbled out to the barn, my armpits sore from the last day's pressure. Queenie trotted over and sniffed the crutches, in case they'd turned into something different overnight. I reached down and scratched her ears.

"Hey, how are you?" Lucy stood up beside Ariel.

I groaned. "Been better, been worse."

Zach, squatting beside a cow further down the row, ignored me.

I shifted the crutches and leaned on them with my forearms, Queenie dancing away, as if the crutches had moved on their own. "Anything I can help with?"

This brought a snort from Zach, but Lucy smiled. "I don't think so. Thanks, though."

"Tess okay?"

"She's at home with Lenny. He has to go into work today, but he said she can hang out at the store, at least for a while. Bart will be there, and she hasn't gotten to spend time with him lately."

Bart Watts, Lenny's business partner at the Biker Barn, their Harley-Davidson store, had become "Uncle Bart" to Tess, and the two got along like they'd been playing together since her birth. He'd sworn to Lucy early on that he wouldn't smoke around his new niece, and I was hoping it might be the catalyst for getting him off the habit. I wanted to keep him around as long as possible, and his promise to Lucy seemed like a good start.

I sank down onto a straw bale to watch Lucy and Zach work. There was always paperwork to be done in the office, but who wanted to do that that early in the morning? I sat for a while, but soon realized that watching other people milk wasn't even close to the same experience as doing it myself. I tried to close my eyes and relax, breathing in the warm, homey smells of the cows, but at that close range it wasn't very smart.

I pushed up from the bale and limped without my crutches over to the bulletin board to see what had been tacked up.

"Got a photo of the new calf already, I see. Thanks, Zach."

He made some sort of noise, but didn't actually say anything.

"Now we just need Tess to decide on a name. She come up with anything last night, Luce?"

"Nope. Nothing yet." She stopped in the middle of the aisle. "Are you supposed to be walking around like that?"

"Why not? It's called a walking cast."

"But aren't you supposed to cover it while you're in the barn?"

A minivan pulled into the lane, sending Queenie into a frenzy, and I looked out, happy to escape Lucy's last mothering question. The van was an Odyssey I didn't recognize. I limped back over to the straw bale to grab my crutches, and headed outside, in Queenie's wake.

Katherine Hershberger hopped down from the side door, then turned to offer a hand to Ma Granger, who slid slowly out. Tricia and Sarah, Katherine's sister and niece, got out the other side, while the men—Katherine's husband, Alan, and Tricia's husband, David—stepped out of the front doors. Trevor, who looked like he'd just rolled out of bed, hair askew and several angry pimples adorning his chin, finally emerged, climbing through the middle seats from the back. It was like those clowns who keep getting out of the VW Bug, except this group looked a lot grumpier. I thumped toward them behind Queenie, who ran enthusiastic circles around the car, finally stopping by Ma, whom she knew. Tricia stood halfway behind her husband, as if Queenie were a threat, while Katherine looked on in amusement.

"What on earth?" Ma stopped, staring at me, her hands on her hips. She reminded me of Lucy, and I figured all these women of good Mennonite stock have that look of consternation down pat.

Katherine winced. "Cow step on you?"

"How'd you guess?"

"We grew up next to a farm. The folks there would end up limping or on crutches every so often. And that was in-between black eyes, broken noses, pulled muscles…" She smiled, shaking her head.

"Well, you're right. I got stepped on. Anyway, Ma, I'm fine. Nothing to worry about."

"Hmpf." She stared at me for a few moments before changing the subject. "I took these folks to The Towne for an early breakfast and thought I'd show them your place on the way home. But I guess you're not up to it."

"Of course I am." If I popped another ibuprofen pretty quick. I looked at the group and wondered exactly what time Ma had roused them for breakfast, since it was barely eight-o'clock. Most of them looked at least kind of awake. "What do you want to see first?"

Alan smiled. "Wherever you like. It's your place." He looked like he was giving every effort to show the early hour wasn't bothering him, but I wasn't fooled so easily. I knew the only thing keeping him going was that coffee cup in his hand.

Katherine, looking rather awake, nodded. "We don't want to impose. So whatever is easiest for you."

"This is all yours?" Sarah looked around at the various barns, her face alive. "Cool."

David, usually the morning person from what they'd said, didn't look it this time. Maybe Ma had dragged them out of bed so early he didn't get his usual exercise. I laughed to myself, looking at the differences—and the similarities—between him and Alan. If I hadn't known better, I might've thought they were the brothers, rather than their wives having the family ties. They had the same coloring, and the same eyes—although it was hard to tell since both men's were half-closed. David obviously had the muscles, while Alan looked like any normal middle-aged man—healthy but not necessarily athletic. Alan, on the other hand, had a graying but full head of hair, while David's was cut military-short, trying to hide the fact that it was thinning. So while they weren't brothers, they easily could've been.

Tricia didn't seem to care where the tour led, and Trevor wouldn't even look at me, so I headed off. Out of necessity the tour was a slow one, with me picking my way around machines, fences, and slippery patches of manure.

"So you run this place yourself?" Alan asked as we stood in the far pasture, which Wendy had vacated the day before. Alan's coffee was gone, and his enthusiasm seemed more genuine the longer we'd strolled around the farm. "Looks like a lot to keep track of."

"I own it. Lucy works for me full-time, and Zach when he can. Mostly during the summers."

"Two women and a teen-ager." Katherine smiled. "I like that."

"Yeah," Sarah said. "Me, too."

Alan grinned at her. "I like it, too. Very enterprising. Was the farm handed down from your family?"

I felt Ma's gaze on me as I looked at my barn. "My folks died young—my dad when I was three, my mom when I was sixteen. Howie, our farmhand, kept it going for me until I was of legal age."

"He doesn't work here anymore?"

I swallowed. "No. He died last summer."

"Oh." Alan stopped smiling and cleared his throat. "I'm sorry."

I shrugged and flattened a thistle with the tip of one of my crutches. I certainly wasn't going to explain how Howie was murdered on this very land, trying to protect it. Trying to protect *me*.

Katherine's voice was gentle. "It's hard to lose a loved one. Especially a parent, or someone who has been like one."

Tricia inhaled sharply and stepped away from our group, giving Katherine a flat look before walking back up toward the house. David glanced at Katherine, his expression guarded, and headed off after his wife.

Katherine closed her eyes, breathing deeply, then opened them. "I'm sorry. Tricia's still very…sensitive about our mother's death. Can't quite handle talking about it yet, even though it's been a few months."

Sarah frowned. "She has to get over it."

"She will." Katherine's voice was firm.

Sarah looked away.

I watched as David caught up with his wife and fell in step beside her. "Had she been sick?"

"Our mom?" Katherine looked at Alan. "She was…it wasn't Alzheimers, but she was beginning to lose herself. It was hard to know— She'd been living with David and Tricia—and the girls—for a long time."

Sarah made a face. "Forever."

"A dozen years ago or so we decided Mom couldn't really live on her own anymore. She was doing things like leaving the burners on, or forgetting to get dressed in the morning. Alan and I both had full-time jobs, so she moved down to Lancaster to be with Tricia and David. It was just at the very end that she moved into a nursing home, and then they discovered she had Stage Four breast cancer. She died only a couple of months later." Katherine looked up the hill toward Tricia, who was no longer in sight. "Like I said, Tricia hasn't been able to put it behind her quite yet."

My mother had died from breast cancer, too. And while I certainly didn't think about it every moment, I wasn't sure I'd ever be able to put it completely behind me.

Ma put her hand on Katherine's elbow and pulled her gently away. "Who wants to head back to the car? I'm tired."

She wasn't tired. But I had to love her for her protectiveness. And not just of me. Of all of us, thinking about our lost loved ones.

Tricia and David were waiting for us by the van, David leaning against it, arms crossed, while Tricia stood a few steps away, watching Queenie as if the dog would attack her at any moment.

Lucy and Zach were done milking, on to cleaning the stalls, and when I stuck my head in the door I saw they'd been joined by Randy, who had taken over my straw bale and was watching them work. I hadn't noticed his Caddy in the drive, but peeking back out I saw it parked to the side, under a tree.

"Hey, Randy," I said. "What's up?"

He glanced over at me and nodded, but kept chewing on the piece of grass he had stuck between his teeth. He turned and looked through the door at the rest of the group, but didn't say anything to anybody. I raised my eyebrows at Lucy, and she shrugged. These teen-agers in the mornings…

I pulled my head back outside and we stood in an awkward circle outside the door, David rejoining us and gesturing for Tricia to come over. I wasn't sure she was going to, but she finally came to stand next to him.

"Sorry." I leaned against the doorjamb. "My tour guide duty ends here. I think I'm done in."

"I could show them more." Zach appeared at my elbow. "Could take them up the silo, or let 'em try out the bobcat."

The mens' eyes lit up at that.

"You go ahead," Katherine said. "I think I'll pass."

"Yeah," Sarah said. "Me, too."

Zach looked at me. "So can I?"

I laughed at the child-like expressions on Alan and David's faces. Even Trevor showed some interest. I stuck my head back into the parlor and shouted to Lucy. "You need Zach anymore?"

She yelled back without looking at me. "You can have him. I'm about through."

"Okay, Zach. Go ahead. Just be careful. Our liability insurance only goes so high."

Alan went a shade paler, and I laughed. "Sorry. Just a joke. You'll be fine."

He looked mildly relieved, but not altogether sure.

"I mean it. Zach will keep you safe." I looked at Zach. "Right?"

"Right." He leaned into the parlor. "Coming Randy?"

Randy grunted and left his straw bale, loping along beside Zach as they led the guys toward the shortest silo.

I turned to the ladies. "What do you folks want to do?"

"They'll really be okay?" Katherine's forehead creased. "Alan's not real good with heights. And Trevor doesn't always think…"

"They'll be *fine*." Geez, were these people completely clueless? So much for teasing the newcomers. "What about you? Anything you're interested in that I could manage?"

Katherine looked at Tricia until she finally met her eyes, and I could see silent conversation going on between them. I ignored Ma, whose expression left no doubt that she thought I should play lady of the house and invite the women inside, where I could be hospitable at the same time I rested my foot.

Katherine tilted her head at her sister, and Tricia turned toward me, her expression tentative.

"What?"

"Can I…would you show us your home? It's such a great example of a period farmhouse."

My eyebrows rose, and I ignored Ma's expression of "I told you so."

"Tricia's interested in interior design," Katherine said. "Rugged and realistic is all the rage, and she likes to get ideas wherever she can."

"You know," Sarah said. "Just for fun."

I squinted toward the house. "I don't know. I wasn't expecting company."

"Oh, Stella, surely it's not that bad." Ma frowned, apparently forgetting she was supposed to be feeling sorry for me.

"Remember I *do* live alone."

"Well, then, I guess you'd better change your habits if you ever hope to cohabitate with that young man of yours."

"Ma..." Heat crept out of my collar, but I wasn't sure if it was from irritation or embarrassment.

"You have a boyfriend?" Sarah sounded almost disappointed.

"Well, yes, actually—"

Ma put her hand on mine. "Come on, honey. Let's go inside, where you can sit down." The woman was relentless.

"Oh, all right. It is a nice house, but I don't have it fixed up anyhow special."

In fact, the decorations were still pretty much as my mother had left them close to fifteen years before when she'd died. Not my thing, decorating. If it was practical, I used it, if not, it pretty much just hung where it had always been.

Once we'd seen the first floor I said I was done. The upstairs was only bedrooms and a bathroom. Nothing special. And I didn't feel like struggling up the stairs or sending the women up without me.

Tricia stood by the door. "Can I just peek up the stairwell?"

Somehow I refrained from groaning, and allowed her the peek. If it wasn't enough, that was just too bad.

"How 'bout some lemonade?" Ma said.

I glared at her. "I don't have any."

"Tea?"

"All out."

Her eyes flickered. "Oh, well. Water will do. I suppose you do have *that.*"

"It's okay," Katherine said. "We can leave now."

Ma looked at me, her patient face on.

"It's fine." I doubt I sounded too welcoming through my gritted teeth, but I tried.

Ma sat us around my kitchen table, bustling around to get glasses and fill them from the water pitcher in the fridge. I suppose she'd thought I'd act as hostess, but then, she did have her fantasies.

As she was setting down the last glass, Lucy came in and pulled a chair up to the table. "Got one of those for me, Ma?"

"Of course." Ma filled another glass while Lucy wiped her forehead and smiled around the table.

"So," she said.

I waited for more, then realized she hadn't actually met the other women. I told everybody who was who, and let them carry on with more detailed introductions. After they'd played the Mennonite Game of seeing what mutual family, friends, and acquaintances they had, Tricia turned to me, her expression more relaxed than it had been earlier. "You have a lovely home."

"Yes, you certainly do." Katherine sounded genuine, if not as enthusiastic as Tricia.

"And you live here *alone?*" From the sound of Sarah's voice I was back to being cool, forgiven for having a boyfriend.

"Yes. All by myself." I took a sip of water and set down my glass, a lump forming in my throat. "Thanks. For the compliments about the house. I like it."

Ma sat down with her own water and looked at me expectantly. I'm not sure exactly what she was expecting. I mean, she *knows* me.

But now that we were just sitting, I realized Katherine's smile wasn't quite as easy as it had been at Ma's the other evening. And her eyes looked tired.

"Sorry to hear about the vandalism," I finally said.

She glanced at me, then away. "Thank you. That was…disturbing."

Sarah huffed. "It was awful. I mean, who would *do* something like that?"

I kept my eyes on Katherine. "You figure it was people who don't like you being a woman minister?"

She gave a little laugh, without humor. "That's the assumption."

Tricia made a noise, but when I looked at her, she was studying the trim around the kitchen door.

"Oh, these *people*," Lucy said. "What is the *matter* with them?"

Katherine smiled gently. "They're just…"

"Behind the times." Sarah shook her head, obviously disgusted.

Lucy leaned forward over the table. "It makes me want to scream. Don't those people read their Bibles?"

Ma let out a laugh, and Katherine grinned at Lucy. "I sometimes think they read them too much."

I blinked. "What do you mean?"

"I mean if you scour the Bible hard enough you'll find something to back up whatever you want. Especially the New Testament. It's filled with letters to specific churches. Corinth. Thessalonica. Collossae. And just like today, each church back then had its own issues."

"Like women talking," Lucy said.

"Exactly. People like to take the I Corinthians scripture literally that tells women to be silent in church—"

"—when Paul was speaking to one *specific* congregation." Lucy's eyes sparked. "The women there were probably just chatterboxes. Couldn't be quiet."

Katherine laughed. "That's right. We all know women like that."

I was searching my memory for the old days, when Ma used to take me to church and send me to Sunday School with Abe.

"What about…isn't there something that says women should have no authority over men?"

"Sure," Katherine said. "In I Timothy."

"And that women are supposed to submit to their husbands?"

Katherine grinned. "Ephesians 5. Colossians 3. I Peter 3."

Lucy thumped the table with a finger. "But *Jesus* told us we were to sell all we have and give it to the poor. Do those people who insist on women's submission do *that*? Or leave their families high and dry to go evangelize? If these people who discriminate against women want to take those anti-women Scriptures literally, they need to take *everything* literally. Including where Paul says there 'is no longer Jew or Greek, slave or free, male and female.'"

I licked my lips and looked around the table. Katherine was watching Lucy with an expression approaching amusement, while Tricia looked a bit like she feared for Lucy's sanity. Sarah kept her eyes on Katherine, as if waiting for her response.

"I didn't mean to start a riot," I said.

Katherine laughed, and laid a hand on Lucy's arm. "I'm impressed with your knowledge about this subject. How did you come to know all these details?"

"Well," Lucy said, sitting back. "I *am* from Lancaster."

Sarah let out a bark of harsh laughter. "And we all know what goes on out *there*."

Katherine smiled, looking at Tricia, but received only a tightening of her lips in response.

Lucy relaxed into a sheepish grin. "It's good you didn't want to go to Lancaster to work."

"I actually did make some inquiries last year," Katherine said, "to see if we could get closer to Tricia's family and…and Mom, but of course nothing came of them."

"How come?" I remembered someone else mentioning Lancaster when we were at Ma's the other evening for dinner. Something about Katherine getting nasty letters.

Lucy let out a huff of air. "Because last year their ministers voted against ordaining women. Of course all of those voting were *men*."

"But the vote was about as close as it could get," Katherine said. "They needed sixty-six percent in favor and they got sixty-five."

Sarah growled, sounding remarkably like Queenie. "So one third of stodgy old men got to dictate the rules and keep the women out. Stupid."

Ma clicked her tongue. "Don't blame it all on the old people. There are lots of young conservatives, too."

"And there was a church that already went against the vote," Katherine said. "Ordained a woman anyway."

"And are they still allowed in the conference?" I asked.

She held up her hands. "The jury's still out."

The door opened and Zach stuck his head into the kitchen. "The guys are done."

Katherine and Tricia looked at each other and pushed their chairs out from the table, Sarah following.

"Thanks for the water," Katherine said, her eyes sparkling. She looked much more alive than she had when we'd sat down. I guess a little controversy will do that for you.

Tricia nodded. "And for the tour."

"Good to meet you all," Lucy said. "I'm going to hang out here and make a phone call."

The women said good-bye to Lucy and I herded them outside, where they met up with the guys, who had somehow managed to survive the bobcat/silo tour.

"Sorry it got a little heated in there," Katherine said as she opened the van door for Ma.

"Well, it was Lucy more than you. And I started it all by asking about your office."

We stopped talking and stood back as a big milk truck pulled into the drive. I held up a hand to wave to Doug, but realized he wasn't driving. And there was a tiny little passenger riding shotgun.

I got to the side door as a woman hopped down. "Patty?"

"In the flesh."

"Then that must be Iris. Doug told me all about you two." I waggled my fingers at the little girl strapped into a car seat. Her shock of black hair stuck straight up, and she blinked her dark eyes sleepily at my fingers. "Just wake up?"

"Hard not to sleep in this big old rumbly truck," Patty said, laughing. "Soothing, kinda."

"So where's Doug?"

"New Jersey. Had to take his daughter to a softball tournament. I said I'd fill in. It's been a while since I've been behind the wheel. Gets old sitting in the office day after day. For Iris, too." She stretched out her hands over the truck seat. "Want to come out, honeypie?"

Iris jiggled in her seat, reaching toward her mother. Patty climbed back in and undid the car seat's buckle, sliding the girl toward her. She backed down from the truck. "Hold her a minute?"

"Uh…"

I looked down at my crutches, and Patty giggled. "Whoops, sorry. What happened?"

"Cow."

"Oh, sure. Stepped on you?" She held Iris out toward Sarah. "Want to hold her?"

Sarah wrinkled her nose.

"Here, I'll take the baby." Katherine came up and took Iris from Patty. "How long have you had her?"

"Almost two months now. Seems like much longer." The look she gave the girl was warm with affection. She reached behind the seat and pulled out a backpack. "I'll put her in here."

Katherine set Iris in the contraption, and Patty squatted down to get the straps over her shoulders. "This way she can see what I'm doing, and I don't have to worry about her getting, um…" She glanced at my foot. "Stepped on."

"I'm too big to put in a backpack," I said.

Patty laughed, and Iris gurgled something in reply.

"So." Patty stood up and turned around. "You have some visitors today?"

I introduced her to the group, everyone taking their turn to shake her hand. Everyone but Trevor, that is, who merely gave a jerk of his head. Iris peered at them over the top of Patty's head.

I gestured toward the truck. "You folks want to see what she does?"

They all agreed, except for Ma, who elected to sit in the mini-van and wait. The rest followed behind as Patty cut the cable tie on the hose door and put the scrap of plastic in her pocket.

I grunted. "Doug always leaves those for me to pick up."

"Yeah," Patty said. "He would."

We all squeezed into the milkhouse, where she proceeded to take her samples of milk in little tubes, explaining that they would be used to test milkfat, and also to check for antibiotics, should her tank end up showing contamination. The cable tie she cut off the hose door was a safety precaution, so she'd know her load hadn't been messed with in-between trips.

Alan and Sarah asked a lot of questions and seemed to be taking in the whole experience, exclaiming over the work and the fact that Patty was driving a truck, as if they couldn't quite believe she was allowed to do it. Katherine and Tricia spent more time doing baby talk with Iris, while David and Trevor stood in the corner with their hands in their pockets.

"Whoa! Full up in the milkhouse." Lucy appeared in the doorway.

I introduced her to Patty, and while they started out talk-ing about the milk load, it soon merged into the trials and joys of single motherhood, and the rest of us eased our way back outside.

"Thanks for taking the time to show us around," Alan said. "And for loaning us Zach, and letting us see how your milk gets collected. We appreciate it. You women are all amazing. And the teen-agers, too, of couse."

I laughed. "That we are. Come back when I'm out of this—" I tapped my cast with a crutch—"and I'll give you a fuller tour. Amaze you some more."

He smiled. "We just might take you up on that."

Ma held out her arms and I leaned into the van the best I could, giving her a one-armed hug while trying to keep my crutches from going out from under me.

"Let me know if you need anything." Her breath tickled my ear.

"I will."

"Uh-huh. Like you let me know about your foot?"

I stepped back and tried to look contrite. It mustn't have worked, because she was frowning as she eased back into the middle of the seat.

The rest of them followed, Alan and David shaking my hand, Katherine reaching for a hug, then appearing to think better of it and simply patting my arm, and Tricia giving a little wave from the other side of the van. Trevor got in without acknowledging me in any way.

Sarah held out her hand, and I braced myself for the grip of steel. "It's so great that you run your own life. I mean, that's so cool."

"Yeah," I said. "It is."

Katherine stopped to pet Queenie good-bye, and that got her a friendly nose in the crotch, making her jump.

"Sorry," I said.

She laughed. "No problem. But that'll teach me to get too close." She brushed off her pants and slid into the van, easing the door shut beside her.

They left in a cloud of dust, Alan waving out his window as they drove away. I eased myself onto the grass beside the house and lay flat on my back. My armpits ached, my foot throbbed, and my shoulders were on fire. What I wouldn't have given for one of Nick's massages.

"Stella?"

I looked up at Patty, Iris' eyes peeking out from behind her shoulder. Sucking sounds came from the backpack, and I could see that most of Iris' hand had disappeared into her mouth.

Patty waved toward the tanker. "I'm all set. Doug should be back next time."

I pushed myself up onto my elbows. "Thanks. Appreciate your coming by. And it was nice to meet Iris."

She looked back over her shoulder. "Say bye-bye to Stella, Iris."

The sucking sounds continued, and the girl didn't even blink.

"Bye-bye, Iris." I tried out a smile, but got nothing in return. Patty laughed and swung the backpack to the ground in a fluid movement, finally getting the girl to pull the fingers from her mouth.

Once Iris was strapped into her car seat and the backpack was stowed away, Patty climbed into the driver's side, slamming the door behind her. She put the truck in gear and roared out the lane, sending a cloud of dust over me. I lifted a hand in farewell as I coughed, then fell back onto the grass, my neck protesting the weird position I'd been in.

I'd just begun to relax when yet another vehicle drove up, cracking the gravel. I repressed my desire to scream and opened my eyes.

Carla waved to me from the passenger seat of a shiny black Toyota Tundra. Her smile was contagious, and I found myself returning it until I realized whose truck she was in. Bryan walked purposefully around the front of the vehicle and put out a hand to help Carla down from her seat.

Carla came to stand over me and hitched a thumb toward the departing tanker truck. "Different driver from usual, wasn't it?"

"Yeah," I said from the ground. "Doug's off taking his daughter to a softball deal in Jersey. His sister Patty's driving today. She runs the place from the office, usually."

"Was there a kid with her?"

"Iris. Just got her from China."

"Nice."

"Yeah. She's pretty cute. So I guess the doc let you out?"

"Just now. Thought I'd stop by and let you know."

I glanced at Bryan, then back to Carla. "You're feeling okay?"

"Feel great. They told me I'm supposed to take it easy, but I'm not on house arrest." She grinned.

"Food?"

She made a face. "Told me to take it easy there, too."

"Hey!"

We turned to see Zach coming from the barn, Randy slouching behind him. Zach smiled at Carla. "You come to see Barnabas?"

"Well, no, but I'd be glad to take a look at him."

Bryan and I both made noises, and she shushed us with an impatient gesture. "I'm not going to *do* anything. Geez. Come on guys, let's go see."

And like the pied piper—although I wasn't sure who was leading whom—Carla and the boys started toward the barn.

Bryan gave one look in my direction and took off after Carla.

Chicken.

Chapter Sixteen

When everyone had finally left my farm except for those who were supposed to be there—Lucy, Zach, and me—I went into the house, struggled to the front room, and collapsed onto the sofa. It didn't take me long to fall asleep.

I woke about an hour later, hot and tangled in an afghan, thinking about Nick. This wasn't surprising. I often think about him, and it often leaves me hot and tangled in the sheets. But this time it was a little different.

When Nick had come back into my life the past December after several months of not knowing what the hell had happened or whether or not I'd ever see him again, that sofa—the one where I lay at the moment—was where he had slept. We'd met the summer before when I'd hired him to paint my barn. I'd developed an enormous crush on him, been hit with all sorts of personal tragedy not related to him, and discovered he made his living as a developer. Not the kind of person I normally associate with, especially after one of his kind had tried to send me into bankruptcy so he could have my farm. Nick had taken off, my reaction to his career anything but calm, and I'd done nothing to look him up.

But there he was, at Christmas. Showing up on my doorstep like the little doggie in the window. Against my instincts I'd let him in, and while it had been anything but easy the past six months, I couldn't imagine being without him again. Ever.

But I *was* without him. A majority of the time. He had his life in Virginia, while mine took place here, a couple hundred miles north. His family was in Harrisonburg, with his house, and his job. And mine was in PA.

I shoved my face into the afghan and inhaled the scent of it. It smelled like home. I pushed myself up, rubbed my temples, and took a deep breath before struggling upright onto my crutches. If armpits could talk, mine would've sounded like a sailor.

Biting my lips against the pain, I stomped out to the barn, left a note for Lucy, and crawled into my truck. Queenie whined pathetically at my feet, and I leaned over the seat to open the passenger door. She changed instantly from pouty girl to happy-go-lucky canine and ran around the truck, jumping into the passenger seat with much more agility than I had at the moment. Or ever did.

We drove uptown to the medical supply store, where I closed the windows halfway and told Queenie to stay. Ten minutes later I had traded Dr. Peterson's prescription note for a pair of new crutches. The luxury model. Padded tops and hand grips, easily adjustable height, and rubber tips with no cracks. I felt ready to take on the world. Well, no. Not really.

The clerk from the store followed me out and tossed the old crutches into the bed of the truck. I thanked him and got into the cab, where Queenie had made more than her share of smeary nose lines on the passenger window. "So," I said to her. "Let's take these old crutches back to Dr. Peterson."

She panted happily.

We drove across town toward the doctor's office, and when it came into view I slammed on the brakes and swerved to the curb, causing a chorus of horns behind me. I waved them past, not bothering to see how many middle fingers were aimed my way, and stared at the scene in front of the brick building, where hordes of vehicles, lights flashing, blocked the drive and parking lot. My stomach hatched an immediate and ferocious batch of butterflies.

Had that crazy, outraged patient from the other day come back to mess with Dr. Peterson?

I checked my mirror and eased back onto the road to get as close as possible to the scene. I found a spot away from the cop cars, in front of another office building, and sat for a moment more, wondering what I should do.

"Well, I have to know, don't I?" I asked Queenie.

Telling her again to stay, I slid down from the seat, got balanced on my new crutches, and trundled along, up to the police tape stretching in front of the drive. Amidst the crowd of cops and who knows who all, I somehow managed to catch the eye of an officer I'd been acquainted with since the past summer, when she'd helped gather up my younger cows when my heifer barn burned down. Her face was tight, her mouth a thin line.

"Ms. Crown?" She glanced at my crutches, momentarily distracted. "Why—"

"Pregnant cow, broken foot."

She nodded, unimpressed.

"What happened?" I asked.

Stern glanced toward the building and I followed her gaze, stopping on the receptionist, who stood alongside the front steps with her arms wrapped tightly around her stomach. Her face looked even paler than the other day after dealing with the mad guy. Another female cop stood next to her, posture straight, eyes darting around the scene, her face as hard as Officer Stern's. The butterflies in my stomach changed into hornets.

"Where's Dr. Peterson?" I asked. "Is she okay?"

Officer Stern turned back to me, her eyes softening. "She's… she's gone, Ms. Crown."

A gush of air escaped me, my relief almost enough to topple me over. I took a firmer hold on my crutches. "Where did she go?"

Stern's mouth twitched. "I don't mean she left, Ms. Crown. Stella."

But of course I knew what she meant. I closed my eyes for a moment, fighting dizziness. "What happened?"

Stern opened her mouth, then shut it. "I'm not sure what I should say. You'll have to wait for the detective, or someone else. I'm sorry." She glanced down at my foot. "Did you have an appointment?"

I shook my head. "No. No, I didn't. I just…I came by to return my old crutches. She loaned me some. Asked me to be sure she got them back." I looked at the building, not really seeing it. "I guess she doesn't need them now."

Stern looked at me sharply. "Ms. Crown, why don't you sit down?"

And the next thing I knew I was on the ground. Stern squatted beside me, one arm around my shoulders, one hand under my arm, holding me in a sitting position. She must've broken my fall, but I wasn't really sure.

She let go of my upper arm. "Can I call someone for you?"

I blinked a few times. "No. No, don't. I'll be okay."

I pulled my crutches toward me from where they'd fallen, then rested my head on my good knee. "I'll just sit for a minute."

"Okay. If you're sure."

She left me to go back to her duties, and I sat. I'm not sure how much time passed before I felt another presence beside me. Willard. He knelt on the sidewalk.

"She was your doctor?"

I nodded, turning my head to see him. "Since last summer." Only a year ago. "What happened?"

He looked at his shoe, blowing up his cheeks, and letting the air out. "You know I can't say much. But Dr. Peterson is—"

"I know. She's dead."

"Yes. I'm sorry." He was quiet, while a breeze came along, cooling my face, which felt wet. I reached up. I was crying.

I wiped my cheeks on the sleeves of my shirt. "Can you tell me anything?"

He shifted, kneeling on his other leg. "Somebody broke in. Messed the place up pretty good. There are patient files all over the place, must be thousands of papers…" His face tightened.

"It looks like she'd been working late. Or really early. I'm not sure which. But when they broke in, she was there…"

I sniffed and wiped my face again. "How? How did she die?"

He looked at me, then down at his shoes. "It's hard to know for sure, but if I had to guess, I'd say she hit her head hard enough it killed her."

"She hit her head? Or someone hit it for her?"

His lips formed a thin line. "I can't answer that yet. But I assume from the way she's lying that she was pushed, and she fell on something sharp. Meadows is testing the corner of a sink in the examining room where we found her. I expect it will match the wound on her temple."

I tried not to think of how she must have suffered. "Was it for drugs?"

He nodded shortly. "Probably. There were some stolen. And other supplies. Hypodermic needles. Scales for measuring medicines. In fact, that's what I was…where I was going. I need to put out a message to all the police within a hundred mile radius, telling them what was taken." He sighed again, this one lifting his shoulders up and down.

I waved toward the building. "But isn't there an alarm system on this place? I'd think a doctor's office—"

"Sure. But alarm systems don't help all that much, a lot of times. Too easy to defeat."

"How?"

"They cut the phone line. It's not rocket science, unfortunately."

I opened my mouth to ask more, but he cut me off. "I have to go, Stella." He pushed himself up from the ground. "You'll be okay getting home? You need me to call Lucy?"

"No. I mean, yes, I'll be fine. Willard?"

"Yeah?"

I looked up at him. "Help me up?"

He reached down and pulled me to my feet, bending over to get my crutches and hand them to me.

We stood for a moment, side by side, watching people go in and out of the parking lot and the building itself. Cops, medical folks, people in plainclothes. Officer Meadows made an appearance at one point, a camera in his hands, and I didn't have it in me to complain about him. I just hoped he knew what he was doing, so he could help nail the bastard who did this.

"I have to go, Stella."

"Sure. Do what you need to."

He left, and I stood for a while longer, watching the receptionist, who still stood huddled beside the building. And who hadn't yet been able to stop her tears.

Chapter Seventeen

After standing on the sidewalk for several minutes I summoned up the energy to walk back to my truck, and I drove home, my mind spinning. What was it Nick had joked about just the night before? That it sounded scary to be a woman up here in Pennsylvania? Or had he said dangerous? Either way, he was right. And it was obvious now that it certainly wasn't a joke.

Dr. Peterson was dead. Carla had been attacked, Katherine's church struck by vandals, and now… My cow Wendy obviously wasn't after me because I was a woman, so I wouldn't count my own broken foot in the mix of events, even though I fit the gender of the victims.

The more I thought about Nick's words, the more I realized they were true. I swung into a driveway and turned around, heading back into town. I might not be able to give Willard the answers he needed, but I needed to tell him what I was thinking.

Gladys looked up as I lurched into the police station. "He's really busy right now, Stella."

"I know. But it's about that. About Dr. Peterson, I mean."

She studied my face, which was probably red from crying. "All right. Okay. Come on back."

She buzzed me in, and this time when I got to his office Willard wasn't staring out the window. He wasn't bouncing his pencil up and down, either. He was holding it still, one hand on each end, as if he was going to break it in half.

"Willard?" I asked. "Got a minute?"

He jerked his head up, his eyes taking a moment to focus on me. "One."

I went in and sat down. "I think they're all connected."

He stared at me. "What are?"

"Carla's car-jacking. The vandalism at the church. And now Dr. Peterson."

"What church?"

"Remember? Kulpsville Mennonite?"

His face cleared. "That's right. I'd forgotten about it. Never got around to calling over there." He looked at me. "But I don't get it. What's the connection? Drugs? Were there drugs taken from the church?"

"Willard…" Wasn't he supposed to be the smart one? "They're all *women*. Women in positions men usually hold. A large-animal vet. A pastor. A doctor. See?"

He sat for a moment, thinking. At least I thought he was thinking. Maybe he was just waiting for me to make more sense.

I studied him. "Was there anything…anything at the office that might make you think it was about that? I mean, I know people were angry about Dr. Peterson taking over her dad's practice."

He looked at me sharply. "Why do you say that?"

I described the encounter at the office the day before, with the comb-over guy who knocked the pens all over the waiting room. "Dr. Peterson—and the receptionist, too—said it wasn't the first time. People are really upset at her dad. And at her. They don't…didn't…want her to take care of them. They wanted the man they were used to."

Willard bit his lips together. I had his interest.

I continued. "And there was a sign."

"A sign?"

The abruptness of his question made me jump. The idea of a sign had struck a nerve.

"There was a sign at the church," I said, "that made it pretty clear the attack was about Katherine, the minister, being a woman. They spray painted the words, GO HOME SINNER on her office wall."

He looked at me more intently, but I wasn't sure he was seeing me.

"Willard, what is it?"

He let go of his death grip on the pencil and began tapping the eraser on his desk. "There wasn't anything for Dr. Beaumont. No sign."

"No. Just a concussion. And a swollen face. Willard, what is it? Did Dr. Peterson get a message, too?"

He looked at his pencil, now stilled, and rubbed his chin.

I sat forward. "*Willard?*"

He dropped his hand from his face and released a drawn out breath. "The attacker went into one of the rooms, Stella. Tore a paper sheet off an examining table. It's now across Dr. Peterson's desk." He looked me in the eye. "It says, 'Women should be the patients. Not the doctors.'"

A chill settled over me, and I could tell Willard felt it, too.

My voice reflected the feeling. "It's the same guy."

"It could be."

"Oh, come on, Willard. It has to be."

"Maybe Dr. Peterson and the church are connected. Dr. Beaumont's car-jacking is a little different."

"Maybe." But I didn't think so. "Do you have anything new on Carla's truck?"

"Actually, yes. We've received a few calls about a man seen walking along Route 63 in Green Lane on Sunday, close to where her truck was found."

"And?"

"We're checking into it. There's not a clear description of him, and there's no way of knowing if he had anything to do with the attack. But it's the only lead we have at the moment."

Better than nothing. I guessed. "And these other two things?"

He carefully set his pencil on the desk, lining it up with his computer keyboard. "I guess I need to be in touch with the police in Kulpsville. There could be a connection between the two. And Stella? Don't tell anybody about the sign, okay? It's best to keep it under wraps for now, just in case."

"Okay."

I wanted to push him. Get him to say he was sure. That he'd take care of it and nothing else would happen to any other women.

But of course he couldn't.

I left him and his pencil and went out to my truck, where I grabbed onto Queenie and tried to keep my hands from shaking.

Chapter Eighteen

Carla wasn't home. I rang her doorbell and banged on the door, but all I succeeded in doing was getting Concord all riled up. Queenie heard him barking and began her own ruckus in the truck. I found some paper and a broken pencil in my glove compartment. Using one of my keys, I scraped enough wood off the end of the pencil that I could write Carla a note, asking her to call me as soon as she got home. I stuck it in the door, where she should see it, and hoped the breeze didn't blow it off.

Concord continued to bark, and I tried to calm him by talking through the door, but that only produced whining, which was harder to take than barking.

"Sorry, buddy. Sorry. Carla will be home soon." I hoped.

My hands had finally stopped shaking, but it was still hard to drive home. The sun hurt my eyes, and the ache from my foot had traveled up to lodge itself in my temple. Or maybe that was just from trying not to let any more tears cloud my vision.

Lucy was at the back of the barn, pulling nails out of a piece of wood. She didn't notice me until I was standing right in front of her, and even then she didn't stop working, except to notice my crutches.

"Those are nice. Feel better?"

When I didn't answer, she stopped what she was doing and looked up. Seeing my face, she dropped the board and stepped toward me. "What? What is it?"

"It's Dr. Peterson."

"Dr. Peterson? You mean your doctor?"

"Yes."

She waited, but I couldn't speak.

"What? What about her?"

"Lucy, she's dead."

Lucy dropped her hammer now, and stared at me, stricken. "What happened?"

I told her.

"Willard thinks it's about drugs?"

"Seems to. But he's calling Kulpsville about the church, to see if maybe they could be connected."

Lucy leaned against a stall and put her face in her hands briefly before looking up. "Are we in danger?"

"Us?"

She held out her hands. "Look at us. Women running a dairy farm."

"So you think that, too. That he's after women."

"What else would it be?"

"Separate cases. A random car-jacker, an angry Mennonite, a drug addict who happened to choose her office."

She considered it. "It could be either. But we need to keep our eyes open. Protect each other."

I looked out the door of the barn, over the manure lagoon and my back pasture, bordered by the developments, which seemed closer every day. Closer to this farm, that had been my haven.

Lucy came to stand beside me. "Does she have family?"

"Dr. Peterson? Her dad, at least. And I think she's married. I haven't seen any photos of kids. And she never talked about any."

Lucy shook her head. "What a waste."

Soon she left me, and I heard the hammer scraping against the wood, and the sound of nails being dropped into a can. I turned and walked back through the barn to my office, where I stood staring at my phone. I sat down and picked it up, dialing Carla's cell phone.

No answer. Where could she be?

I looked at the phone a little longer, and ended up calling Nick. He answered, out of breath.

"Sorry," I said. "Bring you running from somewhere?"

"Actually, I'm on the treadmill. I've got a ton of paperwork to go through and I'm getting all stiff, so I thought I'd loosen up. I only answered the phone when I saw it was you. What's going on?"

I tried to tell him, but my throat closed, and I pushed on my eyes with my fingers to get myself together. The whine of the treadmill on the other end of the phone stopped.

"Stella?"

I took a shuddering breath. "Something awful has happened." And I told him.

He was quiet for a moment, and I listened to him breathing before he said, "You okay? Is Lucy there with you?"

"She's here."

"You want me to come up?"

Yes. "You don't have to. I know you have things to do there. I'll be fine."

"I don't know."

"I'm fine. I'll be fine. I just wanted to talk to you. That's all. Hear your voice."

"Why don't I—"

"You don't have to come. I feel better now. Sorry to bother you."

"You never bother me."

I bit my lip, trying to breathe deeply, trying to get rid of the tight feeling in my chest. "You can call later, if you want."

"Okay. Okay, I will."

"Love you."

"Stella?"

"What?"

"Nothing. Love you, too."

I hung up and looked at the phone some more before getting up. It was lunch time, but I had no desire to eat, so I strapped a garbage bag over my foot and went to work around the farm.

After a short while I realized I had only managed to get in the way of the others and give myself a headache. I figured if I waited another day or so I would be able to do the same work in a quarter of the time with no extra resulting body aches or irritated co-workers, so I took some painkillers and set myself up in the office...again. The amount of time I'd spent sitting at my desk and staring at my computer during the past twenty-four hours was enough to make me stir-crazy.

So when Zach and Randy stopped by, asking me to give them a ride to see Randy's calf at his uncle's farm, I jumped—or stood up very slowly—at the opportunity.

I grabbed my keys and followed the boys out the door. "How come you didn't drive today, Randy?"

He frowned. "My dad dropped me off on the way to work."

"Caddy not working?" I remembered the whining it had made as he'd left the farm the day before.

"It's working fine. Never mind, okay? Can't a guy get a ride to work without playing Twenty Questions?"

He stomped off ahead of me, and I looked at Zach, who gave me a sickly smile. "Sorry."

"It's all right. Just make sure you sit in the middle. I don't want to have to smack him while I'm driving."

So Zach sat between Randy and me, and no smacking took place, or even much conversation. Queenie, who had joined us and taken a spot in the extended portion of the cab, kept sticking her nose in Randy's ear, until he'd finally snapped at her to keep her drool to herself, and she'd stayed over on my side. I reached up to scratch her ears, telling her she was much better off leaving grumpy teen-agers to themselves, but I glanced over at Randy a time or two and wondered exactly what had happened to turn this nice boy into Oscar the Grouch. Was it just the driving thing, or was there more to it? I'd have to ask Zach later.

Randy's uncle lived on one of the few farms left out toward Chalfont. We made it there in a little over twenty minutes, dodging cars and sitting at traffic lights a good portion of the time. His uncle, who was mowing his lawn at a speed faster than what we'd been able to do most of the way over in the truck, waved and kept on going once he saw who it was.

The boys took off for the barn, and I paused to let Queenie jump out ahead of me and run to greet the obviously ancient golden retriever who lay almost flat out on the sidewalk. I hoped Queenie wouldn't be too annoying to the old dog, but it seemed she'd already discovered its limitations, and had trotted restlessly away, sniffing the bushes.

I stumped into the barn, following the path of the boys, and soon found them at a stall, where Zach leaned on the door, watching Randy.

Randy's calf nuzzled the hand I held out to it, and I checked out my former property. He looked good. Healthy and clean. Friendly and manageable. Very cute, with his mostly black body and a white spot right over his rump.

"Looks good," I said.

Randy grunted and continued forking dirty straw into a pile.

"What's his name?"

Randy mumbled something I couldn't understand.

"What?"

"Simeon," Zach said.

I glanced at Randy and opened my mouth to say something else, but Zach grimaced at me, shaking his head. I closed my trap and turned around, taking in the smells and sounds of a beef cattle operation. Quite a different beast from home.

Before long we were ready to go, and Randy closed the door, making sure the hook was secure. He didn't even look at us before walking away.

Zach followed, and I tried to push down my concern at Randy's unusual behavior. By the time we were in my truck, I was about ready to burst.

"So, where are we going now?" I asked.

Zach's seat belt clicked in. "Dropping Randy off at home, if that's okay."

"No problem. And you?"

"Back to the grind at your place." He grinned.

"Okey-dokey." I waved to Randy's uncle and pulled out of the drive. We were a few miles down the road, enduring Randy's sulky silence, when I remembered. "Hey, how was MYF last night? Was it fun?"

Zach shrugged. "It was all right."

Randy mumbled something about "women" and "telling people what to do."

I raised my eyebrows at Zach. He smiled weakly. I decided to let it go so I wouldn't damage my suddenly tense relationship with Zach's best friend.

We dropped Randy off at home none too soon—without even a 'thank you'—and Zach held his hand up before we'd even left the driveway, to keep me from pouncing. "He's hurtin'."

"Obviously. What the hell is going on? It can't all be because your parents don't want you driving with him."

"No." He sighed loudly. "It's a coupl'a things. But mainly his girlfriend's acting weird."

Oh, boy. "That swim team girl? What's her name? Chrissie?"

"Crystal. She's a lifeguard. And she decided this summer that 4-H is boring and she's 'outgrown' the farm stuff."

Stupid girl. "So she's too good for him now?"

"Seems to think so. And Randy's convinced she's met another guy at the pool. She's always busy when he calls, and they haven't seen each other for over a week. He thought once he got his license it would help, but..." His voice trailed off.

"Poor Randy."

"Plus he *is* ticked at my mom and his for not letting him drive me around."

Can't say I was too bummed about that, myself.

"So that was the problem with MYF last night?" I asked. "Was he complaining that Katherine's just another woman to tell him what to do?"

"He seems to think his life is run by women, even at church now. Except the MYF sponsors haven't changed any. There's still a couple of guys doing that. Well, their wives, too."

We drove in silence for a few minutes.

"And how about Trevor?" I asked. "Was he as weird last night as everyone thought he was going to be?"

"Yeah, kinda. But I feel sorry for him. I think he's pretty tired of his mom telling him what to do, too. I don't think he talked to her once all night. And when she tried to introduce him he acted all embarrassed and mad."

Like any normal teen-ager in front of a group.

When we got home Zach thanked me and headed into the barn, where Lucy had already gotten started with milking. I was tempted to follow him, but decided I'd take one more round off. By morning I figured maybe I'd feel well enough to try my hand at work again. If I could possibly sleep without nightmares.

It smelled yummy in the house, and I was surprised to notice I was actually hungry. A peek in the kitchen showed a crockpot full of chicken and vegetables. I was just reaching to take off the lid for a better view when the phone rang. It was Ma.

"You can drive your truck, right? Your foot doesn't keep you from doing that?"

"Yeah, I can."

"Good. Then I need you to go around to the Hershbergers' tomorrow morning and deliver a load of mulch."

"You mean Katherine's?"

"Who else would I mean? Go out to the nursery in Hilltown and get a load of the nice dark stuff. You don't have to worry about unloading it. Alan and David will take care of that part."

"So you already volunteered me?"

"Well, they don't have a truck."

Okaaaay. "Thanks for checking with me first, Ma."

"Oh, what do you have that's better to do? You can handle a bit of Christian charity now and again."

I supposed she was right. And I certainly wasn't brave enough to tell her no.

So I guessed I knew what I'd be doing after milking the next day, whether I wanted to or not.

Chapter Nineteen

After eating Lucy's delicious supper, sharing the table once again with Lenny and Tess and avoiding all conversation of murder and car-jackings, I decided I'd waited long enough to take on the project of showering. So when the house was my own again, I got a clean garbage bag, taped it to within an inch of its life, and stepped into the shower. There were a couple of close calls, and I'm not sure I got all the shampoo rinsed out of my hair, but I felt a hundred percent better. Or at least eighty.

I pulled on an extra large T-shirt and climbed into bed, exhausted from the effort of becoming clean. Once I'd gotten back my breath and stopped sweating from all the exertion, I picked up the phone and dialed Nick's number.

Busy. Crap.

Carla hadn't called, and I wondered if she'd gotten my note on the door. I dialed her number, but got only her machine. I left a short message for her to call, and hung up.

I lay down, and tried Nick again five minutes later. Still busy.

This time when I lay down, I fell asleep until something jerked me awake. I lay still, heart pounding. Did I have a nightmare? Was there wind? Had Queenie been barking? A glance at the clock said it was almost ten. Not late, but dark. I lay frozen, breathing as quietly as I could. Something creaked downstairs, and I heard the stairway door open, rasping on its hinges. I reached over to grab one of my crutches, and eased off the side of the mattress onto my good leg, keeping the bed in-between me and the door.

Quiet footsteps came up the stairs, the wood creaking, and a man-sized shape filled my bedroom door. I raised the crutch.

"Stella?"

I froze. "Nick?"

He stepped forward, and I fell into his arms.

I woke before my alarm, lying on my side, Nick behind me, still in the clothes he'd been wearing the night before. It had taken a while for my shaking to stop after the scare he'd given me, but once my heartbeat had returned to normal I'd told him to stop apologizing, and I'd slept through the night without dreaming.

But now a wave of nausea hit me as I remembered the events of the day before, and I swallowed. When the sick feeling had passed I turned off my alarm and eased out of bed. I needed to get my mind on something other than Dr. Peterson's death, and work would be the best thing, if I could handle it.

I grabbed some shorts and was able to get out of the room without waking Nick. My trip down the stairs was much better than the day before, and once I'd eaten a little breakfast and popped some ibuprofen I went out to the barn, beating both Lucy and Zach. With a little hitch in my breathing I put on the little shoe Dr. Peterson had given me, tied a bag around my cast, and found a place to put my crutches. Then I started down the rows, clipping in the cows who had already found their spots. By the time Queenie had herded the rest of them in Zach had been dropped off by his dad and was in the aisle, ready to start. He didn't say anything, but grunted twice, so I thought that was pretty good.

Lucy arrived after Zach had attached the first milkers, and I was filling feed cups.

I looked up at her. "Well, look who decided to show up."

She glanced at the clock, hands on her hips. "I'm not late."

"Nope. Just not as early as me."

She narrowed her eyes. "So I got up for nothing?"

"Sorry. Didn't know I'd feel up to it." I gestured toward the house. "You can go back to sleep if you want. Your old bed's still there."

She thought about it, but apparently decided sleep was now a lost cause. "Nick's here? I saw his truck."

"Yeah. Arrived last night."

"I didn't know he was coming."

"I didn't, either."

She took a deep breath and pushed her hair back from her face. "I'll go feed the calves."

"Thanks. Sorry again, Luce."

She waved me off. "No biggie."

With three of us around the work got done in good time, even with me being gimpy. By the time we were finished it was close to eight.

"Anybody know what time the Hilltown Nursery opens?"

Zach looked at me blankly.

Lucy smiled, cocking an eyebrow. "Planning some gardening?"

"No. Ma volunteered me to pick up some mulch for the Hershbergers."

Zach looked at me some more. "You want help?" It was a grudging question.

"Thanks, but Alan and David are supposed to be there to take it off the truck. And I can drag Nick along, if he's awake."

I could almost hear the "Good" Zach didn't say.

Leaving them to repair some boards in the paddock, I went into the house and found Nick still sleeping. I eased the door back shut, left Nick a note on the kitchen table, and went outside, where I found a shovel in the heifer barn that Lucy and Zach wouldn't need after milking. It was covered with filth of the kind the Hershbegers probably wouldn't want in their mulch, so I wiped it down with a rag before heaving it into the truck bed. I whistled Queenie into the back seat, and took off for Hilltown.

The nursery manager loaded us up with the beautiful dark brown mulch the Hershbergers had pre-ordered, and sent us on our way toward Kulpsville. A half hour later I found their house on a winding "country" road behind the church. "Country" meaning there were houses only every fifty feet instead of every twenty.

David met my truck in the drive, looking a little more awake than he had the other morning at my farm. "Morning."

I nodded. "Where do you want this?"

"How 'bout you back up to the front of the house? The ground's hard enough these days it shouldn't matter. Just don't run over the guys."

Another look showed Alan and Trevor hunched down between two bushes, messing with something in the dirt. I maneuvered the truck so the open tailgate hovered over the middle of the flower bed, and hopped down from the truck. Queenie jumped down, too, and immediately began running circles with a terrier that shot out of the shrubbery, yapping to high heaven.

Alan, who had clambered up from his knees, winced. "How they can have so much energy at this time of the morning is beyond me." He reached for a coffee cup balanced on the porch railing.

Trevor looked up, but didn't say anything.

"Early?" I said. "I've been up four hours already."

Alan groaned, putting his mug to his forehead. "You and the Incredible Hulk over there."

I glanced at David, who grinned. "Can't help it I'm a morning person. At least I do you the favor of going out for a run and not making noise in the house."

"Can you imagine?" Alan said. "Getting up early just to exercise?"

I looked toward the road, where cars passed every few seconds. "Where do you go so you don't get run over?"

David pointed west. "If I go that way, there's a little road that misses a lot of this traffic. And that early in the morning, I even beat most of the commuters."

"Crazy," Alan said, with feeling.

I laughed. "You're not an exerciser?"

"Give me an air-conditioned gym at a decent hour, and I might consider it."

I remembered the gift certificate Carla wanted me to use, and fought down a wave of anxiety at the thought of sweating on purpose, in front of people.

Trevor stood up and brushed dirt off his knees.

"You in any sports?" I asked him.

He shrugged. "I like soccer."

"Well, that's good around here. Big soccer area, isn't it?"

"I guess. The school's team won State a few times."

Mallory had talked about that. "You going out this fall?"

He looked away. "I'm not that good."

"Sure you are," David said. Then to me, "I told him he could come running with me. Wouldn't take that much to get him in shape."

Alan groaned, and I took a look at his son. David was probably right—Trevor looked pretty fit, from what I could see under his baggy shirt and shorts. But knowing most teen-agers and their sleep patterns, I couldn't imagine David was going to have much luck getting this one up at dawn to pound the pavement. I was surprised he was up now, and it was closing in on nine-o'clock.

"So should we get this mulch unloaded?" I asked.

"Oh," Alan said. "Right."

I grabbed my shovel from the corner of the truck bed and swung onto the tailgate while Alan set his mug back on the porch.

David gestured to my foot. "You sure you should be working?"

I stood up, towering over him. "I'm fine. Doctor said I could start work after a day or two."

"He know what he's doing?"

"*She* does. Or, she did."

"Oh. She. Sorry."

Alan looked up. "What's her name? We need to line up a doctor, and Katherine would prefer a woman."

I took a breath, wondering how to say what I needed to say. They obviously hadn't caught it when I'd changed tenses. "Her name was Rachel Peterson."

Alan looked at me. "Was?"

"Yeah. She…she died yesterday."

"Oh my God," David said. "She's that doctor that was on the news. Someone broke into her office to steal drugs, and she was there. They killed her."

Alan blinked. "Are you serious?"

I sat on the side of the truck bed, the nausea of the morning returning.

"You okay?" David stood beside me, his hand on my elbow.

"Yeah. Yeah, I'm fine." I took a deep breath and stood back up, getting a shovelful of mulch.

Alan stood to the side, thinking. "You know, I'm pretty sure she was on the list one of the church members made up for us. Doctors and dentists and stuff."

David dumped a shovelful of mulch around a plant. "Wasn't she the one taking over her father's practice?"

Alan snapped his fingers. "That's right. Over in Souderton? The one Sarah was urging you to check out."

Trevor's shovel banged the tailgate, and I jumped. A look at his face reminded me of what Zach had said about Trevor and women. Having Dr. Peterson as his doctor would've given the kid yet one more woman to tell him what to do. He didn't have to worry about that now. Unless there was another female doctor on the list.

We left the topic and finished unloading the mulch in silence, Alan bringing a broom from the garage to sweep the last chunks out of the truck's nooks and crannies. "Thanks so much for bringing the mulch. I wasn't sure how to get it here before Mrs. Granger mentioned your truck."

"No problem. I'm glad to help out." And I was, now that I'd done it.

He finished sweeping before taking off his gloves and banging them together over the flowerbed, spraying tiny mulch pieces. I held out my shovel and he took it and gave it to Trevor to hold while he helped me climb down from the truck. "Katherine's over at the church. I'm sure she'd be glad if you'd stop by and say hello."

"Well—"

"In fact, when I mentioned you were bringing the mulch she said to be sure to tell you to come on over and see her office."

Oh, great. More people volunteering my time. "Thanks."

He took my shovel from Trevor and set it in the truck bed. "The church is just around the corner. Less than a mile."

"Sure. I know." I closed the tailgate, and little mulch pieces fell to the ground from the back bumper. I swept the rest off with my hand.

Trevor was giving me the eye, so I whistled for Queenie. "Come on, girl! Time to go!"

After a few more rounds of the yard, and an entirely mismatched wrestling bout—Queenie was bigger, but the terrier ten times feistier—my disheveled collie escaped the clutches of the little bugger and jumped into the truck. I closed her window halfway and pulled slowly out of the yard, finding a space in the traffic to drive away. It was busy enough I didn't feel comfortable looking back to wave.

When I got to the red light at the intersection to Allentown Road, I paused. Left to my house, or right to the church?

"What do you think?" I asked Queenie. "Should we do what we want or try to act neighborly?"

She smeared her nose on the window.

"Oh, if you insist."

I turned right.

Chapter Twenty

I pulled into the parking lot of Kulpsville Mennonite Church and studied the building. An old stone structure, it was probably at least a hundred and fifty years old. A modern addition was tacked on to the west end—probably a wing for classrooms, the way it looked. Thick, mature oaks and maples competed with the church's height, casting shadows across the tall, white-paned windows.

Several cars were parked close to the front door, and I recognized the Odyssey the Hershbergers had driven to our house the day before. Neither of the other two cars were familiar.

I parked next to the minivan, by the front walk, and left the windows partially open, promising Queenie I wouldn't be long. "Really," I said. "This is just a drive-by visit, and I doubt the church folks would welcome a dog running around the property. Even one as good as you."

She flopped onto the seat, very put out.

Stepping into the foyer of the church, I was pleasantly surprised by the coolness of the interior. The stone and trees were doing their job to keep the summer sun from heating up the church.

"May I help you?" A woman peered at me suspiciously from a doorway, where she stood, a stack of papers in her hands. Her eyes traveled from the tips of my cast to my head, lingering on the points of the steerhead on my neck.

"Yeah. Is Katherine around?"

"The pastor?"

Um, *yeah.* "I came by to say hello."

She looked at me for a few more seconds before stepping back and waving me inside the room. "Her office is in here."

I clomped toward her, making her step back even further, and stepped into the room. It looked like any church office—at least the few that I've seen—with a computer, desk, phones, and a watercolor painting with the words "Come, ye that love the Lord" inked in with fancy script. It reminded me of a piece Lucy had owned before the tornado had destroyed her apartment over my garage last summer. What had she called it? A fraktur. Mennonite folk art done by a local artist.

The woman bustled ahead of me, sticking her head through a doorway in the corner. "Pastor Katherine? There's a…lady here to see you."

I heard the rise and fall of Katherine's voice, and the sound of her footsteps.

"Stella!" She smiled and walked up to me, hands out. I picked one of them and shook it.

"What brings you by?"

I leaned against the desk to rest my foot. "Delivered some mulch to your house and helped to shovel it out. Alan suggested I come over to see your office."

"Well, that's great. This is Dorie. The church's secretary." She gestured to the woman who'd greeted me. She looked a little more enthusiastic now that Katherine had accepted me.

"Dorie, this is Stella Crown. The one with the dairy farm I was telling you about."

Dorie smiled and nodded, and I was amazed she hadn't recognized me, seeing how I'd obviously been a topic of conversation. Could it be that Katherine hadn't mentioned my tattoos? Unheard of.

The sound of hammering came from Katherine's office, and I blinked.

"Here. Come into my office," Katherine said.

I walked past smiling Dorie and stepped toward Katherine's room, pausing in the doorway. "Oh, hi, Tricia."

Katherine's sister turned briefly from the wall, where she had just pounded in a nail. "Stella." She picked up a framed picture, which I expected to be the usual picture of Jesus. This painting, however, was different. Much better than that one with him looking all washed out and simpering. This one gave him some color—a darker skin than most portraits show—and some fire in his eyes. The kind of Jesus I'd prefer, any day.

I looked around the room for obvious signs of the vandalism, but didn't see anything. Another glance at the wall told me it was freshly painted, and I could only imagine the offensive words that had been slashed across it only a couple of days before. I wanted to say something about them, try to make a connection with Dr. Peterson's murder, but Willard wanted me to keep quiet about the sign.

I forced a smile at Katherine. "Looks like you're getting settled in."

"I've had good help. Tricia's much better at this stuff than I am."

I gestured toward the Jesus painting. "I thought your artwork had all been destroyed."

"Most of it was. This one, thank goodness, I'd been planning to hang at home, so it wasn't over here." Her face was tight. "But I lost a lot of special things."

I looked around the room, seeing small, unharmed pieces of pottery and a hanging tapestry.

Katherine followed my gaze. "Tricia made a trip to the Kulpsville Flea Market this morning, over in the old elementary school. She found a few things to start my collection back up. It will take a while to replace everything. And some things can't be replaced, of course. But it's a start."

A photo sat on a shelf at eye-level, and I stepped closer. It was obviously the extended family, with Katherine's and Tricia's broods, and a woman who must have been their mother.

Everyone wore red and green, and a wreath hung on the wall behind them. "Christmas photo?"

Katherine smiled. "From a few years back."

"That's your mother?"

Katherine glanced at Tricia, whose focus was on the painting she was hanging. "Before she got sick. You can tell just by looking at her face that she was happy that Christmas."

A sound of scattering nails came from across the room, and we watched as Tricia knelt to pick them up. Katherine stepped forward to help, but Tricia shooed her away.

Katherine sighed, and turned back to the picture. "You recognize Alan and David, I'm sure, and Trevor." She pointed at the girl in front of Alan. "That's our daughter, Tori. And Tricia's two daughters. You've met Sarah, of course, and that's Elena."

"But Elena's little." Young and leggy, like a colt.

Katherine laughed. "She looks much older now. But still in high school. Doing a high school kind of summer job."

"She's a nanny for a couple of bratty kids."

I jumped at the voice behind me, and saw Sarah in the doorway.

"I'm *so* glad I'm past that."

I remembered her saying the same thing at Ma's the other night. She must've really hated baby-sitting as a teenager if she had to repeat herself all the time.

"It's a good job, Sarah." Tricia stepped back from the painting, then toward it again to tip it to the left with her finger. "There. Looks level. Now, I'm going to go plant those geraniums, unless you wanted me to do something else?"

"Sounds good."

"Want to help me, Sarah?"

Sarah blew a bubble with the piece of gum she was chewing. "No. Thanks."

Tricia's face fell, but she rallied, and while she didn't look happy, she at least looked resigned.

Katherine glanced at her niece. "I can help you, Tricia."

"No. No, that's fine. I'll get Dorie to help."

"Oh, okay. Great." Tricia left, and Katherine turned to me. "Sorry about her. About the nails. She's still so sensitive about Mom dying. Thinks it's her fault, somehow."

A weight settled on my chest. I knew that guilt. The guilt of knowing Howie would still be alive if it weren't for me. For my farm. "Why would she think that?"

Sarah rolled her eyes so expressively I thought she was going to lose her balance. "Because she's just so…*Mom*."

Katherine peeked out the office door to make sure Tricia was gone, then came back to stand beside me and spoke quietly, glancing over at Sarah. "I know it was hard on Tricia, taking care of Mom all that time. Especially the last year. It got so bad Tricia felt she couldn't do it any more, and they put Mom in the nursing home. Mom didn't last long after going there, and Tricia thinks she died from unhappiness. Science says it was breast cancer."

"She was also really old."

"Sarah…" Katherine held up her hands, then dropped them. "Tricia just needs some time, I think. But I hope she can soon feel better. She just looks so…"

"Bad?"

"*Sarah*." She turned to me and smiled. "Do you want to see the rest of the church? Or are you familiar with it?"

"I don't think I've ever been here before."

"Then come. I'll show you around."

The three of us walked back past Dorie, who was just getting up from her desk. "I'm going out to help Tricia plant the flowers. Is that okay?"

"Sure. We're going for a little tour. Be back in a minute."

Dorie nodded and glanced at the phone, like it would ring as soon as she and Katherine stepped out, and Lord knew what would happen then.

"Here's the sanctuary." Katherine led us through a double-door into a spacious room with carpeting and padded benches. The sounds of passing traffic were muffled in the enclosed space, and the air felt slightly stuffy. An upright piano sat at the front of the room, along with a drum set and some music stands. The pulpit was up on a raised stage, with a huge cross hanging on the back wall.

I looked up at the ceiling fans and wondered if they only ran them on Sunday mornings. Sarah stood beside me, and I studied her. "It's nice you folks can stay to help out with the move. You have time for that?"

Sarah smiled. "I'm working part-time doing some filing and stuff for a law firm in town. They were fine with me taking a few days off to make sure my aunt got settled in okay."

Katherine put her arm around Sarah's shoulders and squeezed. "I don't know what we would've done without them. We weren't sure *David* would be able to get off work, but he called in a few favors and took some vacation time."

"What does he do?"

"He's a salesman for a fire protection business. They make sprinkler systems, smoke alarms, that sort of thing."

"And Tricia?"

Sarah waved a hand in the direction of where her mother was, outside. "She's just at home. She can make her own schedule since she doesn't have anything she has to do."

Katherine glanced back toward the doors, as if afraid Tricia would suddenly appear. "She used to be a photographer. I mean, she still is, but doesn't actually have a job doing it. She gave it up when the girls were born, and hasn't ever gotten back to it, even now that the kids are getting older. She was really good at it. I keep hoping, now that Mom's gone…" She shook her head and held her hand out toward a side door. "Want to see the classrooms?"

She took me through the rest of the church, showing me the Sunday School rooms, the nursery, the kitchen. I was soon glancing at a clock. "Queenie's out in the truck. I really shouldn't leave her out there any longer."

"Oh, I'm sorry. Let me take you back." Katherine led us back through the church, stopping in the foyer. "Thanks so much for stopping by. It was nice to see you."

"Sure. I hope things go smoother for you now. No more break-ins."

She pointed at the door, where I could see shiny new hardware. "We had the locksmith come out and change the locks. That's about the best we can do. Other than pray that the perpetrator has a change of heart."

Oh, God.

"Well, good luck."

"Thank you."

"See you later, Sarah."

She waved and followed Katherine back into the office.

I exited the door as Tricia was coming in. She gave me a startled look, and glanced back out the door before coming all the way in. "I hope you don't mind, I used—"

Queenie went suddenly frantic, barking and jumping around in the truck.

"What the…?" I pushed past Tricia to get outside. A squirrel sat on the tailgate of my truck, a nut in its mouth, tormenting Queenie. I shooed it off, and Queenie gave a few more yips before settling down. When I turned back to the church to say good-bye to Tricia, she had already gone.

"She's really wonderful." Dorie was watering the new bed of red geraniums next to the church sign, right in front of my truck.

"Tricia?"

"No. Pastor Katherine."

"Oh. Yeah, she's nice."

"More than nice." She shook the last few drops from the watering can, and turned toward me. "She's what our church needs right now." She looked at me expectantly, like it was my turn to say something.

"Um, pretty flowers."

"What? Oh. Yes. Tricia picked them out. The petunias that were here before were…well, they got pulled out."

By the vandals?

"It's nice Tricia can help out."

Dorie's expression soured. "I guess." She fiddled with the handle of the watering can. "I don't know if… She makes little comments here and there. Stuff about wondering if Pastor Katherine can really do the work. If she should stay after…after what happened the other night. Like she thinks she shouldn't be here."

Or shouldn't be doing this job? I recalled the discomfort on Tricia's face when Lucy was spouting off about women in ministry. Or maybe it had more to do with being jealous that Katherine had a career of any kind, since she'd given up photography.

"She's probably just worried about her," I said.

Dorie considered it. "Maybe. I hope so." She peered into the watering can, like maybe it filled itself while we were talking. "Anyway, she'll be gone soon. Although I do like her daughter. She's much more supportive of Pastor Katherine."

Queenie made a thumping noise as she bumped her head against the truck window. I did my own thumping on the way across the parking lot. When I got in the seat and backed out, I could see Dorie filling up her can to water some more flowers around the front of the church.

"Shall we?" I asked Queenie. "I could really use a little nap. And Nick's probably wondering where I disappeared to."

She cocked an eyebrow at me, panting noisily.

We left the church and headed home.

Chapter Twenty-one

Nick's blue Ranger was a welcome sight when we turned into the drive, and my heart jumped at the sight of Nick himself sitting on the side steps. Queenie tried to claw her way out of the truck, having missed him when she was getting her beauty sleep during the night. I parked, somehow managing to avoid getting run over by Queenie as she was first out the door, and let myself down from the cab as quickly as I could, hobbling up the path toward the house. Nick was halfway down the walk before I got there, and scooped me into his arms, Queenie fighting for space between us.

I kissed him, then pulled back to look at his face. "Sleep all right?"

"Slept fine, once I got over feeling guilty for giving you a heart attack."

"Well, you were close to getting a crutch upside your head, so I guess we would've been even."

He smiled. "Want another chance?"

"Nah. I'd have to go back to the truck and get my crutches."

Arms around each other, we went inside the house, and I pulled him to the front room and sat on the sofa where I'd taken my nap the day before. "I'm glad you came."

He reached out to run his fingers down my face. "Me, too. I couldn't see leaving you up here by yourself with everything that's going on."

I took a deep breath and laid my head on his shoulder.

"Besides," he said, "Miranda's driving me crazy."

I gave a short laugh and sat back up. "What's she doing now?"

"You know. Going through my refrigerator. Screening my calls. Trying to talk me out of dating some gal who likes cows better than her."

My jaw tightened. "Well, I *would* like her if she'd—"

"I'm kidding." He pulled me back in his arms. "I'm kidding. I know you do your best with her. As we all do."

I relaxed and let my head fall back onto his shoulder. "Whatever you're doing here, I'm glad. I tried to call you last night before I went to sleep."

"Yeah?"

"Busy."

"Trying to tie up some business on my way up. I know, I know, I shouldn't talk while I'm driving, but I got one of those new ear pieces I can stick on in the truck."

His phone, as if knowing we were talking about it, vibrated on his belt, making me jump. He pulled it out of its holder and looked at the screen. "And guess who's calling?"

"No way. Let me talk to her."

He grinned, but flipped open the phone and put it to his own ear. "Miranda? What's up?" He listened. "Sorry. Can't. I'm in Pennsylvania." A pause, then a barrage of loud talking. Nick held the phone out, away from his head. When he heard silence for a few seconds he risked putting the phone back. "Listen, Miranda, I came up to see Stella. Yes, I know you don't." He smiled at me. "But the thing is, you see, I do."

He does? Of course he does.

"Okay. Tell Mom not to worry. I'm fine. Okay? Bye." She was still talking when he closed the phone and clipped it back on his belt. "That's the problem with cell phones. I can't get away."

"Isn't that what I've been telling you all along?"

"I know. So anyway, you don't need crutches anymore?"

I grimaced, the mention of my foot making it throb. "Actually, I'm pretty sore right now. I should probably take some painkiller and put it up for a bit."

"Well, don't let me stop you."

He left me on the couch and scrabbled through the medicine cabinet in the bathroom until he found the pills. He brought one, along with a glass of water, and sat beside me. "So where have you been? I woke up not long ago and haven't even found Lucy yet."

"You didn't see my note in the kitchen?"

"Wasn't hungry, so I didn't eat breakfast."

"Nick—"

"I'll eat lunch. I promise. Now tell me about your morning."

I explained how Ma had volunteered me for the mulch expedition, and how that turned into a visit to the church. He shook his head. "So it's back to business as usual for the Mennos, huh, even with the vandalism?"

"What are they going to do? Hire security guards?"

He smiled. "I guess not."

"So they go on."

"Well, it's no wonder your foot's tired."

I lay my head against the couch. "What about you? You look good."

"Don't I always?"

"Of course." I grinned. "What I mean is, you look healthy."

"I *feel* healthy. But don't tell Miranda. She won't believe you."

He leaned back beside me and set his feet on the coffee table, next to mine. "So what's your plan for the rest of the day?"

I thought about the farm, and the work that needed to be done. And then I thought about my foot, and the look on Lucy's face when I got in the way and risked more injury. Mine and hers.

"I thought maybe I'd go visit Carla. She's home from the hospital, and I want to make sure she's okay."

He brightened. "Think her boyfriend would be there?"

"Why, you want to date him now?"

He laughed. "I want to meet this paragon."

"You'll probably have the chance, since he's practically stuck to her. Unless I call ahead. Then he'd leave, since he seems to be scared of me."

"Can't blame him. But don't call. Let him be there."

I grunted. "Okay. But if he sees me and takes off running, it's not my fault."

"Whatever you say. You want to go now?"

I considered what it would mean, most importantly that I'd have to get off the couch. "Nah. Let's give my pills some time to work. And maybe have some lunch a little later."

"And what do we do till then?"

"You have to ask?"

No. He didn't.

Chapter Twenty-two

By the time Lucy, Zach, and Tess—who had come mid-morning—joined us for lunch, Nick and I had spent a nice time getting reacquainted and I was feeling much better. Lucy whipped up some sandwiches for lunch, and afterward Zach took Nick out to show him how Barnabas had grown since his last visit. I told Lucy our plans for the afternoon and she tried to hide her relief.

Lucy had brought my crutches into the house before lunch, and I limped over to them. "I'll be back in time to help with milking."

"You don't have to."

"I know. But I want to. In fact, why don't you take the evening off."

"Stella—"

"Really. Nick's milked with me lots of times. We can handle it. And we'll get supper on our own, too. Go home and spend some time with your family."

"You're sure?"

"I'm sure."

She studied my face, and her serious expression turned light. "I'd like that. So would Lenny."

"Give him a call. Tell him you'll be home for a normal supper time."

"Thanks, Stella."

I shooed her away from the kitchen, and she went back outside, where Tess was wrestling with Queenie on the side yard. I stood at the kitchen window and watched as Lucy talked briefly to her daughter, then continued on to the barn. Zach and Nick soon came into view, Zach's hands in his pockets as he did the teen-age shuffle beside Nick's straight-backed posture.

I couldn't help but remember a time just half a year before when Zach resented Nick, thinking he was keeping me from a relationship with his uncle Abe. In reality, it sort of was Nick's fault, since I'd discovered feelings for him I'd never had for Abe. I mean, I loved Abe, but I loved him as a brother, not a lover. Zach seemed to have accepted it by now.

As Lucy passed the guys, Zach made a U-turn to follow her, while Nick continued on toward the house. Glancing up, he met my eyes through the window and smiled. My heart caught in my throat at the sight of him, looking like he belonged here.

The side door banged as I made my way to the front room, managing the crutches better than days before. Nick stood by the door, his keys hanging from his fingers. "Ready to go? And I'm driving. No use arguing."

So I didn't.

Queenie stayed home this time, happy with the companionship of Tess, which was good, since the Ranger was a lot smaller than my F150. And this way Nick could hold my hand when he wasn't shifting gears.

I groaned as we pulled up to Carla's in Quakertown. Bryan's Tundra sat in the drive, and Nick inched as close as he could so he wouldn't block the sidewalk.

"Nice truck," Nick said.

I grudgingly agreed.

Carla came to the door as we made our way up the walk. Her face, while less swollen than several days before, still sported a variety of colors, and I had to look away.

"Nick! What a surprise!" Carla hugged him, and punched me on the shoulder, almost sending me off my crutches. "You didn't tell me he was coming up."

"I didn't know. And since you didn't call me, I couldn't tell you."

"Call you? Were you expecting me to?"

"I left a note."

"Oh, that. I figured you were checking up on me, and since I was fine I didn't call back. What did you want?"

I started to tell her about Dr. Peterson, but thought that standing on the doorstep wasn't the best place. "I'll tell you later."

"Well, I wish I'd known you were coming. I would've fed you lunch, or something."

"You can eat now?"

She smirked. "Barbecued chicken sandwich for lunch. With potato salad."

"That's allowed?"

"I hope so."

I narrowed my eyes, but was stopped from scolding her by the appearance of Bryan behind her. Carla introduced the two men with exuberance, and I watched as Nick took a first look at Carla's new boyfriend.

I tried to catch Nick's eye after their handshake, but he avoided looking at me as Carla ushered us into her house, getting us away from the heat and humidity that had sprung up with the middle of the day. Concord huddled behind the couch, peeking out from behind it as we entered. Carla knelt down and called him softly.

"He's still shaky from his previous life," she said to Nick. I could hear the anger under her voice. "They treated him so horribly. Come on, sugar. Come on out. We're all friends here."

I glanced up at Bryan, who caught my eye for a split second before jerking his head away.

Concord crept slowly out from hiding until he stood, shaking and leaning hard on Carla. She smoothed her hand over his sleek head, talking softly. "This is Nick. He's a good guy. And Stella...well, you know Stella, don't you? Don't worry about her crutches. They won't hurt you."

I set my crutches on the ground out of sight of the greyhound and held my hand out toward him, letting him reach out to sniff it before attempting to pet him. Soon he let me run my hand down his back, but never left the circle of Carla's arms.

"You've sure been going through a lot," Nick said to Carla.

"You said it." But then she went on, telling him all about the attack, the hospital, the lack of adequate nourishment, and how Bryan had stepped up to take care of her. "He's been my knight in shining armor."

Gag.

"And Stella came to see me, too, of course."

Nick looked at me, a smile flickering on his face. "Yes, she told me."

"Oh, and you know what I didn't tell *you*," she said to me.

"Something else?"

She looked at me, puzzled, and I waved her on. "What didn't you tell me?"

"Remember how I was saying I got that pass from a new client to go to Club Atlas for a couple of weeks? That gym where my friend Babs is the manager?"

"Sure."

"Well, she was almost attacked in the parking lot."

"*What?*"

"Real early this morning. She got there about five, and there was a man waiting. Luckily, some of her big lifters showed up just then and scared the guy away. Completely freaked her out."

"Does she know who it was?"

"Couldn't tell. It was dark enough the shadows hid his face, even with the security lights on the building."

"He have a car?"

"She doesn't know. He ran through the back, into the parking lot for the spa next door. And with all the racket the guys made chasing him, she wasn't sure if she heard an engine turning over."

"They didn't catch him, I take it."

"Nope. But she'll make sure from now on that she doesn't show up for work alone."

I looked at Nick, my neck prickling. What the hell was going on around here?

Nick met my eyes. "You don't think it's the same one?"

Carla's brow furrowed. "The same one that what?"

I cleared my throat. "That attacked you."

"What? Why would it be?"

"Because these attacks are happening every day now."

"What attacks?"

I took a breath. I told her about Katherine's church being vandalized. And then I told her about Dr. Peterson.

Bryan, who had been listening to all of this with a darkening expression, shook his head. "That's it. I'm staying here."

Carla looked up at him. "You don't have to, sweetie."

"Yes, I do. If there's some maniac on the loose you need protection."

But who was Bryan to take over? She'd known him for a grand total of what? Three and a half weeks?

"You can stay at my place, if you want." I stared at her, trying to send my vibes of discomfort into her head.

She gave a half-hearted laugh. "Come on, you guys, you make it sound like I can't take care of myself. I've got Concord, after all."

Great. A quivering, aging greyhound. That's what she needed.

"This guy's already come after you once." Bryan wasn't giving up. "He might come after you again."

"He will not."

"You don't know that. And it sounds like he's getting more violent, not less. Killing the doctor. And he probably would've killed your friend at the gym if the other guys hadn't gotten there."

They faced off, Carla's stubborn countenance against Bryan's crossed arms and clenched jaw. Her arms around Concord tightened until the dog whimpered. Carla released him, and her shoulders loosened. "All right. Maybe it would be a good idea."

"I don't think—"

Nick widened his eyes at me, and I snapped my mouth shut. Fine. I stood up. "I guess we'll be going."

Carla frowned. "So soon?"

"Got to get back to the farm."

"Oh. Well, sure. Give Barnabas a pat for me. I'll come out to see him again soon."

"You're going back to work?"

"Saturday." She looked relieved. "I'll be glad to get back to it."

Bryan didn't seem so sure, but that was his problem.

We said our good-byes and I lurched out to the truck, throwing my crutches into the bed before climbing in. We were a couple of miles down the road before Nick said, "He seemed nice."

"Hmpf. He treats her like she's going to break. She's a tough woman. She can take care of herself."

He glanced at me, his eyes sparkling. "Maybe she likes it."

"What?"

"Being treated like a princess."

"I don't think so. She got pretty pissed at him back there."

"But she gave in."

He let that sit for a few seconds before he said, "Not every woman is as tough as you, you know. Not even your friends."

I looked out the window, watching the passing developments. Carla had always seemed so independent. So much in control of herself. Her life. Maybe that was changing.

And, I had to tell myself, Nick had come to stay with me. And I was glad.

I shook my head, realizing my discomfort had another level. "I just don't like him."

When I looked back at Nick, he was grinning.

"What?"

He tried to stop smiling. "Nothing."

"*What?*"

Now he laughed out loud. "It's just…I don't think he likes you too much, either."

I crossed my arms and stared out the windshield, wondering again when it was ever going to rain.

Chapter Twenty-three

We sat in my office, the window air conditioner chugging away, trying to ease the heat and humidity. I took an ibuprofen and leaned back in my office chair, feet on my desk.

"It's *got* to be about women," I said.

Nick stood in front of the window unit, his shirt sticking to his chest. "Sure seems like it."

"I mean, Carla, Katherine, Dr. Peterson, and now this Club Atlas lady? It seems obvious. But why them?"

We were quiet for a few moments before I said, "I guess that should be obvious, too, just like I told Willard."

Nick's eyes were closed. "What should?"

"That these women are threatening someone. Think about it. All of them have jobs that are traditionally men's. A vet. A pastor. A doctor. Now a lady who runs a predominantly male gym. I mean, who's next? Some poor business owner who just so happens to be female?"

Nick's eyes were open now. "You mean like you?"

I sucked in a breath. "No."

"Why not?"

Because I'd already been through my share of sabotage and pain and heartbreak.

"Because who else would want to be a dairy farmer? I mean, come on. It's not like I'm taking one of the more...*desirable* male jobs. There are hardly any farmers left *at all* because it's such a shitty lifestyle."

He was still looking at me.

I dropped my feet to the floor. "I'm calling Willard. He probably knows about Club Atlas, since it's in his jurisdiction, but I want to make sure."

He knew.

"We're on it, Stella." I could imagine his pencil bouncing up and down on his desk.

"On what, though? The event at the gym, or the fact that women are being targeted?"

"Was there a sign?"

"A what?"

"You know, like at the church, and the doctor's office. A sign with a saying."

"I don't know. I didn't investigate it."

"Well, there wasn't. No sign."

"There wasn't for Carla, either."

Silence.

"Okay," he said. "It's not that I won't consider a connection. I just want to be sure."

"Well, be sure sooner rather than later."

"Yes, ma'am." He didn't say good-bye.

"What?"

"I spent the morning in Warminster."

"Okay. Doing what?"

"Attending Dr. Peterson's autopsy."

Oh. "I'm sorry, Willard. I don't mean to be an ass."

"It's okay. You can't help it."

"What did you find out?"

"Pretty much what we expected."

I waited.

"You sure you want to know?"

"No. Not really. But yes, tell me."

"It was the head injury."

"From hitting her temple on the corner of the sink."

"Yes."

"So she was pushed."

"Or tripped. There's no way to know at this point."

An accident? Or murder? Both, really.

"It was a direct hit," Willard said. "She probably died instantly. No prolonged suffering."

A small consolation.

"So you think I might be right? About it being the same guy?"

"Stella, I just don't know. We have to check out the possibility that it was one of her patients. Or a druggie."

"I know, but—"

"I'll talk to you soon, Stella."

I hung up, closing my eyes and breathing deeply.

"Stella, what is it?"

I told him.

Nick stepped away from the air conditioner and pulled his shirt away from his chest. "What about your theory?"

"Willard thinks I'm wrong."

"He said so?"

"Not exactly."

"Wrong about what?" Lucy stood in the doorway.

"About why women are being attacked."

"What?"

I told her about Babs.

She frowned, the lines around her eyes deepening. "It's getting really scary." She looked out the window, then back at me. "So what do we do about the farm?"

"What do you mean?"

"I mean this place is owned and run by women. What makes you think we won't be a target?"

Nick looked at me, like "*See?*"

A flood of memories hit me. The days—and nights—of watchfulness the past summer, taking shifts with Howie, rage simmering just below the surface. The sabotage, the dead cows, Howie, lying in his own blood...

"Okay," I said. "Suggestions?"

"Queenie," Lucy said. "She always lets us know when someone's on the property."

Except for last night when she'd missed Nick's truck.

"She helps. But at night she's coming inside. She can watch from the window. She's done that before." She'd also been dog-napped, and I wasn't taking any chances. I rested my elbows on the desk. "And nobody stays at the farm alone. There's got to always be at least two people here. Not including Zach."

"Agreed."

"And at night?"

I sighed, resting my face on my hands. "Like we said, Queenie will keep watch from downstairs. We'll leave the window open a little so she can hear. And we'll flip on the barnyard lights."

Lucy chewed her lip. "You think that's enough?"

I could stay up. Sit outside like I did last summer. Fall asleep out there where I'd be vulnerable. Make Nick sit out with me, when he needed his sleep to stay healthy.

"It'll have to be."

She looked at me a little longer. "So should I still take the evening off, or do you want me to stick around?"

"You can go. Nick's here with me. We can do the milking, and keep an eye on things." I looked to make sure he was with me, and he nodded.

"All right. But if you need me, you just call."

"Will do."

She glanced at the clock. "I'm going to finish up what I was doing, then head home."

"Sounds fine."

She still stood there.

"Lucy, go."

She bit her lip, looked at the floor…and finally left.

Chapter Twenty-four

Milking went smoothly, if a little slow. Nick had helped enough times he knew the routine and was able to do the things I couldn't quite manage. The cows accepted him, and he avoided getting peed on or falling in a slippery patch of manure. I stayed upright, too, to both of our surprise. We were finally done and resting on the side yard, talking about how we could go about getting ice cream from Dairy Queen and still keep an eye on the farm when a Camry pulled into the drive, Queenie running circles and barking in front of it. I sat up quickly, staring at the driver. What was *he* doing here?

But it wasn't just Abe Granger, my childhood best friend and almost-could've-been boyfriend who stepped out of the car. The passenger door also opened to reveal a familiar face.

"*Missy?*"

She smiled and raised her hands, like *Ta da*. "It's me."

It sure was. She wore the same fashionable, light-colored clothes I remembered from the summer before, free of farm dirt and grime. White sandals, a tank top, and a short skirt. Long blonde hair, tied back from her tanned and conservatively made-up face. Pretty. No…*cute*.

Nick hopped up to greet the two of them, but I didn't feel like struggling to get upright while they all watched, so I stayed where I was.

Abe came around the car to shake Nick's hand and offer Queenie a rub before stopping in front of me and looking down at my leg with an amused expression. "So what's up with you, Princess?"

I groaned. "Ma didn't tell you?"

"Nope. Did you get mad and kick one too many butts?"

"Ha, ha." I held out my hand. "Help me up."

He did, and gave me a hug. "Good to see you."

"Yeah, you, too. But I didn't know you were coming down."

"Neither did anybody else." He looked over at Missy. "We, um, had some news we wanted to share."

Oh, no.

He held out his hand and Missy walked over to take it, wrapping her other hand around his arm and smiling into his face.

Abe looked at me. "We're getting married."

I stared at him, my mouth open, until Nick stepped up. "Congratulations. That's great news." He shook Abe's hand again, and gave Missy a kiss on the cheek.

Abe continued looking at me.

"Yeah," I said. "Congratulations."

Nick put his hand lightly on my back. "So when's the big day?"

"December twenty-four," Missy said. "A Christmas Eve wedding."

"That sounds nice. Here or in New York?"

"At home. New York. We thought if we did it at Christmas Abe's family would have a better chance of getting there, with kids home from school and everything."

"Sure," Nick said. "That's a good idea."

It was?

Abe was *still* looking at me, but I didn't know what to say. I didn't even know what to *feel*.

"Hey," Nick said. "We were just talking about getting some ice cream from Dairy Queen. You folks want to join us?"

Missy brightened. "Sure."

He looked over at me. "How about Missy and I go get it?"

"Great," Abe said.

I gritted my teeth. "That would be fine."

"Good. Let me just run and get my wallet."

He was back in a few seconds, and Abe tossed Missy the keys to the Camry. "Here you go."

She paused, keys in hand, then smiled, looking from me to Abe. "Requests?"

We gave her our orders, and they left. I sank back onto the ground, Queenie sitting beside me, snuffling at my face with concern.

"I'm okay, girl," I said, pushing her gently away.

Abe sat next to me. "So what did happen?"

"Huh?"

"To your foot."

"Oh." I explained.

He shook his head. "The things you get into..."

That was nothing. But I didn't feel like telling him everything *else* that had been happening.

I took a deep breath and let it out. "So you're getting married."

"Yup."

"You proposed?"

"Yeah." He pulled out a piece of grass and started breaking it into little pieces. "I took her to a really nice restaurant and had the waiter bring out the ring with dessert. You know, in case I chickened out during the main course." A smile flickered on his face.

"I thought you were going to wait until next Valentine's Day."

He tossed away the grass. "I changed my mind."

"How come?"

He pulled his knees up, hugging them to his chest. "Because I'm ready now."

I looked at the barn and listened to the sound of a cow, mooing in the paddock. "Which means what?"

"Being ready? That I'm tired of waiting. I want to get started with the rest of my life."

The dusk-to-dawn light flickered on, and I squinted up at it.

Abe tilted his head back, too. "We are almost thirty, you know."

"Yeah. I know."

Queenie insinuated herself between us, and our hands met as we both reached out to pet her. Abe grabbed my fingers. "I need you to be happy for us."

I looked at our hands, then at his face, tense and serious. "She's really who you want? She makes you feel…complete?"

He didn't hesitate at all before saying, "Yes." Then, "I love her."

I squeezed his hand. "Then I am happy for you, Abe."

He blinked. "Really?"

I smiled and squeezed his hand back. "Really."

He let go of my hand and hugged me, Queenie making a little squeak before scooting out from under us. Abe finally let go and slumped backward onto the ground, where he started laughing.

"What?"

He laughed some more. "Now that's over, I can have fun telling everybody else."

"You haven't told anybody?"

He shook his head. "Just Ma. She said I'd better come out and tell you next, before you heard it from somebody else, or I'd wish I'd never been born."

I grinned. "She knows me pretty well."

"Plus, I was so scared to tell you I knew I couldn't enjoy telling anyone else until I got it over with."

I frowned. "Really?"

He stopped laughing. "Really."

I rubbed my face, ending up with my face in my hands.

"Stella?"

I threw my hands up. "I don't mean to be such a bitch. Good grief. Scaring my best friends half to death."

He smiled again. "I know you don't *try* to be scary. You're just…intense."

I thought of Carla, and how I'd been terrorizing Bryan. But then, I didn't *know* Bryan. Not like I'd gotten to know Missy.

"But, anyway," Abe said. "Now Missy and I can spend the rest of the evening telling my brothers."

"After you eat your ice cream."

"Of course."

Nick and Missy soon got home, bringing the ice cream, slightly melted from the drive home. I watched as Missy and Abe shared a look, and her shoulders visibly relaxed. They really had been worried.

Nick handed me my Peanut Buster Parfait and smiled. "Hungry?"

I took it. "Starving."

We ate our sundaes sitting on the grass, talking about the wedding—they were, thank God, going to spare me the humiliation of dressing up as a bridesmaid—and catching up on all of our lives. They asked Nick only a few questions about his illness, and he responded casually, underplaying the whole experience. Abe cast a few worried looks my way, and I tried to act unconcerned. No reason to get everybody all worked up, especially with Nick playing it cool.

Sooner than I would've liked we'd finished and Abe was pulling Missy to her feet, saying they had a lot of people to visit before the evening was through.

Nick helped me up, too.

I reached out to give Abe one more hug. "Thanks for coming by to tell us."

"Sure."

"And Missy, welcome to the family."

She gave a little cry and flung her arms around me. I could feel Nick's hand on my elbow, keeping me from tipping over. Abe's eyes crinkled, and I gave Missy's back a little pat.

"By the way, Missy…"

She stepped back, suddenly tense again.

"You never did show us your ring."

"Oh!" She giggled and thrust her hand out, ring sparkling even in the dim light.

"It's beautiful," I said.

And it was.

Nick and I stood in the drive, his arm around me as we waved good-bye until their taillights had disappeared into the night.

"So," Nick said. "They're getting married."

"Yup. They are. And they seem pretty happy about it."

He stuck his hands in his pockets and looked at the stars. "Stella?"

Oh, God. Oh, no. "Yeah?"

He smiled and looked down at the grass, rolling back and forth on his toes before meeting my eyes. "You did really well taking the news."

I shook my head. "What?"

"You did a good job. With Abe and Missy."

"Oh. Well. I'm happy for them."

He looked at me some more. "So am I." He gazed into my eyes for a few more seconds before taking his hands out of his pockets and slapping them together. "Now, if you'll excuse me, I'm going to go take a shower. Not used to smelling like a barn, you know."

"Right. Sure."

And he went inside.

I looked down at Queenie. "What was that that just happened?"

She had no idea, either.

Inside, I puttered around for a few minutes, throwing away the ice cream trash, picking up the living room. I was in the bedroom choosing a T-shirt to wear to bed when Nick's phone rang. I hunted around for a moment before finding it on the floor next to his dirty jeans. I flipped it open.

"Hello?"

"Stella?"

Oh, great. I should've looked at Caller ID. Dumb, dumb, dumb. "Hi, Miranda."

"Where's Nick?

"In the shower."

She paused. "Really?"

"Yes. He helped with milking."

A growl. "I should've known. You're making him feel *useful*."

"Excuse me?"

And suddenly she was crying. "You're making him think you *need* him up there. That he should be there instead of here."

"Miranda—"

"Well, you can try all you want, but this will always be his home. Where we are. Mom and Liz and me. We care about *Nick*, but all *you* care about are your stupid cows."

"That's not true, Miranda."

But she had already hung up.

I sank onto the side of the bed and stared at the floor.

"Stella?" Nick stood in the doorway, hair wet from the shower, towel around his waist. He saw his phone in my hand. "What is it?"

I shook my head.

"Stella." He sat next to me, smelling good like soap, drops of water clinging to his shoulders and chest. "What's wrong?"

"Miranda hates me."

"Ah." He sighed. "She called?"

I nodded. "She says Virginia will always be home for you, no matter how hard I try to steal you away."

"And what did you tell her?"

I gave a short laugh. "She didn't give me a chance to say anything."

He smiled. "Sounds about right." He took the phone out of my hand and set it on the bed before taking both my hands in his. "You need to remember something."

I waited.

"Miranda can say whatever she wants. She's my little sister, and she's going through a rough time. She loves me, even though she has a weird way of showing it." He stroked my hand with his thumb. "But remember, I'm here with *you* right now. Because I choose to be. I'm not in Virginia, with Miranda."

I rested my head on his damp, warm shoulder. He *was* here with me. In *my* home. And for the moment that would have to be good enough.

Chapter Twenty-five

When Doug drove the tanker up to the milkhouse the next morning I had to take a second look. "That's not your usual rig, is it?"

He jumped down from the cab, his expression dark. "No. It sure isn't."

"What's going on?"

He cut the cable tie from the hose plug with extra force and flung it even farther than usual down the drive. "Someone decided to slash the tires last night."

"What? Isn't the truck somewhere protected?"

"As protected as it can be. The whole fleet is in the truck yard behind the office, in a locked wire fence. Can't fit 'em all in a building, you know."

He stomped off toward the milkhouse and I followed. "So how did they do it? A knife? A Saws-All?" Those tires were huge and thick. It would take more than a little blade.

Doug took the samples from my tank, unscrewing and screwing the tops and lids jerkily, spilling drops of milk onto the concrete floor. "Cordless drill."

"A drill?"

"Made holes in the sides of all the tires. If the bastards would've at least damaged the treads, we might've been able to plug 'em and use 'em some more. But no, they had to go after the sides."

Wow. "Just the one truck?"

"Nope. Started with it, then moved onto the next one. Got three tires on that one done before something interrupted 'em." He looked at me with exasperation. "It would've taken them over an *hour* to get all that done."

He went back out and dragged the hose into the milkhouse to hook it up. "I guess we should be glad they didn't do anything worse to the trucks themselves. Those tires cost two-fifty each, but if they would've gone for the tanks…" He ran a hand through his hair. "Those are upwards of ninety-two *thousand*. And that's not including the semi."

I shook my head. "So the truck will be okay?"

"Sure. It'll take all freakin' day to get those tires replaced, but it'll be fine."

"Insurance?"

He checked the hose, then stood back up. "It covers vandalism. But geez, if I could get my hands on whoever did it…"

The milk tank emptied, and Doug pulled out the hose, closing the tank lid and taking the hose back out to the truck. He yanked a new cable tie out of his pocket and fixed it around the hook, checking it twice to make sure it was tight. "Now I'm all paranoid, worrying about somebody getting into the milk."

I must've looked concerned, because he waved his hands in the air. "Don't worry. I've got it covered. I'm just a little nervous today."

"Don't blame you."

He climbed up into the cab, and it hit me.

"Hey, Doug? How was your daughter's softball game the other day?"

He smiled. "Her team got creamed. But that's okay. She had fun."

"Well, good to see you back."

He shut the door and pulled out the drive.

I turned right around and made a bee-line for my office.

Lucy and Zach looked up as I passed through the parlor, but I didn't stop until I got to my office, picked up the phone, and dialed. My call was answered in the middle of the first ring. I interrupted Gladys' usual spiel.

"Gladys, I need to talk to Willard."

"Stella?"

"Sorry. Yeah. Is he there?"

"Sure. Let me put you through."

There were only a few bars of Muzak before Willard was on the line.

"There's been another attack," I said. "And you can't say it has nothing to do with women."

"Tell me," he said.

So I explained how Patty had driven the truck on Thursday, and had even had her baby girl with her as she made her rounds.

"I don't know, Stella…"

"Oh, come on. Don't you *tell* me they're not connected."

"But you said she doesn't usually drive the truck."

"No, she usually runs the office. And can obviously drive the truck when she needs to."

He was quiet for a moment. "Okay, where did this happen?"

"Hatfield."

"All right. I'll call the police there to get more information. But don't get your hopes up. I'm not convinced this is part of the same thing."

But I was. And I was damn well going to find a connection before somebody else got killed.

Chapter Twenty-six

"It all started with Carla."

Nick sat across from me, feet resting on the front of my desk, laptop balanced on his lap. He looked up. "Huh?"

"These attacks. Carla began it all. But *why*? People don't usually get mad at Carla. I mean, how can you be mad at someone like her?"

"Because she picked the wrong boyfriend?"

I ignored him. "And if they don't want a woman taking care of their animals they can just ask for one of the guys. It's not hard. There are two men who do the same work she does."

"Well, maybe she's thought about it more by now."

He was right. I picked up the phone and called her house, miraculously getting her and not her watchdog. And I didn't mean Concord.

"People that were mad at me?" She sounded unsure.

"If the attack wasn't random. If it was somebody that was upset with you for some reason."

"I can't think of anybody."

"No one who lost a lot of animals recently, or a really valuable one?"

She was quiet for a bit while she thought. "I had to put down a horse a few weeks ago. A pretty high-priced stud. But he was getting old, and the owner is the one that said he thought it was time to give the poor thing the rest he deserved. And a whole litter of pigs died last week, but it was because the mother accidentally suffocated them. I don't think the farmer blamed me."

"What about folks that might resent your being a woman vet?"

"You're thinking this because of the other attacks."

"Right."

"I've been trying to come up with something about that, actually, and see if I could think of anybody. But if they don't like me they just ask for Bruce or Tim."

Exactly. "Everything okay over there?"

"Sure."

"Bryan's treating you well?"

"Very."

Another idea struck me. "What's Bryan's last name? I don't think you ever told me."

"Really?"

But then, maybe she had, and I just didn't remember.

"It's Walker. Bryan Walker. Why?"

"Just wondered."

It did sound familiar. I guess I'd just blanked it out.

"If you think of anybody else who might've had it in for you, let me know."

"I'll try. But it just doesn't make any sense."

"I know. Talk to you later."

I hung up and immediately swiveled to my computer and typed in "Bryan Walker" on the search line at Ask.com.

Nick glanced up from his laptop. "What are you doing?"

"Googling Bryan."

"But you're using Ask.com. Can you still call it Googling?"

I stuck my tongue out at him and he grinned. "May I ask why you're doing this?"

"Why do you think? To get the dirt on him."

"Okay. But what if there isn't any?"

"Don't worry. There will be."

But there wasn't. I found "Bryan Walker" in all sorts of guises: Game creator, baseball fan, Kentucky lawyer, Amazon reviewer, doctor, and deceased. Even as a player for the New York Rangers and a disgusting YouTube video made while he was drunk and sitting on a toilet. I must say I was relieved when that wasn't the same guy. For a brief moment I thought I had found him under a listing for North Wales, a town close to mine, but it turned out it was talking about North Wales as in Europe, and the guy was a professional tennis court cleaner. Not our guy.

Finally, a mention under Montgomery County Community College. A member of the class of '95, and then a blurb of him being on the basketball team at North Penn High School, 1992-93 season.

Nothing else.

"Well, crap."

Nick looked up again. "No luck?"

I grunted, and deleted his name from the search line. I typed in gender + attacks + Pennsylvania + the last two months and the year. Nothing. I substituted "female" for gender, and then "woman." Both of them got a few hits, but nothing new. Some things that had happened in other parts of the state, too far away for me to consider, and then the things we already knew about.

I swiveled back around to face Nick. "Nothing before Carla. And hardly anything after. It just seems so weird that Carla would've started it all."

Nick was looking thoughtful.

"What?" I asked.

"What if…I know it sounds backward, but what if she *wasn't* the start of it?"

"But there's nothing before her attack."

"But what if something else was the catalyst. She's just the first thing that happened. Or at least that we know about."

"Okay. Let's look at everything else. Katherine, Dr. Peterson, Club Atlas, and now the truck line. They all happened *after* Carla."

"But…when did Dr. Peterson's father announce his retirement?"

"You mean—"

"This could be something that's been brewing a long time."

"All right." I turned back to the computer and looked up Dr. James Peterson. And there it was. The announcement of his retirement. Two months before.

"Too long ago," I said. "If that was the catalyst, why wait till now to act on it?"

"Maybe somebody didn't need a doctor till now. And when they went in they couldn't have him."

I nodded, thinking.

"And," Nick continued, "when did Katherine get the job at Kulpsville?"

I tried to remember. "She said they came down for interviews during the past year. I don't know for sure when it was decided, but it had to be at least a few months ago. But they didn't move here until last week sometime."

I glanced at the calendar, then got up and went to the door. "Lucy?"

Something banged far down the barn, and I walked out to the parlor. "Luce?"

But it was Zach and Randy, sorting through some old wood. Mostly old fencing and stall boards.

Zach acknowledged my presence with a jerk of his chin, but Randy didn't look up at all.

"What are you guys doin'?"

Zach stood and hitched up his jeans. "Looking for some cool-looking boards to make signs."

Signs. "What kind of signs?"

"You know. For the fair. That have our calves' names on 'em and stuff. People usually use cardboard, or just paper, but we thought wood would be neat. We could paint 'em."

"That'd be nice." I mentally took inventory of the farm's castoffs. "Have you guys checked out the feed barn? I'm pretty sure there's some old wooden barn siding out there. You could use whatever of that you want."

Now Randy looked up, but at Zach, not me.

Zach brightened. At least as much as a cool teen-ager will allow himself. "I'd forgotten about that. Thanks. Come on, Randy."

I watched them go, then called after them. "Zach! Know where Lucy is?"

He shook his head, then stopped. "I think she might be in the house."

The house?

I limped up the sidewalk, moving faster than I'd been able to since stupid Wendy, and stopped inside the door of the house. It smelled great.

"Luce?"

"In the kitchen!"

I went in and stood, taking in the smell, watching Lucy stirring something. "What are you making?"

"Lunch. Lenny and Tess are going to come join us." She looked up from the stove. "You didn't make plans, did you?"

"Huh-uh." I walked over and took a peek into the pan. "Ribs?"

"Just browning them. I'll put them in the oven and cook them for another hour or so before lunch."

"Wow."

She went back to stirring. "So, did you need something?"

"What? Oh, yeah. Do you know exactly when the Hershbergers moved in?"

She clicked her tongue while she thought. "A week ago. At least, that's when Lenny went over to help unload the truck."

I must've looked surprised, because she said, "Ma called him." Ah.

She was still looking at me. "Why?"

"Just wondered. Thanks."

"But—"

"Can't wait for lunch!"

Back in the office, I relayed the information to Nick. "So they came only a day before Carla was attacked. Doesn't seem like enough time to get anybody so worked up they'd go after a completely different person. So what does that mean?"

He shook his head. "I have no idea."

"I remember Katherine saying their family—or at least she and Alan—went to church. She didn't preach, because she wasn't actually starting work until Monday, but they decided to go, anyway. So people would've seen her."

I paced behind Nick, and he craned his neck to see me. "There's no sense to any of this."

"Nope. None."

My stomach growled, and Nick grinned.

"Can't blame me," I said. "You should smell the kitchen."

"Lunch ready?"

"No, she said at least another hour."

"So what should we do?"

I stopped pacing. "Talk to the one person we haven't yet."

"Who's that?"

"Babs."

"Babs?"

"The lady at Club Atlas."

"Oh. Sure."

I leaned over and closed his laptop. "So let's go, before I walk back into the kitchen and demand lunch now."

He laughed. "Someone's feeling better."

"Yeah." I pulled him up from his chair and landed a kiss on his mouth. "So you'd better watch out."

He put his arms around me and squeezed. "I don't know, I'm feeling pretty good myself."

I put my arms around his neck and returned his hug.

A throat cleared. "Uh, Stella?" Zach stood in the doorway, averting his eyes.

I leaned back from Nick, but didn't let go. "Yeah?"

"We found these." He held up a piece of an old barn door, and Randy, standing behind him, had some wooden shingles.

"Great. They're all yours."

"Really?"

"Sure."

"Thanks."

I looked at Randy, expecting some thanks from him, but he turned and disappeared from the doorway. I frowned. He might be disenchanted with women—at least the teen-age variety—but this woman was going to have to teach him some manners soon if he didn't shape up.

"So shall we?" Nick said, letting me go.

I shook off my irritation with Randy and went outside with Nick.

Chapter Twenty-seven

Club Atlas was busy when we arrived. We waited, hanging back, while the lady—Babs, I figured—dealt with some walk-ins. Two big-haired ladies with brightly-colored Spandex outfits and clean, white tennies. I wondered if Missy, Abe's *fiancée*, belonged to a club. I had to think she did.

When the wonder twins went on their way toward the treadmills Babs welcomed us with a smile. Her clothes, while fashionable, were more practical. Black warm-up pants, with a red Club Atlas polo shirt. Couldn't see the shoes, but I'd bet they were high quality. Her arms were toned, her biceps filling out the shirt's short sleeves, and her face glowed with health. I made a mental note never to get her mad at me.

"Can I help you?" Her expression said she didn't think we were there for a work-out, but she wasn't discounting it altogether. "Physical therapy, perhaps?"

I was wondering how she could possibly know about Nick's illness when I realized they were both looking at me.

"Oh, my foot? Just broken. It'll be fine."

Amusement sparked in her eyes. "All right. Looking at a membership?"

I glanced at Nick, but he was obviously waiting for me. What the hell was I supposed to say? That she didn't know me from Eve but I wanted to know about yesterday morning?

"I know you don't know me from Eve, but I was wondering if you would tell us about yesterday morning."

Her eyebrows rose, and she looked sideways, as if to make sure the heavy lifters were close by.

"We're friends of Carla Beaumont," I added.

Her face cleared. "Carla? Oh, poor thing. She's had a bad week."

"Yeah."

"At least she has that nice man to take care of her."

I took a moment to swallow some bile and Nick's elbow gently poked my back.

"Uh, that's right," I said. "You know Bryan?"

"Sure. He comes in here a lot."

"Really? But he's a stick."

She laughed. "Not everybody's a power lifter. He runs. And runs and runs and runs."

Huh.

"Anyway, we're trying to help out Carla. She can't think of who might've attacked her, and we were thinking there might be a connection with what happened to you."

Her nose wrinkled. "I can't see how."

So I explained.

She took her time considering it, and her expression turned more anxious once it all clicked. "I guess it makes sense."

"So, is there anything you can tell us? He didn't leave you any...sign, or anything, did he?"

"Sign?"

"Like something saying you shouldn't be here because you're a woman."

She shook her head. "No. He didn't leave anything."

"Did he *say* anything?"

"Nope. I saw him—"

"Where?"

She looked at me. "Come on." She came out from behind the desk and walked us out the front door. "See that Miata? That's mine. I always park there, under the light, since it's dark when I come in. He was standing over there." She pointed to the side of the building. "You can't tell now, but there's a shadow at that corner, cast by the security light. The only reason I noticed him was because he moved." She shivered.

"So what did you do?"

"Grabbed my car keys so they stuck out between my fingers and said, 'Hello.'"

"He didn't answer?"

"Didn't have time. Just then two cars pulled in, and it was a few of my regular guys. Their headlights caught him, and he took off. A couple of them tried to run him down, but they're lifters, not runners." She smiled. "Now if *Bryan* would've been here…"

Yeah, whatever. "Did you see what he looked like?"

"Just a generic shape. A big one. He wasn't in the light, except for that short time in the headlights, and all I noticed was him putting his arms over his face. And light hair, I think."

An image of David, Katherine's brother-in-law, flashed through my mind. But that was hardly fair. There were lots of big guys around a gym, and a good percentage of them would have light hair.

"Clothes?"

She studied me. "You really need to know all this?"

I shrugged.

"Athletic clothes. Warm-ups, shoes. A ball cap. Can't tell you anything specific."

A ball cap. Carla's attacker had a ball cap.

"The lifters had no idea who it was?"

"Nope."

I looked at Nick, wondering if he had anything else to ask. He didn't.

"Well, thanks," I said.

"Sure. If you think of anything else, give me a call. I'd love to find out who it was so I wouldn't have to worry in the mornings."

"You're not coming alone anymore, are you?"

"Nope. I worked it out with the guys, and they arranged their schedules so one of them always shows up at the same time."

"Nice."

"Yeah. They are."

She was headed back toward the door when I remembered. "Carla says she got a free pass from a new client. You hand those out a lot?"

"Actually, we do. To everybody who comes in looking, folks new to town, those deciding if they want to switch gyms. You two want some?"

I was just saying no when Nick said yes. Babs jogged inside and came back with two passes. One for each of us. Oh, joy.

"Great," Nick said, after she'd gone back inside. "Now we can come work out together.

"Yeah," I said. "Fantastic."

Nick grinned and put both passes in his wallet.

Chapter Twenty-eight

Lenny and Tess were at the farm when we got home. Tess came running out to greet us, Queenie on her heels, and Nick picked her up and swung her around while she squealed.

When he set her down I ruffled her hair. "Hey, Pumpkin."

"Why aren't you using your crutches? Is your foot all better?"

"Well, it *feels* better."

"Mom said you were kinda crabby when it hurt."

Nick turned a laugh into a cough.

I took a breath through my nose, then said, "I think we all get kinda crabby when we hurt, don't you?"

"Oh, sure. You should've seen Mom when she had the stomach flu last winter. I didn't want to even talk to her." She leaned closer. "But that was also 'cause she smelled bad."

Now Nick did laugh, and I felt a whole lot better.

"Come in for lunch, guys!" Lucy was framed by the kitchen window as she yelled out at us.

"We'd better not tell your mom we were talking about this, okay, Tess?"

She looked surprised, but agreed. "Okay."

The table was set for five.

"Zach's not eating with us?" I asked.

Lucy set the steaming plate of ribs on the table. "The boys went back to Randy's place. I guess he has some paint they were going to use for their signs."

"In Randy's car?"

"Why? What's wrong with his car?"

"Nothing." That I knew of. "It's just that Zach's parents don't want Zach riding with Randy."

She filled my glass with milk. "Didn't know that."

"How come?" Tess asked, already with a milk mustache.

Lucy wiped it off with her thumb. "Probably because Randy's a brand new driver."

"Yup," I said. "And a boy, at that."

"Hey, now," Nick said.

"You know what I mean."

The floor shook and Lenny appeared from the living room. "Hey, all. Smells great, hon."

She sat, and we sang the blessing—"God is Great" set to "Rock around the Clock," accompanied by snapping fingers. I spared everyone's ears and snapped while everyone else sang.

"So, Lenny, Lucy tells me you helped the Hershbergers move in last Saturday."

He took a piece of fresh bread and smeared a slab of low-fat margarine on it. I guessed Lucy was trying to reduce that gut of his. "Sure did. Ma called the night before, trying to round up movers. I was glad to help out."

"Did many people show up?"

"Lots, actually. A whole group from their church, including the MYF, and her brother-in-law. Katherine and her sister mostly told us where to put stuff."

I took a bite of ribs and spent a moment savoring the rich taste. "Awesome, Luce."

She grinned. "Thanks."

I swallowed and took a drink of milk. "What about the church? Did you take stuff over there, too?"

"Yup. They'd packed it all so her work things were in the front of the truck. We took out their personal things and moved on to the church. There wasn't all that much. Books and artwork and stuff."

Stuff that had all been ruined.

"Did their son help? Trevor?"

"High school age, right? I guess you could say he helped, but mostly he just hung around and watched us work. The one time he did try to help carry a big dresser he stepped on their dog."

I winced. "Hurt it?"

"They were afraid he broke its ribs. Ma had 'em call Carla, and she came out to look at it."

I froze. "Carla was there?"

"Yeah. She was on-call that weekend and figured with them moving and all it was easier for her to drive out instead of making them go to the office."

And she had a whole supply of vet stuff right on her own truck. At least until the next day.

They were all looking at me, Nick with more understanding then the others.

"What?" Lucy said. "You think it had something to do with her..." She glanced at Tess. "With her truck?"

"I don't know." I looked at my plate and considered how cold it would get if I got up to make a phone call. I decided it didn't matter. I crossed the room and dialed Carla's number. This time neither she nor Bryan answered. I left a message for her to call me—saying I meant it this time—and sat back down.

Somehow the food wasn't quite as appetizing as before.

I had finally found a connection.

Chapter Twenty-nine

Detective Willard was in court for the day, and Gladys wasn't sure she'd see him again before tomorrow. She promised to leave a message on his cell phone to call me as soon as he could.

I didn't know what else I could do, until I thought of one more connection between Carla and the Hershbergers. Well, not a *connection*, exactly, but a way someone would've known about them both.

"Nick?"

He blinked up at me from the couch, where he had just lain down to take an after-lunch nap. I studied him, hoping not to see the bloodshot eyes he got when he was feeling really sick. I was glad to see what would pass as normal tiredness.

I sat on the arm of the sofa. "What kind of information do you think I could get on Bryan at his old schools?"

He squinted. "What do you mean?"

"Like if I went to the office, would they tell me anything?"

He scrunched a throw pillow against his chest, resting his arms on it. "Maybe the year he graduated, but nothing interesting, I'm sure. What are you trying to find?"

I swiveled to put my feet on the couch, and rested my elbows on my knees. "I don't know. Anything that would give me a clue to his background."

Nick sighed. "Why are you having such a hard time trusting Carla on this?"

"Because she just *met* him. She's known him less than a month and he's sleeping over at her house. I don't like it. I want to find out more about him. And what if…"

He waited.

"What if he's the one doing all this stuff?"

He blinked. "Now you've lost me. Why would he torment women? And kill a doctor that's not even his?"

"Do we know that for sure? That she wasn't his doctor?"

"Stella…"

"I don't know why he'd do it. But that's what I'm saying. He sees Carla every day. Every night, too, while he's staying at her place. He could easily know about the Hershbergers through her, since she went on a house call there."

"And the church?"

I lifted my shoulders, and dropped them heavily. "There could be a connection."

"Sure. There could be." He took a deep breath and sat up. "Okay, I'll go with you."

"No. Stay here."

"But—"

"You need to sleep. And I don't want to leave Lucy here, alone with Tess."

"But if I'm asleep—"

"Your truck is still out there. It looks like more people are here."

"If you're sure."

"I'm sure." I got down and hobbled over to get my keys. "I shouldn't be too long."

"Be careful. Here." He held out his cell phone. "Take this, just in case."

"In case what? Miranda calls and wants to have a nice, sisterly chat?"

He laughed and pressed it into my hand. "Just you wait. Some day you'll be surprised. You might actually end up liking each other."

"Yeah. Sure. Like that's gonna happen."

I thought maybe I should kiss him good-bye, but he was already lying down again, and his eyes were closed. I shut the door quietly on the way out.

After telling Lucy where I was going, I made my way to North Penn High School. The building was huge, and it took me a few minutes to find a parking place and trek to the office.

"Can I help you?" The secretary gave what was probably supposed to be a smile, but came through as something else. Poor woman looked harassed.

"I'm doing some research and was wondering if someone might talk with me about a student who graduated here some years ago."

"Oh, like a historical paper?"

Yeah, right. "Something like that."

She glanced around the office, but no one else was listening to our conversation who could jump in. "Who are you researching?"

"Bryan Walker. He graduated in the early 90s. '93, I think."

She pursed her lips and shook her head at the same time, which made her look pretty funny. I didn't laugh.

"I wasn't here then, yet." She turned. "Viola? Hey, Viola."

An older woman looked up from her computer, sliding her glasses up onto her nose to look at the secretary. "Yeah?"

"You were around in '93, weren't you?"

"I've been here since '85."

The secretary pointed at me with her thumb. "This lady wants to know about someone named— What was his name?"

"Bryan Walker. He graduated in '93."

"What do you want to know?" The older lady again. Crabby and blunt.

"Whatever you can tell me."

"There's copies of the school yearbooks in the library, but other than that you're on your own. I couldn't say anything even if I could remember it, and let me tell you, with three thousand kids in this school every year I don't remember many of them. They've got to be really bad or really good to make an impression."

"So he wasn't either?"

"Not so's I remember. But then, like I said, I couldn't tell you if I did."

She turned back to her computer, her back to me. The secretary shrugged. "There's your answer."

Great. "So where's the library?"

She pointed out the door. "To the left. Down the hall. Can't miss it."

"Thanks." A whole helluva lot.

"Wait!" She stood up. "You're going to have to sign this—" A Visitor list. "—and wear this." A clip-on badge that said, "VISITOR."

I did both, and left.

The library was teeming with kids, which shouldn't have surprised me, but it did. Somehow I didn't figure students into my trip to the school except for sitting quietly in class, texting each other. It's hard to imagine teenagers actually going into a library, but I suppose they have to sometimes, when their teachers make them.

The librarian was a young woman with short hair and a pixie nose, who looked happier to be in a school library than seemed possible. A plaque on her desk said, "Ms. Richardson." She smiled. "Can I help you find something?"

"School yearbooks."

"They'll be in the reference section. Over there. Second shelf from the top."

"Thanks."

"Let me know if you need anything else."

Like a reason to justify my hesitation about Bryan? She didn't look old enough to remember when he'd attended school. Although maybe as a classmate.

"Did you go to school here?"

She looked surprised. "No, actually, I grew up in Illinois."

"Oh. Never mind, then."

The annuals were easy to find, but picking Bryan out of the crowd proved a lot harder. As the crabby office lady had said, there are thousands of kids at North Penn High School, and it took a major event for someone to stick out.

I had the advantage of the Internet search, so I picked out the '92-'93 yearbook first, and found him on the basketball team. And the cross-country team. Of course. Hadn't Babs said he goes to the gym to run? (And run, and run, and run?) A peek in the yearbooks around that one showed he actually graduated in 1994. His senior picture, serious, with him in dark suit and tie, looked just like him. He'd only added a few wrinkles. And his hair was now a bit thinner.

While looking at that year's cross-country section I was struck with an idea. I put back that yearbook and grabbed the most recent one. The basketball coach was different now, but one glance at the cross-country team showed the same guy. Older now, with gray hair, but the same. Royce Byler. Then and now.

Talk about commitment.

I slid the annual back into its slot and returned to Ms. Richardson, the librarian. She looked just as happy as before.

"Can you tell me where I might find the cross-country coach?"

She pondered this for a moment before turning to her computer and typing briskly. It didn't take long.

"He's teaching freshman health right now. Class will be over in—" She glanced up at the clock on the wall. "—twelve minutes."

"And where would that be?"

She looked back at the computer. "Second floor. All the way down the hall. Room 47."

I thanked her and left the library, finding the stairs after a minute of searching, and the classroom exactly where she said it would be. Through the door's window I could see the coach/teacher at the dry erase board, scribbling something no one could possibly read. Then I stepped back and leaned on the wall to wait.

Ten minutes later I about had a heart attack when the bell rang and the door slammed open, almost crushing me. Guess I should've stood on the other side.

I waited for the rush of kids to stop before stepping into the doorway. Royce Byler was still at the board, but this time he was erasing the illegible scribbles. He glanced up, taking in my VISITOR tag. "Help you?"

"Yeah. You're the cross-country coach?"

"Sure am. You interested in helping out?"

Uh. Right. "No, I'm doing some...research...and wondered if you might remember a runner named Bryan Walker."

"Bryan? Sure. He was one of my best for a couple of years."

"Just a couple?"

He shrugged. "Things happen."

"Like what?"

The eraser stilled, and he studied me. "Who are you, again?"

"Name's Stella Crown. Just trying to find out some information about him."

"Because...?"

Honesty? Seemed the best route, as I'm a terrible liar.

"My friend recently started dating him. I'm looking out for her."

A smile tickled his lips. "Watch dog, huh?"

"Sort of."

He finished wiping the board and leaned against it. "Bryan was a good guy. Strong runner. Good student." He hesitated.

"Was?"

"Oh, he's still a good guy. He just had some struggles. His dad died during his sophomore year. Left him with his mom and three younger sisters. He was never the same after that. Much more serious. Actually worked harder at running, if that were possible, but his heart wasn't in it. During the fall of his second year, before his dad died, I'd thought he'd be able to get an athletic scholarship to college, when the time came, but that never happened. I'm not sure he even went to college."

"He did. MontCo. At least for a year or two."

"Probably didn't run, though."

"Don't know about that."

He pushed himself away from the board and looked at his watch.

I paused, then asked, "How about girls?"

"Like girlfriends? No. At least none that I knew about. And he didn't joke around, even with friends. When we'd go on trips with the women's team he'd be the guy in the front of the bus sleeping. And those meets that lots of parents would come and take their kids home with them? He'd be one of the two kids returning on the bus. Sad, really."

"You know his mom?"

"Just to look at. She rarely came to a meet. Had those three younger daughters, you know."

Students began trickling into the classroom and Byler's attention wandered toward them.

I backed out of the way. "Thanks. I appreciate it."

"Sure. I hope it turns out well. He really was a good kid. I hope she's a good one, too."

Uh-huh.

I waited for a break in the flow through the door, and made my escape.

Chapter Thirty

"So when someone's dad dies it turns him into a killer?" Nick wasn't too happy.

"Of course not. Don't be stupid. But look at the circumstances. He's left alone, at fifteen, with a mom and three little sisters. He's suddenly the man of the family, and the normal high school stuff is over. Cross country, the thing he loved the best, becomes something he does alone."

"Cross country's all about being alone."

"But not without support. His mother never even came to his meets. Can you hand me that hammer?"

Finding the boys digging through lumber that morning had reminded me of some stalls that needed repairing. After I got home I found Nick awake and needing something to do, so I dragged him out to the barn, where the two of us tried to do together the work of one person. It felt good to do something physical and see some actual development, even if it was slow going. My brain was tired.

Nick put the hammer in my hand. "What about at MontCo? What did they have to say?"

"Nothing." After North Penn I'd driven out to Montgomery Community College, where I'd found out exactly zilch about Bryan. Nobody really remembered him, he'd participated in nothing extra-curricular, and the yearbooks had one of those generic "No photo available" graphics in place of a headshot. "Waste of time."

Queenie, who was lying a few feet away, supervising, leapt to her feet and went racing out of the barn, barking. I hit my thumb with the hammer, then stood up too quickly, getting a head rush in conjunction with my throbbing thumb. I squatted back down.

"You okay?" Nick knelt next to me.

"I'm fine. Can you go see who it is?"

A minute later Carla was standing over me.

She was smirking. "Now what?"

I stood up, slower this time, and held out my red thumb. She winced.

I put my hand down and clenched my thumb in a fist. "How's your head?"

"Real good, actually. I feel pretty much back to normal." She was grinning like all get out.

I peeked behind her, but didn't see the skinny running cowboy. "Where's Bryan?"

"Work."

"So how'd you get here?"

She grinned even wider. "Come see."

It was a brand spankin' new F250. Shiny silver paint, tires with the little rubber tags still on, and not one scratch or dent or fleck of dust to be seen.

"Wow." I didn't know what else to say.

"Went and got her this morning. Isn't she beautiful?"

I stepped a little closer and took in the perfect leather interior. "You're allowed to drive?"

"Got the okey-dokey this morning." She put a loving hand on the hood. "Bryan took me right to the dealer, and I picked her out."

"She's gorgeous."

"Not that I didn't love my old one."

"Of course not."

We had a moment of silence.

"What about a Port-a-Vet?"

She turned around and leaned against the warm truck. "Had to order that special. Should get it by early next week. I'll have to drive down to Philly to pick it up."

"Need me to come?"

"No, thanks."

"Bryan?" I tried not to sound whiny.

She laughed. "No. I can drive myself. They'll put it right on the truck and I can drive it home."

"Oh. Right."

She stepped away from her truck and looked at Nick's Ranger. "Kinda makes yours look like a little baby."

Nick grinned. "At least I don't need a ladder to get into mine."

"Yeah. It is kind of high, isn't it? Higher than my old one."

Another moment of silence.

"So," Carla said. "Got any ice cream?"

We dug through the freezer and found an old tub of cookies-and-cream. Carla scraped off the top layer and said the rest would be fine. Nick and I watched her eat right out of the box.

"So Willard called me this morning," she said around a mouthful.

"Yeah?" Before court, I guessed.

"Have you heard the latest?"

I shook my head.

"I thought you were always in the loop."

I'd thought so, too. "Anyway…" I rolled my hand.

She took another bite. "Anyway, a guy called the police to say that not only did he see someone walking along Route 63 in Green Lane on Sunday, but he stopped and picked him up. He gave a description to the police, but from the description it could be anybody. The guy had on a jacket—"

"In this weather?"

"—and jeans. Sunglasses. And, unfortunately, a Phillies cap."

Damn. There went the whole regional loyalty thing. "White guy?"

She nodded.

"Hair?"

"Brownish. The guy *thinks*. He didn't study him real hard because how was he to know the guy was a criminal? Besides, they just talked about the Phillies for a few miles and the rider wanted out." She looked at Nick. "Guys and their observation skills."

He held up his hands. "Don't blame me. I'm not responsible for *every* guy."

Carla pointed at him with her spoon. "I'll bet you a million bucks if it had been a blonde with big boobs he woulda remembered *that*."

"Yeah," Nick said. "But he wouldn't have any idea what they talked about."

She laughed.

"Hey," I said. "You went out to the Hershbergers to check on their dog last weekend."

"Who?"

"The Hershbergers. They were just moving in."

"Oh, that's right. A cute little terrier. Some kid had stepped on him. I wasn't sure how it was going to turn out, but the poor thing was just bruised. Why?"

"Carla…that's the *Hershbergers*. The new minister at Kulpsville Mennonite. The one whose office was vandalized."

She stared at me, mouth open. I was glad there wasn't any ice cream in there. "I am so…dense. I just didn't connect it from what you said before. And I was busy that day. I was headed to Freddy Hill for a dislocated hip when I got the call, and just swung on by their house. We didn't talk about why they'd moved. I mean, how many people move to this area every day? Zillions. I don't even think I saw the woman."

"Who did you see?"

"I don't know. Moving people."

"Like…"

She closed her eyes. "Well, Lenny was there. Can't miss him, since I know him… There was another big guy. He and Lenny were moving a huge bureau, just the two of them." Had to be David, the brother-in-law. "And lots of other people."

"Teen-agers?"

"Actually, yeah, now that you mention it. Pretty many of them."

The Kulpsville MYF.

"Oh," Carla said. "And some college girl. The Hershbergers' niece, maybe? Seemed pretty excited to see a woman doing my job."

"Yeah. She's into that. Going to be a lawyer. Change the world, you know."

"More power to her."

I thought about Carla's truck. "Did you have the medication on board that day?"

"You mean the Ketamine that got stolen? Yeah, I had some. During on-call days you never know what you'll need, and I usually take some."

"And was your Port-a-Vet open so anyone could see in?"

"I don't know. It wasn't locked, since I was using it. Anybody could've gotten in it, but I'd think they would've been noticed." She studied my face. "Why does all this matter?"

"Because of the connection. It's the first one between you and any of the other women. What if someone there saw you?"

"Like a church teen? Or the family? Come on."

"Well, it had to be somebody."

"Yeah, Stella, a random mugger."

I stared at her. "You really think so?"

She took another huge bite and gave it time to melt in her mouth before swallowing it. "Willard told me about the signs at the church and the doctor's office with the nasty stuff. I didn't get anything like that. All I got was the concussion and the stolen truck. And the stolen drugs. Don't you think the drugs are all the connection we need?"

She wasn't getting it.

"So, does Bryan know your routine?"

"What do you mean? I talk to him about work. And he talks to me about his."

"But does he know about your being on-call and how you take the drugs with you?"

Nick inhaled sharply at the same time Carla slammed her bowl down on the table. "What exactly are you trying to say?"

"Just that—"

"That you can't stand it that I got a boyfriend and you didn't know about it. Well, just for your information, Miss *Nosy*, I don't have to get permission from you. I don't have to get permission from *anybody*. So you can just take your accusations and your suspicions and your…your *jealousy*…and stick them in somebody *else's* business."

And she thundered out of the house—without finishing her ice cream—and down the drive, swerving to miss Queenie and sending gravel flying.

Nick looked at me. "Well, that went well."

I glared at him and dropped my head down onto the table.

Chapter Thirty-one

"Oh, shit," I said.

I turned off the bobcat and watched Bryan's Tundra pull up beside the barn. Once Carla had left I needed some personal space, and I'd managed to scrape most of the paddock, a bum leg not making much difference with a machine. Nick, who seemed a little annoyed with me, helped Tess, who'd decided to stay after lunch, to clean out the calf hutches. I had a feeling more calf-petting than cleaning was getting done, but they seemed to be having fun.

I slid down from the bobcat and limped out to the fence to see what Bryan wanted. Probably to yell at me for the way things had ended up with Carla. Queenie had stopped barking by now, and was busily smelling Bryan's pant leg.

I leaned on the gate. "Help you?"

He jumped, then took a deep breath before coming toward me, Queenie following. Bryan didn't look mad, but then, I really didn't know him.

I leaned over the fence to scratch Queenie's head. "What's up?"

Bryan looked behind me. "Is Carla here?"

"Nope. She was, but she left a little while ago."

He frowned. "I can't find her. She's not at her house."

"Try her cell phone?"

"Yeah, but it's not on."

Probably because she didn't want me calling her. Even if I did want to apologize.

I looked at his work shirt, with the name tag: *Hi! I'm Bryan. How can I assist you?* "Aren't you supposed to be at Home Depot?"

"I was. The boss over-scheduled, so I volunteered to leave so I could take care of Carla." He looked at a loss, and I wondered what he ever did before he met her. Like, a month ago.

"Think maybe her phone being off is a sign?" I asked.

"Of what?"

"That maybe she'd like some alone time?"

"Alone time?"

I swallowed a growl. "You know, like time without someone hovering over her shoulder from dawn to dusk."

He opened his mouth, then shut it into a firm line. "I can't imagine what you know about it."

I blinked. "About what?"

"Anything. Me and Carla. Taking care of someone. Letting someone take care of you."

"I take care of—"

"Sure. Of course you do. You want to take care of everybody. But do you ever let anyone do anything for *you*? You may not know it, but some people *like* being taken care of."

Exactly what Nick had been saying about Carla yesterday. "But maybe it's too much."

"I'll tell you what's too much. *You*. You go around trying to tell Carla what to do, hating me because Carla has someone else in her life now, not letting her enjoy having a man to care about her. But you're a bad one to say anything. You're so bent on doing everything yourself you wouldn't be able to accept help even if it was offered. Oh, yeah, Carla's told me about you."

And what exactly had she been saying? I stood frozen, wondering what the hell was going to come out of his mouth next. He plowed on.

"I don't know what Nick's thinking, being with you. All you do is boss him around and make him feel like less of a man. One of these days he's going to realize he wants something more than a one-sided relationship. He's going to want to be with a *real* woman, who has a soft side and makes him feel needed. Who looks up to him and wants him to be the strong one. So you'd better count your days with him. Because they're numbered."

His face went suddenly white, probably at the realization he was actually talking to me—a regular speech, at that—and he turned on his heel and stalked to his truck. The engine gunned into life, and he spun a U-turn and raced out the drive, as Carla had done not long before. I watched as the dust settled back onto the ground, thankful no one else had been close by to hear his rant. I leaned my elbows on the fence and rubbed my face.

Was I really such a monster?

I turned to head back to the bobcat, and stopped. Nick stood about a stone's throw away, his face a blank.

I looked at him, my breathing heavy through my mouth.

"He doesn't know me," Nick finally said. "Or you. Not really."

I studied his face. "You don't think so?"

"No." A small grin appeared. "If he did, he would've been much more afraid of talking to you that way."

If I'd have been closer, I would've slugged him. Instead, I said, "You don't want me to be more of a real woman? With soft edges?"

He laughed. "If you were any more of a real woman I'd be dead by now." He walked over and put his arms around me. "You are stubborn. And independent. And—"

"Crabby, according to Tess."

"Well, you can't help that."

I punched him lightly in the gut.

"But you're *my* woman. And it's going to stay that way."

I rested my head on his shoulder, the tight knot in my stomach starting to unravel. I stepped back. "Do you think he's our guy?"

Nick blinked. "What?"

"Look. I haven't felt right about him since I met him. And now we know how his life changed when he was a kid, forcing him to take care of his mom and sisters. What if that's what he wants now? What if he thought he was getting a *real woman*, but he's finding out she's not what he expected? No matter what he says, she's pretty independent, too, just like me. She's got her own career, her own house, her own friends. She doesn't *need* him. Not like he's talking about. What if he got frustrated and something snapped? And he's not just taking it out on her—he's taking it out on all of these other women, too?"

Nick watched me, shaking his head.

"What?"

"You really want it to be him, don't you?"

I put my hands on my hips. "It could be."

"Sure. It could be. It could also be me. Or Zach. Or Lucy's pastor Pete. Heck, it could be a *woman* for all we know."

"Carla saw a man."

"She thinks."

"The guy in Green Lane picked up a man."

"Who could've been a regular hitchhiker."

I let out a rush of air. "Look, Bryan's new on the scene. He's got a warped sense of what a woman should be."

"Most men do."

I stopped. "Do you?"

He smiled. "Probably. But then I did grow up with two sisters."

I closed my eyes and rubbed my temples. "So you think I'm crazy?"

"Nah. No crazier than usual, anyway."

I didn't know what else to say. So I turned and stomped back to the bobcat. When I got there, my foot throbbed. I'd have to learn to walk softer when I was pretending to be mad.

Chapter Thirty-two

I finished up with the bobcat and went inside to get a drink. Nick was sitting alone at the kitchen table, a glass of lemonade in front of him while he read the newspaper.

"Where's Tess?"

He looked up. "I don't know. Off somewhere."

"You're done with the hutches?"

"Yeah." He watched me pour a glass of water and throw down an ibuprofen. "How're you doing?"

"Pretty good, actually. Hurts a little, but this should take care of it."

"Good."

I looked at him. "I don't like the sound of that."

He smiled. "I have a plan."

"Uh-oh. What?"

"Don't say no before you think about it."

"No."

"What?"

"I can tell I'm not going to like it."

He sighed. "Can you at least listen?"

I leaned against the counter and downed my water. "I'm listening."

"Let's go to the gym."

I stared at him. "Are you crazy?"

"Nope. Well, stir-crazy, maybe."

"So let's go somewhere else."

"Like…"

The mall? The grocery store? The zoo? "A movie?"

"I said I'm stir-crazy. I don't want to sit around any more." He blinked doe eyes at me. "Pleeeeease?"

"You sound like Tess." I filled up my glass and drank some more. "I don't have anything to wear."

He laughed. "You have a pair of tennis shoes in your closet. I saw them."

"But—"

"And you're wearing a pair of shorts right now. And a T-shirt."

"People don't wear Harley shirts to gyms."

"How do you know?"

Well… "Are you sure you even should be working out? Can your body take it?"

His face darkened. "Now you sound like my sisters."

Oh, crap. "Sorry."

"Come on." His voice was pleading. "Let's go. You don't even have to do anything. You can just watch me, if you want."

Now there's something worth saying yes to.

So I changed my shirt—to a clean Harley one—and Nick drove us to Club Atlas, passes in hand. Wouldn't Carla be surprised. If she ever talked to me again.

Babs wasn't there, but the extra-perky-muscular-healthy specimen behind the desk was plenty good at making us fill out all sorts of forms and signing away our rights to sue for injury or dismemberment or who knew what else. After several worried glances at my cast, he took us on a tour of the place, pointing out the various torture instruments, more widely known as cardio and strength-training equipment. We viewed the sterile locker rooms, the aerobics floor with wall-sized mirrors that assured I would never participate, and ended up at the free weights. At his fourth offer to set us up with personal fitness plans I managed a loud enough snarl he left us alone.

"Nice place, huh?" Nick was actually having fun.

"Really great."

He grinned. "There's a weight bench. Sit on it while I sweat."

"Sounds like a good plan."

So I watched and he worked. I could get used to that.

"Hey. Stella?"

I looked up to see David, Katherine's brother-in-law. Behind him, looking more animated than during the rest of the week I'd known him, was Trevor.

David glanced at my work-out gear. "You a member?"

I laughed. "No. Just trying it out. Well, *he's* trying it out." I pointed to Nick, who was grimacing through some terrible set of squats. "My boyfriend, Nick."

A surprised expression flickered over David's face, but he hid it quickly. He was probably in league with Bryan in not believing anyone would want to date me. He caught Nick's eye in the mirror and they did some sort of guy hello.

Trevor was already picking out some hand weights by the wall. I gestured toward him. "You guys regulars?"

David smiled. "For the week. I've been coming in daily, and was able to convince Trevor it would be fun."

He laughed at my face.

"Well, maybe not fun, but at least beneficial. He's a natural athlete. I just need to convince him of it. Maybe if I can get him fit he'll go out for soccer this fall."

"I guess he needs some kind of an outlet."

"Yeah. This move has been hard on him."

We watched as Trevor began a series of biceps lifts.

David clenched his fists and bounced on the balls of his feet.

I waved toward the weights. "Don't let me keep you from your fun."

"What? Oh. Thanks. I guess I will get started." He walked over to Trevor and took off his sweatshirt to reveal a muscle tank. He also revealed just how huge his arms and chest actually were.

"Hey, now, you're not checking out the other guys?"

Nick was beside me, grinning.

"No need to. But good grief. *Look* at him."

"Yeah. He's big." Nick took a breath and bent over to stretch his legs, tilting his head toward me. "But look at his back."

I looked. "What about it?"

"Look closer. But don't be obvious."

What the…? And then I saw it. "Acne? He's got acne on his back."

"Shh. You know what that means."

I did. Steroids.

"So his muscles aren't real?"

Nick shrugged. "Guess it depends on your definition. Ask Marion Jones or Floyd Landis. Or anyone involved with Major League Baseball."

I studied Trevor. "You don't think he's getting Trevor onto them?"

Nick shifted to his other leg and stretched some more. "No way to know. I don't see any signs, but then, it takes a while."

"Well, David should be going home soon."

"I hope so, seeing that."

"Hey, David!" I called.

Nick tensed, and stood up.

David looked at me in the mirror as he steadied himself under a heavy bar.

"How long are you and Tricia hanging around?"

He adjusted the bar, wincing. "Actually, we're leaving tonight. Sarah and I need to get home. Get back to work. And Tricia's worried about leaving Elena for so long. She's only in high school, you know."

So Trevor should be safe. Unless David had already gotten him started.

"Well, it's been nice meeting you."

"Yeah. You, too."

"See you, Trevor."

But he didn't hear me. His grunting was too loud as he did some awful-looking ab exercise.

I grimaced at Nick. "You are done, aren't you?"

"I guess I am now."

"We can stay."

He smiled. "I think you've been through enough. Let's go." Sweat dripped from his hair, and he rubbed one of the gym's complimentary towels over his head. "How about we go home now, so I can take a shower?"

"A good plan."

"And next time, we'll bring a change of clothes."

I looked at him, and groaned.

Who said anything about a next time?

Chapter Thirty-three

"You rang?"

I looked up from Esmerelda's hind end to see Willard in the doorway of the parlor. "I did."

He came over, greeting Lucy on the way, and offered me a hand up, which was good, since standing was a multi-tasked event when rising from a stiff-legged squat.

Willard wore a suit, the tie loose, his shirt's top button undone. Looking at him made me feel wrinkled and tired.

"You just now going home?"

"Yeah. Long day at court. And after checking my messages I had to go back to the station."

"You could've just called me."

"What? Oh, I'm not talking about your message."

"Gee, thanks."

He grinned. "It was the message about Carla's truck that caught my attention."

I sucked in a breath. "You found the guy from Green Lane?"

"No. But we got something that might help us track him down."

I waited.

"Fingerprints."

"*Fingerprints*? You mean that dolt Meadows actually got something?"

Willard chuckled. "He actually did."

"Amazing. What did he find?"

"One of those fingerprints from the rear view mirror was a match to one in Dr. Peterson's office."

I stared at Willard. "So I was right."

"You were. And I'm not afraid to say it."

My knees went suddenly weak, and I put an arm over Esmerelda to keep me upright.

Willard took a step toward me, but I held out my hand. "I'm okay. But, *damn*."

I really had believed my theory, that all of the attacks were connected, but that was different from receiving hard proof. "So who was it?"

"We still don't know. The prints aren't in the system, so whoever it is has never been arrested or worked for the government."

"What about the Kulpsville church? Any matching prints from Katherine's office?"

"I have a call in to the cops over there. If they have any prints we'll compare them."

I thought about Club Atlas, and realized there wouldn't be any prints there. It didn't sound like that guy had touched anything in the parking lot.

"So what was your call about?"

I jerked out of my thoughts and remembered why I'd wanted to talk to him that morning. "I found a connection."

"Between what?"

"Carla and the church."

"I'm listening."

I told him about the Hershbergers' dog, and how Carla had been called to check on it. "Tons of people were there that day who would've seen her."

"Oh, well that helps."

"It *does*. It means there's somebody who's for sure had contact with both women. Who knows what Carla and Katherine do. Who they are."

"And who exactly would be that 'somebody'?"

"Well, someone from the church. The youth group. Katherine's family."

He was looking at me with an expression of skepticism. "That it?"

"Not quite." Lucy chimed in. "Lenny was there. Want to suspect him, too?"

"Don't be stupid." But I had to admit—my theory sounded pretty weak once I was saying it out loud.

"It's okay," Willard said. "Your ideas don't have to be stellar all the time."

"But it *is* a connection."

He nodded. "Sure. It is."

"Whatever." I turned back to the cow.

"Need something to eat, Detective?" Lucy stood next to him, wiping her hands on a towel. "I brought Stella some leftover chili. Plenty for three."

"Three? You staying?"

"Oh, no, I gotta get home to the family. But Nick's here. He'd be glad to see you."

"He is? That's great. But I'll have to pass on the supper. I'd like to stay, but I need to check in with my family, too. My wife probably has a plate in the fridge for me, and my kids need their dad for at least an hour during the day, even if they are teen-agers." He patted Esmerelda on the haunch and stepped back. "Thanks for calling, Stella. I appreciate how you keep me in the loop."

Even if my theories are stupid.

I eased back down to the floor to switch the milker to Bambi. "Well, why wouldn't I tell you stuff? I want you to catch this guy."

"Right. I'll be in touch."

"Nick's in the house if you want to say hi on your way out."

"I'll do that."

"Hey, Willard?"

He stopped.

"It's illegal to take steroids, right?"

He blinked. "Not if they're prescribed. Are you—"

"But if they're not? If you're just taking them to get big?"

He came back, stood over me. "What's going on, Stella?"

"I just want to know. It's not me. You know that."

He put his hands in his pockets, breathed out loudly. "They're considered an illegal drug. It would be misuse of a controlled substance. You'd be penalized however the judge saw fit."

"Kids and adults?"

"Now you really have me worried."

I waited.

"Sure. Schools often have their own policies, but the law takes care of things, too."

I rubbed my finger over the shiny silver milker.

"You going to tell me what this is about?"

"Not yet. I'm not sure of anything."

He stood there a little longer, until he stepped away. "Keep me—"

"In the loop. I know."

He left, but Lucy stayed, looking down at me. I could feel her eyes burning the top of my head. "Anything you want to talk about?"

"No."

"You're sure?"

I finished putting on the milker and let Lucy help me up. "Yes, Lucy. I'm fine."

"Uh-huh."

"Really."

"Okay." She was halfway down the aisle when I called her. She turned around.

"Do you think Bryan could be the one?"

"Taking steroids? He's skin and bones."

"No. Not that. The women thing."

She looked at me. Shook her head. Kept on going down the aisle.

"So I shouldn't tell Willard about him?"

She kept going, but said, "You want to get a lawsuit slapped on you, go ahead. But you have nothing."

"He's—"

"You've. Got. Nothing. Except an over-active imagination and a boatload of protectiveness."

Crap.

We finished up and Lucy took off for home, not saying anything else about my Bryan-as-Bad-Boyfriend-and-Neighborhood-Killer theory. I went inside, took a shower, and Nick and I tried to relax by watching a baseball game, which the Phillies weren't in. By the fourth inning I still couldn't get into it (who cares about the Yankees and the Red Sox?), and Nick was fast asleep, his head nodding onto his chest.

I got up and went outside to whistle for Queenie, who came running into the house, showing her enthusiasm for the invitation by running over to Nick and licking his face clean of all germs. Who wants to play? Nick opened his eyes enough to realize he was on the couch and I wasn't the one doing the licking.

He sat up and yawned, patting Queenie absently. "I'm going to bed. You coming?"

"Soon."

"You need help getting up the stairs?"

"No, you go ahead. Might want to wash your face first."

He shuffled off, closing the stairway door behind him.

I held out my hand. "Come on, girl."

Queenie and I found a pot big enough to hold some water for her during the night—I just wouldn't tell Lucy how I was using the kitchenware—and I opened the living room window a smidge so she could hear anything—or any*one*—lurking outside. I turned off the inside lights and switched on the outside ones, illuminating the yard and barn, and we sat, looking out the window, Queenie's head in my lap while I stroked it.

"So I don't know, Queenie. I'm being a jerk about Bryan, I guess. It's just… Bryan's mad because I'm not warm and soft, although why he's so concerned about Nick's welfare, I'm not so sure, unless it's just a guys' team kind of thing. Zach's friend

Randy is pissed because his girlfriend likes some swimming pool stud, but you know, it's high school. Trevor basically had no say in changing his life completely right before his senior year of high school because of his mom's new job, and I'm sure that went over real well.

"How do you think Alan, Katherine's husband, feels about it all? Think he cares that she's determining where they live? That she's causing controversy? Her sister seems to think she should quit. But then, maybe Tricia's ticked because she had to give up her job to stay home with kids and her mother. What was her career before? Photography? And who knows if David would let her get back to it. It sounds like he's a bit more conservative when it comes to that stuff. Except when it came to illegal prescription drugs and getting buff."

"Patients are mad about having a woman doctor, someone's slashing the truck company's tires—which I'm sure is because of Patty—Babs can't even go to work on her own…"

I bent over and rested my head on Queenie's. She was warm and soft, and before I knew it my eyelids were beginning to droop.

"You're lucky you don't have to worry about it. Men and women stuff. Relationships. You're a girl, and no one expects you to act any differently as a dog because of it. You can bark and run around and nose people in the crotch, and it's just because you're a dog, not because you're a *female* dog." I sat up and looked at her. "Although I'm not so sure about the nose in the crotch thing."

Her eyebrows twitched.

I gave her one last good rub. "You be good. Let me know if anyone comes around." I really doubted they would, as all of the attacks had been when the women were alone, or not expected to be around. In a quiet parking lot, a deserted church, a truck yard at midnight, a supposedly empty doctor's office…

Upstairs, Nick was sound asleep, his breath coming in little puffs against his pillow. I slid under the sheet next to him, his face a quiet sculpture of shadows and angles, his arm tucked under his chest.

Perhaps I wasn't a typical woman. But then, who was?

I watched the face of my sleeping, wonderful man, who didn't seem to care how I compared to others of my gender. My eyes eventually closed, and I slept.

Chapter Thirty-four

There was a misty rain falling when I woke up. Queenie was happy to get outside despite the wetness, and ran around in fast circles during the short time it took to cover the distance between the house and the barn. The cows, enjoying the cool morning, were congregated outside, and had to be strongly encouraged to join us in the parlor.

My foot felt the best it had since Wendy crunched it, and I was able to get around pretty well, which was good, since Zach takes weekend mornings off. If Nick didn't wake up in time to help, milking would take a bit longer than usual, but I felt at least like I could do it. In a few weeks the cast would be able to come off. I wondered who would be doing that. Would Dr. Peterson's dad be taking over office hours again? Would he bring a new doctor in? And, the big question—would it be a man or a woman?

I got the girls clipped in and stood at one of the windows to take a breather. From where I stood I could see the very end of one of the neighboring developments, but other than that it was my house, my heifer barn, my yard. Nick's truck. If I tried hard enough I could imagine that it really was just my farm, in the midst of rolling fields and crops. Truly alone.

Which made me think about how alone I actually was. Nick asleep, me out in the barn in the dark morning, the commuters not even buzzing past yet. I'd always been a morning person, and was glad about that, but today it felt a bit…creepy. I went back into the dry barn and tried to lose myself in work, but my mind wouldn't go on autopilot. The matching fingerprints Willard had discovered, but couldn't find in the database, kept me wondering why someone would do these horrible things after a lifetime of law-abiding living. Or of just not getting caught.

I tried to concentrate on the cows and the homey smells, the sound of the grain in the cups. Tried to lose myself in whatever symphony was on the radio, but when Queenie sat up in her corner, her ears perked, my blood pressure elevated instantly to racing speed. My shovel, which I'd taken off my truck and set in the barn after getting mulch for the Hershbergers, leaned against the wall, and I hobbled quickly toward it, grabbing the handle. Just in case.

Queenie trotted to the doorway, a low growl in her throat, and she shot out, barking. A man's voice said, "Whoa, it's okay. It's okay." His voice was strained, and I could hear fear in it.

I stepped into the opening of the door. And recognized him. "David?"

His eyes flicked toward me, but went back to Queenie, whose teeth were bared. David held up his hands, as if in surrender, knowing his bulging steroid muscles wouldn't be much help against the teeth of a dog.

I gripped the shovel tighter, and said, "Come, Queenie."

She wasn't happy, but she obeyed, and stood quivering at my heel.

I laid my hand on her head. "She's not used to people show-ing up uninvited this time of day. Neither am I."

He took a deep breath and let it out, fists on his hips. "Yeah, I'm sorry. I didn't mean to scare anybody." He looked from side to side, as if making sure there wasn't anybody else hiding in the barnyard's shadows.

I took in his Spandex shorts and tank top, and his hair, matted from the rain. "I thought you were going home last night."

"We were, but decided to stay one last evening. We got to talking, and before we knew it, it was too late to drive home, even though it is only an hour and a half. It's still early enough today. I can get to work at a decent time if we leave after breakfast, and Sarah can work this afternoon."

"And what are you doing here?"

"You mean at your farm?"

Duh.

"Nothing. I mean, I wanted a new route. Thought I'd come out to your place since I knew you had an early morning schedule, too."

"Awfully far to run. Especially in this rain."

"Oh, I didn't run. I rode that." He pointed to a bike, lying on the drive. "It's nice to change up every once in a while. I get tired of running every day."

So take a day off. "Look, David, I need to get back to work."

"Great. Can I help?"

I glanced up at the house, wondering if I should wake Nick, thinking I was probably just being paranoid that David had come to do me in, that he'd visited several other women or their workplaces in the past week. And I did have Queenie to watch my back. "Why don't you just relax, if you're staying. I have my routine."

"Oh. Okay."

Queenie kept herself between David and me as we walked into the barn. I leaned the shovel against the closest straw bale and headed back into the aisle of cows, turning so I could see what David was doing. He picked up the shovel and moved it to the side of the bale so he could sit down. Queenie lay down at the end of the row, where she could see both me and David. Good girl.

I felt no reason to talk to David, since I certainly hadn't asked him to visit, and I hoped the lack of conversation would give him the hint and he'd take off. No such luck. He started the conversation, instead.

"Tricia said you did stop by the church then, the other day, after bringing the mulch."

I jumped at the sound of his voice, right by me on the other side of Sleeping Beauty. I glanced at Queenie, and saw she was standing up now, keeping an eye on our visitor as he moved about the barn.

"Yeah. Katherine gave me the tour. Tricia was busy decorating."

"She enjoys that."

I stepped back to the bucket and got a rag to clean off Esmerelda's teats. "I hear Tricia is quite the photographer, too. Or used to be."

"She's still good at it."

"But doesn't do it as a job." He was quiet, and I looked up at him from where I squatted between the cows. "She used to, didn't she?"

"Sure, before our kids were born. Then she stopped so she could be home with them. And then her mother moved down."

I stood up. "And now?"

"Now, what?"

"That the kids are older. That her mother's gone. Will she go back to photography?"

He put his hands in his pockets and rocked on his feet. "So, you've been talking to Katherine, have you?"

"She just said Tricia used to work as a photographer."

"And that now the kids are older she should get back to work? She keeps telling Tricia that."

"And Tricia doesn't want to?"

"She has a good job. At home. She likes it. It's where she wants to be. For now."

I studied the rag in my hand. "She's interested in interior design, too."

"Because she's enjoyed decorating our home, not as a job. What is this? You trying to convince me to let her go back to work?"

"Not at all."

"Because it's her decision."

Uh-huh. "Just making conversation."

He moved down the line, looking at the cows, stepping carefully around the dirt in his clean cross-trainers. Which reminded me of Missy, Abe's brand-new fiancée, who had met Abe at work.

Somehow I doubted she would be quitting her job to stay at home and take care of him. Like he needed that.

"She's got them all brainwashed."

I squeezed water out of my rag and knelt beside Ariel. "Who does?"

"Katherine. Alan and Trevor follow wherever she goes. At least Alan does it because he wants to. Trevor doesn't have a choice. The church, and even the Grangers, seem to be under her spell. You'd think the Granger mother had grown up recently, the way she goes on, instead of in the era when women always stayed home."

I kept my voice level. "Ma's had to raise that family of boys mostly on her own, and she's done a great job."

He held up his hands. "Hey, don't get me wrong, I know she's a hard worker. It just seems she'd have a more old-fashioned way of viewing things."

I switched the milker to Esmerelda. "So you have a problem with Katherine's new job?"

He hesitated. "It's not what I'd choose for my wife. And I don't think Alan would've, either, if he'd had a say in it. Not that he'd ever admit that."

"So you have a problem with women in authority?"

"Not in general. But in the church—"

"How about doctors? Or veterinarians? Or driving trucks?"

"What? I don't—"

"Hey."

David and I both looked over to see Nick in the doorway. His eyes met mine with a question, and I gave a subtle nod.

David looked with confusion at Nick, who had leaned over to pet a much happier Queenie, then back at me.

"You remember Nick," I said. "From the gym."

"Sure. But I didn't know he lived here."

Nick smiled, not bothering to correct him. "That your bicycle out there?"

"Yeah."

"I have one a lot like that. How do you feel about—"

And they were off, talking technical bike talk, and moving outside to look at David's model, which was probably good and wet by that time. I guessed I should've had him bring it inside when he'd arrived, but oh well.

A few minutes later Nick came back into the barn, without David.

"He gone?"

"Yeah." He grabbed a rag and went to the opposite aisle to help. "What did he want?"

"I don't know."

He paused, his forehead furrowing.

"I know," I said. "I was worried, too. But I had Queenie."

At the sound of her name, Queenie looked up from where she'd lain back down at the end of the aisle. I told her what a good girl she was.

Nick still stood there. "I don't like it."

"I don't, either."

And I noticed the shovel, leaning against the wall beside the bale of straw.

"I'll be right back."

Willard's home phone rang three times before he picked it up, his voice groggy.

"I have some fingerprints I want you to check against the ones from Dr. Peterson's office," I said. "And I'll bet you twenty bucks they're going to match."

Chapter Thirty-five

The rain had stopped by the time Willard came by to pick up the shovel, so I went out to meet his car and tell him about David's early morning visit.

He frowned. "I guess there's nothing criminal about it. Even if exercising at that time of day ought to be against the law."

"Exercising any time of the day should be against the law."

He shook his head. "Slacker."

"So you'll test the shovel?"

"Sure. Where is it?"

I took him to it, having left it where it was so I wouldn't smudge the prints, and he picked it up carefully by the blade. I followed him back out to his car, where he set the shovel in the back seat on some plain brown paper.

I stepped away from the car. "Let me know, okay?"

"I will. I'll have your favorite cop go over it when he comes in."

"Meadows again?"

"He's the man with this stuff these days. He'll run the prints through our computer, and we could possibly have an answer by lunch time."

"David will be long gone by then."

"Nothing we can do about that. But we know where he lives, right?"

Right. "Somewhere in Lancaster. We can ask Katherine and Alan if we need to. And I guess we hope he doesn't get pissed off by any more women before we bring him in."

"Keep this under your hat, Stella. You don't know he has anything to do with any of these attacks. I'm only checking these prints as a favor to you."

I looked at the ground for a moment before saying, "He's the one on steroids."

He gave a little shake of his head. "What?"

"Remember last night when I was asking about steroids? He's the one."

"And you know this how?"

"He's huge, for one thing."

"And…"

"He's got acne on his back. And thinning hair."

"All things that could be explained by something else."

"Willard… He's obsessed with exercise. I mean, look at him."

"I would, but I've never seen him."

"Oh. Well, he is."

"Okay. But it doesn't mean he's a killer."

I grabbed my head, trying not to let my anxiety out at Willard. "Steroids make people crazy. Their tempers flare. They're unpredictable. Right?"

"Right."

"So…" I held my hands out.

"So you could be right. Let's get the prints checked before we go any further, okay?"

"Fine."

He looked at me, his expression one of fatherly patience, even though he wasn't old enough to be my father. "I'll be in touch."

He got in the car, started it, and rolled down the window. "And Stella?"

"Yeah?"

"You're welcome."

I rolled my eyes as he drove away, knowing he was doing me a favor, but also knowing I had a good chance of being right.

I found Lucy out at the calf hutches, where Tess was feeding Wendy's girl.

She watched me until I got close. "He take the shovel?"

"Yeah. But he doesn't believe me."

"Well—"

"And Meadows is going to do the comparison. He'll probably screw it up on purpose."

"Stella, you have got to stop—"

I was kept from pouncing on her by the sound of a car pulling into the lane. Randy's Caddy. With Zach in the passenger seat.

I met them by the barn, meaning to ask, like a nag, what Zach was doing in the car, and whether his parents knew where he was. But when Randy looked at me, I froze. "What the hell?"

Zach didn't look happy. "He's an idiot."

Randy glared at him as well as he could through his swollen right eyelid. His nose and eye were black and blue, with an ugly yellow color seeping in, and the way he stood it seemed his ribs were sore. And I know all about sore ribs from my bike accident the summer before, so I recognized the stance without any doubt.

"What happened?"

Randy wasn't answering, and Zach didn't add anything more.

"Okay," I said. "I'll guess."

Randy shook his head and turned away, but the pain caught him, and he stopped.

"You went to talk to your girlfriend, who doesn't have time for you anymore." He didn't look at me. "Stop me when I get something wrong, okay? You went to talk to her, but made the mistake of going to the pool when she got off work."

"He waited for her at home." Zach.

"Okay. So you went to her house and caught her after work. But she wasn't alone."

"It was the guy from the pool." Zach again.

"I hadn't gotten there yet. So the other guy is there, and he's acting all possessive of…"

"Crystal." Zach was being very helpful.

"She's acting weird, probably all worried because you caught her, and feeling guilty, too. At least I hope so."

I looked at Zach, and he shrugged.

"So she's dithering around, saying a bunch of stuff about why he's there and asking you not to get mad, and the guy is looking at you all pleased with himself, so you get torqued and haul off and hit him. He fought back."

I watched Randy for any signs of agreement. I didn't get any. And Zach didn't say anything, so I assumed I was right.

"So is this a case of, 'Yeah, I'm a wreck, but you should see the other guy?'"

They gave me blank stares.

I sighed. "Is the other guy better or worse off?"

Randy glowered. Zach grimaced.

So much for that.

Randy stomped off into the barn the best he could, which I'm sure he regretted and stopped as soon as he was out of sight.

Zach stayed behind with me, and I gestured to the Caddy. "Your parents know he's driving you around?"

"Yeah." He made a face. "They're not real happy about it, but they like Randy, and decided to give it a try, as long as I promise to keep him driving safely."

Oh, great idea. One teenage boy keeping another one in check on the road. Can you say "impossible?"

"Do they know about the fight?"

"Well. No. Are you going to tell them?"

I hesitated, but said, "It's not my place, Zach. It's yours."

He shoved his hands into his pockets and looked toward the barn. "Yeah, I know."

"So why don't you go and make sure Randy's not taking his love life troubles out on anything in my barn."

"Okay. Thanks."

"You're welcome."

Oh, Randy, dumb kid. Didn't he know a fifteen-year-old girl who can't tell a great guy when she has one wasn't worth it?

But then, I'd never seen the other guy.

I went into the house and found Nick at the kitchen table with his laptop, which was plugged into my phone jack. I grabbed a Pepsi from the fridge—it was only morning, but who was going to stop me?—and sat across from him. "What'cha working on?"

"Business stuff."

"Anything interesting?"

He laughed. "Actually, no. It's all the paperwork my sisters won't do. I figure they're running the place in person right now, the least I can do is the boring work."

My stomach dropped. "You need to get home."

"No. No, that's not what I'm saying."

I got up and went to the sink, looking out the window. "I don't want to keep you here, if you need to go."

"You're not keeping me here. I mean, I'm here because of you, but not because you're making me."

"And your sisters hate me."

"Just one of them. And she doesn't hate you."

His phone, sitting beside his computer, began buzzing, scooting across the slippery tabletop. He looked at the screen. "I need to take this."

"Sure. Fine. Go ahead."

He reached out to me as I left, but I dodged his hand. I didn't need any sympathy touches.

Well, maybe I did, but I didn't want them.

Lucy was still at the calf hutches, cleaning them out, while Tess had gone off to see if any of the barn cats wanted to play.

Lucy looked up. "Boys okay?"

"What? Oh, Zach and Randy?" I told her about Randy's face.

She let out a short laugh. "I'm sure his folks were happy about that."

"They let him ride with Randy."

"I don't mean Jethro and Belle. I mean Randy's parents."

"Yeah. It's a wonder he's not grounded. His parents being Mennos, and pacifists, and all."

She leaned on her pitchfork. "Maybe they figure he's learned his lesson and won't do it again."

"Right. Teenage boys are great at self-control and getting the educational aspect of each experience."

She forked up another dirty clump of straw. The hutches weren't too bad, since Tess and Nick had taken care of them a couple of days before, but calves do keep pooping, and you want to keep them clean.

I turned over an empty five-gallon bucket and sat on it.

Lucy glanced up at me, but didn't say anything.

"Tess name the calf yet?"

Lucy laughed. "It's between Tinkerbell and Perdita right now."

"Perdita?"

"The mother in the original *101 Dalmations* movie."

"Oh. Right."

She looked at me a little longer before heaving the dirty straw onto a pile.

"Lucy?"

She stopped. When she saw the look on my face she put down the pitchfork and came over to kneel beside me.

"Lucy, I…I don't know what's going to happen."

"With what?"

"Nick. His illness. Our relationship. This." I gestured around us at my property.

Actually, I knew what would happen if I sold the farm. It wasn't hard to figure out. Some developer would buy it, I'd be stinking rich, and my house would become the centerpiece of a brand new batch of townhomes, or condos, or gigantic multi-million dollar dwellings. If my house even survived. I had to hope they'd preserve it as a piece of history, but there's no telling if that would include the barns. The yard and garden would be gone, and the field would be swallowed up in an instant.

Lucy cleared her throat. "And you're wondering what my commitment is." Her voice was soft, tentative.

"I guess."

She rubbed a hand across her forehead, one elbow resting on her knees. "What do you need it to be?"

"I don't *know*." I pushed myself up from the bucket and walked a few paces away, where I looked past my back cornfield toward the nearest cookie cutter house. "I don't know what I'm asking. If I'm really asking anything." I turned around and looked at her.

She stood up. "You don't have to ask me anything. I'll just tell you what little I do know."

"At least one of us knows *some*thing."

She gave a soft laugh. "I know I'll do whatever I can to support you, whatever that might be. If it's continuing to work as your farmhand, I'm more than happy to. I love working here. You know that. Even if you're not here most of the time, if you're in Virginia, I could probably do it."

"And if...if I sell the farm?"

"I wouldn't buy it."

I doubled over, as if she'd hit me, as if I'd been Randy, fighting his teenage foe.

"I'm sorry, Stella. It's just not where I am anymore. Not that I've ever been in a position to buy it. I don't have the money."

I straightened. "I know. I *know*." I walked over to the hutches and put my hand under the chin of Wendy's calf. She looked at me with her mild, gentle eyes, while tears pricked my own. "I don't know what to do, Luce."

She came up beside me. "There's only one thing I can tell you."

"And that is?"

"That I'm not the one you need to be talking to. But then, I think you know that."

But knowing something needs to be done, and actually doing it, are two completely different things.

Chapter Thirty-six

Nick found me out there a while later, still petting Wendy's calf.

He leaned over the fence and scratched her ears. "She have a name yet?"

"Tinkerbell or Perdita."

"From *101 Dalmatians*?"

"How did you know that?"

He smiled. "I always liked that movie."

"Nick—"

"Willard called."

"What? What did he say?"

"He wants you to call him."

"He wouldn't tell you what he found?"

"Nope." He grinned. "He only trusts you."

"Yeah. Whatever. You're off-line, I take it? I can use my phone?"

"I'm off."

We walked back to the house together.

"Stella?"

"Yeah?"

"Were you going to say something back there?"

I took a few more steps. "No. Nothing that can't wait."

I'm not sure he believed me. But then, of course, he was right not to.

Gladys put me right through to Willard.

"Stella, can you come in to the office?"

"Why?"

"Because I was a knucklehead."

"Oh, Willard, what did you do?"

"I forgot we need your fingerprints. We've got a ton on this shovel, and a set of them is probably yours, right?"

I groaned. "Probably most of them. Although I did wear gloves when I was using it."

"How about anybody else at the farm?"

"Well, Lucy uses it, and Zach— But I wiped it off before using it the other day. It was pretty well covered with manure and I figured the Hershbergers wouldn't want that in their mulch."

"So that limits the prints to whoever else handled it since then, including you. That helps. Dan's wondering if you can come this morning."

"Dan?"

"Officer Meadows."

Oh, great. "I'll come right now."

"Super. Thanks."

"Hey, Willard?"

"Yeah?"

"You are going to be there, right?"

"Yes. I will even hold your hand, if you want. The one not being fingerprinted, that is."

"I don't think that will be necessary."

"Okay. See you in a few."

I hung up and told Nick.

"Want me to come along?"

I looked from him to his computer. "You don't need to. Willard says he'll hold my hand."

Nick didn't look so sure about that, but as Willard is a happily married man, and there would be others present—cops, even—he relented.

Not that he was really worried.

Queenie came along for the ride, and happily rubbed her nose on the window while we drove into town. I found a shaded parking spot across from the police department and left the windows partly rolled down, telling Queenie I'd only be a few minutes. She lay down on the seat with a huff, apparently wondering why I'd brought her along if I was just going to leave her in the car. She should've been used to it by then.

An officer I didn't know buzzed me in, and I clumped toward Willard's office. He met me at his door.

"Heard you coming."

"I know."

"Like a herd of elephants."

"Where do I go, Willard?"

"Crabby elephants."

"Willard…"

"Over here."

Officer Meadows—*Dan*—was at a desk in the back room, and looked up when we entered. I tried not to recoil against Willard, but since he had to nudge me in the back, I guess I wasn't entirely successful.

"Over here." Meadows stood stiffly and went to a waist-high counter, where he'd laid out a fingerprint card next to an ink blotter. "Ready?"

It wasn't until that moment that I realized he would have to touch me to get my fingerprints. I hesitated.

His shoulders slumped, and his jaw unclenched. "Come on, Ms. Crown. Stella. I promise I won't hurt you."

Willard gave me one last push, and I was at the counter.

"Right hand, please."

Meadows rolled each of my fingers, my palm, and then all four fingers together. It took about three minutes. "You gonna take my mug shot, too?"

His eyes flicked up to mine, and when he saw I was joking, he gave a little smile. "Not today. Unless you have something to confess."

When I declined he led me to a sink, where I scrubbed my hands with a special soap that had gritty little pieces in it. It got rid of every speck of ink. If I had soap like that at the farm I'd always be clean—but it would take all my skin off after a few days.

"How soon do you think you'll have something?"

Meadows let out a loud sigh. "I don't know. There's a lot of prints on here. It could take a while. How many people handled the shovel?"

"David Stoltzfus. And his brother-in-law, Alan. And Alan's son. Trevor." An image of Trevor, sullen, quiet, athletic under his baggy teenager clothes flitted into my mind. He went to the gym with David. Had his uncle gotten him on steroids? Was he another guy ready to explode?

Meadows was talking to me.

"Sorry. What?"

He stopped and began again. "So we're talking about at least three people other than you."

I looked at him. "For what?"

"*The shovel.* Fingerprints."

"Oh. Yeah."

He looked at Willard. "I'll check them all. If there's a hit we'll need to get them each in here."

I looked at the clock. Way after breakfast. "David's probably gone."

"Gone?"

"Back to Lancaster."

Willard cleared his throat. "We can at least bring the others in to eliminate them."

Meadows nodded. "That will have to work for now. If we get a match."

I liked what I saw in Meadows' face. He actually cared. "Well, good luck."

"Thanks."

We stood, looking awkwardly at each other, until I turned to Willard, who was smirking at me.

"Guess that's it, Willard."

He held out a hand to have me go first down the hallway. "See? I told you you could play well together if you tried."

"Whatever."

"Have a minute to stop in?"

"Sure."

When we were both seated and he'd picked up his pencil, he said, "So tell me how David Stoltzfus is connected to all of the women."

"Oh. Okay. Well, Carla's easy. He got to know her when she came to the Hershbergers' the day they moved. Trevor had stepped on their dog, and Carla was on call. Katherine, well, that's obvious. And he always goes for a run before the commuters are even out. It would've been easy for him to trash her office."

"Do you know about Sunday? When Carla was attacked?"

"You mean does he have an alibi? I have no idea. I do know Katherine and Alan went to church, along with David's daughter, Sarah. But I don't think David did. Or Tricia." I remembered the dinner at Ma's, Katherine flicking a look at her sister when they talked about attending church. I'd interpreted that as a little rebuke for not going with her.

"Okay. Go on."

"Dr. Peterson was on a list of doctors recommended to the Hershbergers by church people. And Babs is a trainer at Club Atlas, where he's been going to work out."

"And the trucking company?"

I had to think. Was there a connection? Yes. "He was at my place the day Patty came with Iris. Ma had brought him and the family to see the farm."

He nodded, and actually used his pencil to write something down. When he was done, he looked up. "You really think he was at your place to cause trouble this morning?"

"Why else? It's not like we're friends. And he'd already seen the place. He acted all funny when he got there, like he was looking for other people, but Queenie held him off. And then Nick came out."

"Well, I have to say it does make sense."

"Yeah."

"So we'll see." He studied me. "Something bothered you in there. You completely left us for a minute while Dan was trying to talk to you."

I took a breath. "It's the teenage son. I think David might have gotten him on steroids, too."

He raised his eyebrows.

"David took him to the gym. Keeps saying what an athlete Trevor is. And Trevor's got acne."

"Like the majority of teenagers."

"Yeah. I know."

"But I'll keep it in mind."

"Okay."

"I guess that's it then."

"You'll—"

"Call you as soon as Meadows gets any results. Thanks for coming in. We appreciate it."

And I was dismissed.

Chapter Thirty-seven

I couldn't get David and the steroids out of my mind, so I said something I never would've imagined coming out of my mouth. "Come on, Queenie. Let's go to the gym."

The gym was hopping. Not something I would've expected on a late Saturday morning in the summer, but maybe these people were all like Alan and just wanted to exercise somewhere air-conditioned. Since it was so busy I was able to slip past the front desk without being stopped by the two very healthy men in the Club Atlas polo shirts. I thumped my way back to the weight training area and checked out the guys working there.

Two especially caught my eye—one whose upper body looked way out of proportion with his lower body, like Popeye, and one who showed the tell-tale smattering of pimples on his back. He also had some on his face, so I thought him a good bet, since forty-somethings are usually past the acne stage.

I waited to approach him until he was done with his set and was drinking from his water bottle. I limped over and sat beside him on the weight bench.

He glanced at me in the mirror, taking in my cast and tattoos before looking at my face. I tried out a smile. "Could I ask you a quick question?"

He didn't say anything, but continued to look in the mirror, so I took that as a good sign.

"I'm looking for someone who could get me some help with strength-training and muscle-building. You look like you might know someone. Any chance you could give me a name?"

His water bottle made a sucking sound as he emptied it, and he tossed it to the floor, bouncing it off the wall. "Lots of trainers in this place. They have the red shirts."

"I'm not talking about them. I'm talking about another kind of help."

I held my breath as he studied me, and hoped he wasn't going to pick me up and smack me over the nearest apparatus.

He blinked slowly. "I don't know what you're talking about."

I looked at the floor and rubbed my forehead. "I'm not a cop, man. I'm not working for a cop. I mean, look at me. Do I strike you as someone who would be in with cops?"

He looked at me some more. Not all of his brain functions seemed to be working together, so it took a while.

"A friend of mine has been in here this week," I said. "Big guy. Fair hair. Came in with his nephew a time or two. He told me I could find help here."

Now that seemed to register. "Guy from Lancaster?"

I tried not to show my relief. "That's him. So, can you give me a name?"

His eyes moved in the mirror, and I followed them to a man at the other side of the free weight area. Not huge, like this guy, or like David, but strong.

I nodded. "He'll help me out?"

The guy grunted. "He helps me. Calls himself Snake."

"Okay. Thanks, man."

I could feel his eyes on me as I made my way across the matted area. I hoped his were the only eyes, and not those of the employees, wondering just what I was doing walking around in street clothes in their gym.

Snake saw me coming. He met my eyes when I was halfway across the space and gave his head a little jerk, back toward the locker rooms. I changed course and walked down the hallway, out of sight of the front desk. Snake met me there a minute later, maneuvering so his back was to the wall and he could see out onto the weight floor.

"You want to talk to me?" He wiped his face with a towel, his eyes not meeting mine.

"Yeah. I'm looking for someone who could help me with some—"

"Strength-training?"

"That's right."

He nodded. "Saw you and your boyfriend in here the other day. You here for him?"

I blinked. I hadn't noticed this guy when we were here. I guess my attention was all focused on Nick being sweaty and gorgeous. And then on David and Trevor and the issue of steroids.

"Yeah," I said. "It's for him."

Snake eyed me. "He didn't look like a body builder."

He was right. "It's actually not for that, Snake. You see, he's sick. Has MS. We heard that st… That the things you have might be able to help him."

He nodded, sucking in his cheeks as he thought. "Doctors won't prescribe them?"

"You kidding? They have their own kind they give him, and only a set amount. We think more could help him." I had no idea if I was making any sense, and knew it wouldn't really work medically, but figured if this guy was selling steroids he didn't care about people's health. He just wanted to make a sale. "You were also recommended by another weight lifter who was here that same day. In fact, he gave me the idea."

His eyes went fuzzy, then focused again. "Oh, the guy from Lancaster."

That seemed to be the one thing these guys remembered about David.

Snake nodded. "It doesn't surprise me that he suggested it."

"Yeah, he's gotten good results. He's huge."

"I don't mean for body building. I mean for health issues. Didn't he tell you he was getting them for his wife?"

Fire hit my chest and moved down to my stomach. I tried not to look shaken. "Oh. That's right. What does she have? I don't know them that well."

His face wrinkled up. "Cancer of some kind. I forget what, exactly. Said she got it from something called DES. Don't know what that is. But docs wouldn't help them either. So he turned to me."

Lovely.

Snake glanced down the hallway, then back at me. "I can help you, too."

"Really? That's great." I clenched my teeth together, fighting my cramping stomach. "I'll tell my boyfriend, and he'll get in touch with you. Should he just come here?"

"Early morning or late at night is best."

"Early morning?"

"Before the gym opens. Better make it plenty early, though. The Lancaster guy and I just about got caught last week."

So I'd been right. It *had* been David. But he hadn't been here to attack Babs.

"Thanks, Snake. We'll be in touch."

"My pleasure." He gave me a smile, and slipped into the men's locker room.

I walked down the hallway and out of the gym, ignoring both my burning stomach and the trainer who was calling after me, asking if he could be of assistance.

Chapter Thirty-eight

"I've never heard of DES."

Neither had Queenie.

"And poor Tricia. No wonder she looks so miserable and worn out all the time."

I tapped my fingers on the steering wheel. "Come on, Queenie. We have some investigating to do."

The Indian Valley Public Library was just down the street. I drove there, hoping I'd make it before it closed. I pulled into the parking lot with fifteen minutes to spare.

"Be right back, Queens."

She looked out the passenger window, showing her complete lack of interest in whatever I was doing if it didn't include her.

The librarian looked irritated as I signed up for a computer. She obviously was ready to close down the machines and head out for the day. I promised I wouldn't be long.

Once I was logged on I punched in "DES," not knowing what to expect. I got hundreds of hits, and clicked on a main one—DESaction.org. It was a gold mine.

DES, or diethylstilbestrol, however the hell you pronounced *that*, was an estrogen supplement given to pregnant women from the 30s to the 70s, with the belief that it prevented miscarriages and premature deliveries. It was finally taken off the market when it became clear that not only didn't it work, but it caused terrible health problems, namely a higher rate of breast cancer in the users, and a high risk of a rare cervical cancer in the babies whose mothers took the drug.

If you were a DES daughter and didn't know your mother took the drug you weren't getting the special testing necessary to find the cancer. Apparently, the usual exam we women all have to live through once a year isn't good enough. And if you hadn't gotten the test and were diagnosed only when symptoms began you didn't have much chance of overcoming the disease.

The timeline made sense. Tricia's mother would've been pregnant during the 60s, years the drug was heavily in use. And Tricia's mother herself died of breast cancer.

Katherine had to be worried, too, that she might get the disease. I wondered if she'd gotten the special exam, or had started now that Tricia was ill.

"We need to close this terminal down now, ma'am." The librarian hovered over my shoulder.

"All right. I'm done."

I could look up more at home.

I climbed into my truck and stroked Queenie's head while I considered what to do. The first step was obvious. I drove down the block and stopped at the police department.

The same officer was at the desk. "Back so soon?"

"Yeah. Willard still here?"

"I think so. Let me check." He called on the intercom, then buzzed me through. "You just caught him."

"Thanks."

I found Willard in the big room with Meadows, who was sitting at a large-screened computer, studying fingerprints. Willard held his briefcase in one hand and his keys in the other. "Make it quick. I've got a date with my wife."

I dove right in, telling him what I'd discovered.

"DES?" His forehead furrowed. "You ever hear of that, Meadows?"

Meadows shook his head.

"Think about it," I said. "David's obviously getting desperate. He's looking for alternative medicine for Tricia. Takes Carla's truck, which had drugs. Goes to Dr. Peterson, who also has drugs, and she won't help him, so he…he kills her. Tries at the gym. It all fits."

"And the church? The milk truck?"

"I don't know. He's just mad, I guess. But he's on steroids. He's prime for going into rages." I looked at Meadows. "You match his prints yet?"

"I haven't had that much time since you left. I'm working on it."

"I know, I know. Sorry."

Willard looked thoughtful. "It does make sense, Stella. Maybe you have caught the guy, after all."

He clapped Meadows on the shoulder. "Meadows is on it. We should know this afternoon."

"Well. Good." I hoped for everyone's sake he was right.

Chapter Thirty-nine

"Up for one more stop, Queenie?"

She blinked at me, ever the patient companion.

I turned the truck onto Telford Pike and in fifteen minutes found myself in Kulpsville. Slowing when I neared the church, I saw Katherine's car and pulled in.

All of the doors were open, so I walked in and tapped on the door to her office. She called for me to come in.

"Stella! What a nice surprise!"

She might not think so later.

I glanced at the computer, where she was sitting, hands perched on the keyboard. "Got a minute?"

She took her hands away and turned to face me. "Of course. Have a seat. I'm just putting the final touches on my sermon for tomorrow. Want it to be extra good, being the first one and all." She smiled, but looked a little anxious at the thought.

I hesitated for a moment, wondering what I was going to say and why I was actually there. What would it help? I finally said, "I'm sorry to hear about Tricia."

She frowned. "Tricia? What about her? She already called to say they made it home to Lancaster."

"I mean, about her being sick. I didn't know."

She raised her eyebrows. "Sick? Tricia's not sick. At least, she wasn't when she left this morning."

I went cold. Did she really not know? "I mean about her…cancer."

Katherine's face went white, then blotchy red. "I'm sorry. I don't know what you're talking about. Tricia doesn't have cancer."

I swallowed. Was I wrong? Was Snake completely off-the-mark? "I heard…someone at the gym told me she was…that she has it."

"At the gym?" She snorted. "You mean one of David's body building buddies?"

I nodded.

"I wouldn't exactly take what they said to heart." She gave a crooked smile. "Why would they know and not me? Her sister?"

"I don't know." And I couldn't explain it. As soon as Nick was sick, his entire extended family knew, as well as his neighbors and everyone in my neck of the woods. And now his family wouldn't leave him alone.

"I guess I got bad information. I just…I was in town and wanted to say I'm sorry that I didn't know." I stood up. "I'll go. Sorry to disturb you."

Her face had gone hard. Well, hard for her, anyway. Even in that state it was kind. "You never disturb me. You're always welcome. And thank you for thinking of me."

"Sure."

She made a move to rise, but I waved her down. "I can see myself out. Thanks."

I didn't quite run, but by the time I reached my truck, the front door of the church hadn't even shut.

Chapter Forty

I sat in my truck, staring at the church and thinking about sisters who don't tell each other their secrets. And how bad communication could destroy a relationship. I sighed, knowing there was something I should do, but not wanting *at all* to do it.

"Think Carla's at home, Queenie?"

Queenie angled her eyes toward me.

"I know. She probably doesn't want to see me."

I didn't exactly want to see her, either, but I had to try.

We drove to her place, only to find it dark and empty, except for Concord, who did his usual whining behind the door.

The next stop was the veterinary practice. I'd forgotten this would be her first day back at work since the car-jacking.

"She's out on a call," the receptionist told me. "Doylestown."

Ugh. "Know when she'll be back?"

"Not for hours, I would think. She has another appointment after this one. Want me to give her a call?"

"No. I need to see her. I'll catch her later."

"She's popular today." The receptionist smiled.

"What do you mean?"

"That new boyfriend of hers was in here, too, looking for her."

"Oh, yeah? What did he want?"

She gave a short laugh. "I didn't exactly ask."

Of course not. But why didn't he just call her? Unless she'd left her phone off again.

Back in the truck. My foot was starting to hurt.

"If it's David, it's not Bryan, right?"

Queenie looked uncertain.

"Yeah, I don't know, either. But still…"

I drove to the Home Depot. Scanning the vehicles in the parking lot, I couldn't find Bryan's Tundra. I even went to the side, where employees usually park. I found an empty spot, and took it.

"I'll be right back, Queenie."

The customer service girl, who didn't look like the kind to be hauling heavy tools, said Bryan wouldn't be in until later that afternoon.

And he was out looking for Carla.

For the first time I found myself wishing I had a cell phone.

I raced home and maneuvered my way to the garage. My driveway was beginning to look like a parking lot. Lucy's Civic, Randy's Caddy, Nick's Ranger…and Miranda's Lexus, parked around the back.

Oh, God.

I stormed into the house, ignoring the eyes that bored into me as soon as I got in the door. Nick's computer was still on the kitchen table, plugged into my phone jack again. I took it out and dialed Carla's number.

"What do you want, Stella? I'm busy."

"Hey. Carla. Are you alone?"

"No, I'm not alone. What do you think? I've got two farmers accompanying me on a herd check."

"Okay."

"Why?"

"Um, did Bryan find you?"

"Stella, I'm working. He's working. It's real life now. Not like the past several days."

"He's looking for you."

"And you know that because…?"

"Your receptionist told me."

A pause. "I'm not even going to ask why you were talking to her about Bryan. Can I get back to work now?"

"I just—"

But she'd hung up.

I went to the fridge and pulled out another pop, drinking half of it before I'd even shut the door.

"A new kind of air conditioning?" Nick stood in the doorway.

I shut the fridge. "What's your sister doing here?"

He gave a tight-lipped smile. "She wants to get to know you better."

"Uh-huh." I took another swig. "She convince you to go back to Virginia yet?"

"Stella."

I finished off the Pepsi and tossed the can into recycling. "Okay. Fine." I went into the living room where Miranda sat on the sofa.

"If you're staying, you can have the second bedroom on the right upstairs. Feel free to make yourself at home."

And I went back outside.

Lucy was coming toward the house. "Thought with this big crowd I'd make some sloppy joes for lunch. Sound good?"

"Whatever." I kept walking, past the barn, through the paddock, past the manure lagoon. Out to the back pasture, where the mother-to-be corner was empty. I sat on the grass, my back against the single tree, and stared at the line of houses bordering the fence.

I heard footsteps, and Queenie shoved her head onto my lap, licking my face.

I pushed my forehead against hers. "Oh, Queenie. Maybe we're better off just the two of us, huh? We sell the farm, become millionaires, and travel the world without worrying about anybody else."

She slumped down onto my lap.

"Yeah. Sounds awful, doesn't it?"

We sat there for a while, me picking burrs out of her fur and thinking about Nick, and Miranda, and women who don't tell their own sisters that they're dying, until my stomach began to growl. Queenie looked up at me.

"Okay. Let's go."

The rest were gathered around the kitchen table, where Lucy was saying grace. An empty chair sat between Nick and Randy, and I took it.

"Randy has a black eye," Tess said, when the prayer was over.

"Tess!" Lucy looked horrified. "We don't need to—"

"Miranda wants to know what he did."

Miranda gasped, and her face bloomed red.

Randy's face was about the same color, and he put a hand to his forehead.

Nick grabbed my knee under the table, and I knew he was trying not to laugh.

"What?" Tess looked at her mom, who was sitting with her mouth open.

"It's just, we don't…"

"I got in a fight." Randy dropped his hand. "I was stupid, I lost my temper, and…" He pointed at his eye. "That's what happened."

Miranda grimaced.

"But," Randy said, "you should see the other guy."

I let out a laugh, and Randy looked sideways at me. And grinned.

Tess' eyebrows crinkled. "What?"

Randy shook his head. "Nothing. But it was dumb. I shouldn't have done it. I should've just…"

We all waited.

"I don't know. But something else."

I glanced at Miranda, who avoided my eyes. I guessed we should "something else," too, before things got any worse.

Lucy looked closer at Randy's face. "Did you go to the doctor?"

"Nah. He would've just told me to ice it, anyway."

"Who's your doctor?"

"Dr. Peterson."

I sucked in my breath. "Rachel's dad?"

He looked confused. "Who?"

"Never mind."

I met Lucy's eyes, and dropped the subject.

We finished lunch without any more touchy conversation, everyone full after Lucy's quick make-in-the-pan chocolate cake.

Zach looked at Randy. "You ready?"

"Sure. Thanks for lunch, Lucy."

I watched as Randy scooted his chair in. "Where are you off to? Simeon?" His calf.

"Nah. We're going to…to the pool."

I raised my eyebrows. "To swim?"

"Yeah. I figured I'd better. And it'll feel good on my eye, anyway."

"Good plan."

"We're off, too," Lucy said. "If you wouldn't mind cleaning up the kitchen. Lenny and I told Tess we'd take her to see the new Disney movie, and there's a matinee at two. I'll be back for milking."

I looked at Nick, and he nodded.

"We'll do milking tonight," I said. "Why don't you folks take the rest of the day."

"Again?"

"We've got extra help." I had to swallow a laugh on that one.

"If you're sure."

"Yup. Thanks for lunch."

"You're very welcome." She left, taking Tess with her.

"Hey, Stella?" Zach was back. "Can you give us a jump? Randy's car won't start."

Nick stood. "I'll do it."

"But—"

And he was gone. Miranda still sat at the table, looking at her half-empty plate.

I opened the dishwasher and began putting silverware into it. Miranda's chair soon scraped back, and she started to bus the rest of the plates.

"What's the problem with the kid's—Randy's—doctor?"

"What?"

"I saw the look you gave Lucy when he mentioned it. Dr. Peterson, was it?"

I looked at her. "His daughter was murdered this week. She was *my* doctor."

"But that's awful."

"Yes. It is."

Nick came back into the kitchen. "I'm going to follow the guys to the welding shop." Zach's dad's place.

"Why?"

"The Caddy doesn't sound so good. I want to make sure they get there."

"Can I come?" Miranda.

"I'll be back in a few minutes."

And he was gone again. The ass.

We didn't talk anymore, and the kitchen was soon clean. I got the dishwasher going and turned to lean against the counter.

"So why are you here, Miranda?"

Her mouth twitched. "Why do you think?"

"To convince Nick to come home."

"Like I could. You think he'll listen to me?"

"So why else?"

She crossed her arms. Uncrossed them. "Because Mom made me."

A flash of anger went through me. "To check up on him?"

"No! No. She wanted…" She ran her fingers through her hair, then flung her hands to the sides. "I'm supposed to see where you're living and…and…"

"*Get to know me?*"

Her lips twisted into a sort of smile. "Yeah."

"Who does she think she is?"

She gave a little laugh. "She thinks she's my mother."

I looked out the window. "Well, I guess we'll see how it goes."

"I guess."

"I'm going to work."

"Here?"

"Yes, here. It's my work."

"Oh. Right."

"You want to come?"

She glanced down at her clothes. "Should I change?"

Just like Missy.

"Yes. I'll meet you out in the heifer barn."

"Okay."

Queenie didn't greet me at the door, so I figured she must've gone with Nick. I walked to the heifer barn, which was mostly empty this time of day. Empty of cows, but full of shit. And the shovel was gone.

Another trip, to the big barn to get that shovel and tape a new bag over my cast. I also grabbed an extra pitchfork for Miranda.

Back in the heifer barn I began scraping the dirty straw toward the conveyer belt that would transport it to the manure lagoon. It might be a new barn, but the heifers made the new barn just as dirty as the old one.

I stopped to take a breather, wiping sweat from my forehead, when I heard the door open.

"Got a pitchfork here for you, Miranda."

"Thanks, but I think I'll pass."

I looked up at the sound of a man's voice. Alan Hershberger.

"Hey."

He smiled, and I figured he mustn't have talked with Katherine since I'd hit her with the bad news. "Hey, yourself. Working on your own today?"

My stomach tightened, and I looked behind him. "How about you? You alone, or did you bring the rest for another tour?"

"I'm alone. Looking for Trevor, actually. He took off this morning and I don't know where he went. He won't answer his phone."

He sighed and looked around the barn, hands in his pockets. "Stinks in here, doesn't it?"

"Well, it is a barn." I waited. "Look, Alan, Trevor's not here. Why would he be?"

"I don't know. He liked the tour the other day."

Right. And Miranda would soon sprout wings and fly on back to Virginia.

"He said something about maybe doing some work here. Checking in to see if you needed someone."

My incredulous reply was interrupted by the ringing of the phone. I scooted past Alan to pick up the extension, leaning the shovel against the wall.

"Royalcrest Farm."

"Stella? It's Willard."

"You have news?"

"Well, sort of. Do you happen to know if the Hershbergers have a cell phone?"

I glanced at Alan, and he was looking at the shovel I'd brought from the barn. "I don't know. Why?"

"We got a match on the fingerprints, so we need Alan and his son to come in so we can eliminate them and get David back here. Nobody's answering their home phone."

I swallowed. "So I was right."

"It appears so."

I looked at Alan, sorry for what he was about to go through. I spoke into the phone. "Well, I don't know about a cell phone, but Alan's standing right beside me. You can talk to him."

"He's there?"

"Looking for Trevor. Here." I held out the phone. "It's Detective Willard. He needs to talk to you."

"Who?"

"A cop."

"Not about Trevor?" He grabbed the phone, a panicked parent, and I got my shovel and went back to cleaning, keeping one ear on Alan's side of the conversation. I didn't turn my back.

Alan soon hung up, his face a mask of surprise. "Seems I need to go to the police department. Get my fingerprints taken. I mean, he says I don't have to, he can't require me to, but…"

"Did he say what for?"

He looked even more shell-shocked. "To eliminate me as a suspect in the murder of Dr. Peterson."

I did my best to look surprised. "What? Why?"

"I…I don't know why. Or how they even got anything to check. I haven't gone to the doctor since we've been here. And even if we had, my fingerprints aren't in any database anywhere that they could match them." He scrunched up his eyes. "And they want *Trevor* to come in, too."

"Well," I said. "That's weird."

"Yeah." He had pulled out a cell phone—so he *did* have one—and was holding it up to his ear.

"Trevor, wherever you are, I need you to call me. Please." He hung up.

"Who's here?" Miranda stepped in the door and stopped short at the sight of Alan.

Alan glanced out at the driveway. "I thought…" He held out his hand. "Alan Hershberger."

She hesitated, then took his hand. "Miranda Hathaway. Nick's sister."

"Nick?"

Miranda looked at me.

I sighed. "My boyfriend."

"Oh. I didn't know you…" He stopped.

"Yeah. All right."

"I'll be going then. Thanks."

"Good luck."

He gave a last little wave and headed out.

"What's his problem?" Miranda watched as Alan got in his car and left.

"No problem." Well, actually… "He's just trying to find his son."

Miranda looked at the barn, hands on her hips. "You don't really expect me to clean this."

"No, not really."

She frowned. "What do you mean by that?"

"Exactly what I said."

It took a moment, but she got it. She snatched the pitchfork from the wall. "I can shovel crap as well as anybody."

"And dish it out, too," I said. But I said it quietly. She was holding a pitchfork, after all.

Chapter Forty-one

"So it really was David?" Nick asked.

"It looks like it. We'll know for sure once Alan and Trevor get their prints analyzed." I laid my head against the back of the sofa. We were sitting in the front room, the afghan cushioning our heads. I had my foot, throbbing with the exertion of the day, up on a stool, and held my cold glass of lemonade against my forehead. "They're going to have a lot to work through in the next few days, with all of this, plus Tricia's illness that she didn't tell anyone about."

"If it's true."

"If it's true. And if it is, why didn't she tell them? I mean, you told your family first thing."

"Family is different for different people." He reached over to take my hand, and held it against his thigh. "Speaking of that, thanks for dealing with this whole Miranda thing. I didn't know she was coming."

"I know. And you're welcome. I was actually glad she was here earlier, because it felt…uncomfortable when Alan thought I was here alone."

He looked at me. "Alan? But I thought it was David who's been hurting women."

"I know. But he's a man, and he was acting kind of weird."

"I thought those things went together?"

I laughed. "Sometimes."

"What are you two laughing about?" Miranda came in and plopped down in a chair.

Nick's hold on my hand tightened. "Weird men."

She raised an eyebrow.

Nick smiled. "Never mind."

"So what's the plan for supper?"

"Supper?" I rolled my head sideways to look at her. "We just had lunch."

"Yeah, like four hours ago." And she hadn't eaten very much.

I tried to think about what was in the fridge. "I guess we have a frozen pizza. And Lucy gave me some applesauce she froze last summer."

Miranda gaped at me. "You have got to be kidding." She turned to Nick, her voice pleading. "Can we go out for supper? Please?"

I closed my eyes.

"What do you think, Stella?" Nick's voice was soft in my ear. "I'll pay."

I looked at him. "It's not that. I'm just…tired."

His eyes showed his disappointment, which was mirrored in Miranda's expression.

"You two go."

"No, Stella."

"I mean it. I could use a quiet night."

"But the milking…"

"It won't be the first time I've done it alone. Go ahead. And if you get back in time I'll let Miranda help clean out the stalls."

She paled.

Nick wasn't buying it. "I don't want to leave you here alone. You know, with everything…"

"But we know who it was. It's over."

"They don't have him in custody yet."

"What's he going to do? Drive over from Lancaster to come get me? And why would he? Willard hasn't called him yet. And even if he did, David wouldn't know the prints were from my shovel."

"I don't know…"

"Oh, come on. I've got Queenie here. She saved me the last time he came. And I can keep my rifle handy."

Miranda's expression was almost desperate as she waited for Nick's decision.

He studied my face. "If you're sure."

"I'm *sure*. Now git."

Miranda jumped up from her chair and held her hand out to Nick.

He still hesitated, so I pulled my hand from his and pushed him away. "Will you go already? Before I get mad?"

"I'll have my phone."

"Of course you will. Now go away."

They finally went.

I stayed where I was, except for getting up to pop an ibuprofen, until it was time to go out to the barn. Once I got there, I took one look at the parlor and went to my office, where I called the police station. I couldn't wait any longer. The other officer was gone, so Meadows answered the phone, sounding harassed.

"It's Stella. Any luck?"

"None of them match."

"You mean neither of them. Alan or Trevor."

"No, I mean *none*. David went to the Lancaster police a couple of hours ago, where they got his prints and sent them. They don't match."

Oh, *shit*. "So there's somebody else."

"Apparently so."

I clenched the phone, my heart racing. "Who?"

"How am I supposed to know? Who else touched that shovel?"

I tried to think. I squeezed my eyes shut and pushed on my temple, going over the past day. The shovel hadn't been anywhere other than the Hershbergers' and the back of my truck until I'd brought it into the barn in the evening. Maybe I'd missed some prints when I'd wiped it down. It's not like I was trying to wipe off evidence—just the extra cow crap that had stuck on it. So the unidentified fingerprint could be anybody's—Lucy's or Zach's or Nick's or even Tess'.

"Those are the only ones I can tell you for sure. I don't know who else it could be other than the folks who work here. And I thought I'd wiped it clean."

I could hear his sigh over the line. "Then we're out of luck."

"I'm sorry, Meadows."

"Yeah. Well, if you think of anybody, call me, okay?" And before I knew what was happening, he was rattling off his cell phone number. I grabbed a piece of paper and scribbled it down, marveling at the way life works. My archenemy, and here I was, able to call him at any time, day or night. I promised to keep in touch, and hung up.

I looked around the office. It was quiet. Too quiet. I was alone, except for Queenie, and Dr. Peterson's killer was still on the loose, knowing who knew what about my shovel and how I'd gotten involved. A rush of adrenaline swept through me, and I picked up the phone to call Nick. The phone system sent me directly to voice mail, and I tried not to sound panicky as I left a message, telling him Meadows' news and that I wouldn't mind if he and Miranda would order their meals to go and get their butts back home. Once Nick ended his present call his phone would ring, telling him he had a voice mail. I hoped the call was a short one.

I looked at Meadows' number in my hand. Should I call him? Nope. Couldn't stomach it. Even if he had become less repulsive in the last few days, I still wasn't ready to ask him to come hang out in my barn.

How about Willard? Now him I wouldn't mind calling. I tried the police department, but got the answering machine, informing me it was after business hours and I should call 911 if there was an emergency. I wasn't having an emergency. Yet. I looked up Willard's home phone number and called there. Brady answered.

"He's out."

"Out?"

"Yeah. He came home, grabbed Mom, and they drove off to some birthday party. Adults only. Not that I wanted to go. I mean, Mallory's here, and—"

"While your parents are gone?"

"Well, they know she's here, it's not like—"

"I'm joking, Brady. Chill. Your dad have his cell phone with him?"

"I'm sure he does. Want me to call him?"

I looked around the office again. Me and Queenie. And my rifle. "Nah. I'll be okay. Thanks."

I hung up, telling him to be good, and looked at the clock. Nick would get my message soon and come home. Right?

I took the paper with Meadows' number into the parlor and pinned it to the bulletin board, where it wouldn't get lost. It would also serve as a bit of humor if I ever needed it. Just the thought of it…

Also accompanying me to the parlor was my rifle. I'd told Nick I'd keep it near me, and now that David was off the hook and the other guy—whoever he was—was still out there, it felt good to have it close by.

I turned on the radio and got the herd in, Queenie nipping at the heels of the slowpokes. I'd put feed in the bowls and turned on the milker when Queenie ran out of the parlor, barking. I looked out, expecting to see Miranda's Lexus. It wasn't there. Instead, I saw an unfamiliar Buick LeSabre.

I glanced down the aisle toward my rifle, where it was hidden behind a beam, and was moving toward it when I recognized the driver. She walked over and stopped in the door of the parlor.

I couldn't hide my surprise. "Tricia?"

"Hi, Stella. Milking alone?"

And suddenly it came to me. The shovel. I'd been to Alan and Katherine's, where I'd taken the mulch and helped scoop it out. I'd left my shovel in the bed of my truck when I left their house, and parked right in front of the flowerbed at the church, where Tricia planted the geraniums. She'd stopped me as I was leaving the church, telling me she'd borrowed something, when Queenie went crazy, barking at the squirrel. I'd never heard what it was she'd borrowed.

But now I knew.

"I thought you went home to Lancaster." I inched toward my rifle, but she matched my steps, coming closer.

Queenie was tense, watching every move. Confused. But ready.

I was kicking myself.

Tricia had every connection the guys had had. Seeing Carla on moving day, knowing what doctors were on the list, visiting my farm when Patty drove the milk truck. The drug dealer at the gym. And most of the attacks were early in the morning. When David would've been out running and wouldn't have noticed she'd left their bed.

Tricia shrugged. Casual. "We *were* at home. But you know, when my husband is suspected of murdering someone, it makes me kind of crazy."

"He was?"

She smiled. "Don't play stupid, Stella. It was your shovel they were testing, after all."

Oh.

"Yes, they told us. Once none of the guys' fingerprints matched, the cop in Lancaster figured it didn't matter anymore. Don't blame him, though. He's young and dumb."

"So you came back? David wanted to talk to the local cops himself?"

"Oh, David's not here. He's in Lancaster, at work. Catching up on the last week of e-mails and office stuff. You know."

"Sure." I held her gaze. "So what is it you want?"

"What do I want? Now there's an interesting question. *What do I want?* The problem is, no matter how I answer that, what I want isn't going to happen, is it? I'm not going to see my daughters graduate, be at their weddings, grow old with David, or know my grandchildren. And as for the photography or interior design careers Katherine keeps pushing on me, they're certainly not going to happen, either, are they?"

So I was right. She really was dying.

Down the row behind me I heard a cow shift, and a rush of urine hit the floor as she relieved herself. Tricia didn't bat an eye.

"So you're here to…" I left it open-ended.

For a moment she looked uncertain, but a shake of her head brought her back. "Get closure on some unfinished business."

She took a quick couple of steps to the side, grabbing the pitchfork that rested there, and was back at the end of the aisle, giving me no time to lunge for the rifle. She held up her weapon and came my way. I backed between the cows, watching her. With my foot in a cast there was no way I could outrun her, especially with the slippery floor covering left by the cows. I prayed desperately that Nick had gotten my voice mail and was on his way home.

Queenie growled, a low, menacing sound. Tricia slid her eyes once toward her, but kept her attention on me.

I held up my hands. "Tricia, think about what you're doing."

"Think? You want me to think? I'm going to die sometime in the very near future, leaving everything important behind me, and you want me to *think*? About what?"

"What this will do to your family. You don't want to end up as a murderer, do you?" *Even though she already was one.* "Think of how this will affect your daughters."

"My daughters already think I'm a dud. At least, Sarah does. She thinks the only women who matter are the ones out doing their own thing. Some important career."

"All college kids think they know everything. You know that. They think they have the answer for changing the world. Sometime soon Sarah will look back and see you did the most important job of all when you stayed home to raise her."

Tricia shook her head. "Not in time for me to know about it."

"She might come around quickly. Especially if you tell her about being sick."

Her eyes sparked. "What would you know? You don't have kids."

And never would, the way this was going. "No. But I *know* kids."

"So what? That makes you an expert?" Her nostrils flared, and the point of the pitchfork rose toward my neck. I hoped Queenie wouldn't scare her now, or that dirty point would come right my way.

"*They're* all important." Tricia sounded sad.

"Who?"

"Those women. You know. The vet, the doctor, the truck driver. *They're* all out there getting the glory for their *important jobs.*"

"So that's why you attacked them? *Killed* Dr. Peterson?"

"Don't be an idiot." She sniffed, and wiped at her nose with her sleeve, not letting go of the pitchfork. "It just worked out that way, that they were all women. And I didn't mean to kill that doctor. She wasn't supposed to be there. She was supposed to be home. But no, she was working at an ungodly hour of the morning, when *normal* people are still home sleeping. She surprised me, and I… she wouldn't help me. David had gone to talk to her about it earlier, try to get her on board with some alternative medicine, and she wouldn't help him, either. So I…I pushed her. She hit the edge of the table, and…I thought, being a woman, she might see my side of things. Maybe it would've been better if it had been her dad."

She shook her head slowly. "If only *one* of them would've helped me…" She closed her eyes, but opened them before I could move. "The vet lady, what's her name?"

"Carla."

"Yeah, well, she didn't really get a chance to help. I saw her truck when David and I went out for brunch."

I remembered Willard asking me about David's whereabouts on Sunday, when Carla was car-jacked. I'd known he and Tricia didn't go to church, but mistakenly had thought of Tricia as her husband's alibi. I'd never considered that *he* would need to be *hers*.

Tricia was still talking. "I recognized the truck from the day before, and knew there were drugs in it. When David went to the bathroom I grabbed his ball cap and slipped out to see if I could open the back of the truck. There could've been something helpful."

"But there wasn't."

"She came out before I could check, so I took off with the truck."

"And when you checked later?"

"Nothing but Ketamine. I thought that might come in handy later, when I need…sedation."

Queenie, in a crouch, slunk toward Tricia, her teeth bared. Tricia made a wild swing toward her with the pitchfork, and Queenie ducked out of the way, pivoting backward, behind Jasmine, who stood completely ignorant of the atmosphere, as did the rest of the herd. The pitchfork was back on me.

I gestured to the parlor, keeping my movements small. "I don't have any drugs here. Nothing that would help you, anyway."

She gave a short laugh. "Do you think being sick has made me ignorant? I know that."

"Then why—"

"You're the only one who can connect me to the shovel. No one else knows my fingerprints are on it, except that stupid Dorie woman at the church, and she doesn't have a clue about what's going on, does she? About my illness or the steroids or *anything*. No one did, until you opened your big mouth."

"I would've thought you'd tell Katherine yourself, since she's also at risk from your mother taking DES."

She waved the pitchfork. "This cancer is rare. There's no way she'd get it, too."

"You don't know that."

"You had no *right*—"

The phone split the air with its shrill jangling. Tricia jerked the pitchfork upward. "They'll just have to leave a message."

"No problem."

I wondered who it was. Nick? Willard? A telemarketer who had no idea what she was interrupting?

Queenie was peeking out from between Jasmine's legs, her eyes trained on the pitchfork. If the tool made any movement toward me, Queenie would be on it in a heartbeat. I had to hope she would get the handle in her teeth, and not the tines in her face.

The phone stopped ringing.

"One question, Tricia."

She twisted the fork in answer.

"If you're the one who took Carla's truck, who was the guy in Green Lane? The hitchhiker?"

She shook her head. "I have no idea. An angel sent to confuse the authorities?"

"But he was wearing a ball cap."

"As do millions of other people." She grinned. "And I wouldn't abuse the Phillies that way. David's hat was for a minor league team from Ohio."

Oh, much better.

"Anyway, David saw me take off in the truck and followed me with our car. Picked me up after I crashed the truck into the side of that building. No one even thought about looking for a woman. The public service announcements on the radio were only asking about men."

"Because Carla was sure her attacker was a guy."

"She was *sure*?"

I thought back. We'd always assumed it was a man, because Carla had assumed it. Babs was certain the person at the gym had been a guy, and I'd put it down to the same attacker. But Carla had said only that the person who stole her truck was tall, with a ball cap. That she'd gotten the *impression* it was a man.

"Why didn't your family realize you were gone the morning you killed Dr. Peterson?"

She smiled weakly. "David was out running. The rest were still sleeping. Alan and Katherine have never been early risers, and the kids…well, you know how they are."

"But David knew?"

"He got home before I did. And when he saw me…he knew something had happened. I told him." She blinked hard, like she was trying to keep focused. "It was…he had a hard time with that."

"Did he have a hard time with Katherine's office, too?"

Tricia swallowed. "That was…I was just so angry. No one would help me. Mom took that drug and *I'm* the one who got sick. Katherine has her perfect life with her perfect family. Her perfect, *meaningful* career."

Perfect, if you consider the teen-age son who hates your guts, and the people who think you're going against God's will.

"And the milk truck? Why vandalize that? There weren't any drugs there."

Tricia's eyes flicked to the side, and back. "That was just…that woman was so *happy*. Had that beautiful little girl, the rest of her life ahead of her…"

Rapunzel, standing next to Tricia, raised her tail, and Tricia followed my eyes. It took only a split second for her to realize what was about to happen, and only a moment longer for Rapunzel to do her thing. Tricia raised her arms to her face as she spun away, and I lunged toward her, my face to the side to avoid the tines of the pitchfork. My hands found the handle as we crashed to the ground in the gush of urine, my elbow hitting the cement at the same time Tricia's head made a hollow, smacking sound. She looked up at me, her eyes glazed, and shook her head, frantically trying to clear it.

I blinked, trying to ease the sting of the ammonia in my eyes, and pulled the pitchfork from Tricia's hands, throwing it to the side. She used that moment to go for my face with her nails. Grabbing her hand, I pushed it toward the floor while she kicked and squirmed, doing her best to wrench her other hand from my grasp.

Queenie danced around us, whining and barking, unsure what she should do, waiting for an opening. Tricia's arms and legs were so entwined with mine Queenie didn't have much chance of seeing which part belonged to who.

"Stop, Tricia," I screamed. "Just stop!"

She made a growling sound and flung herself sideways, pulling me over, my shoulder smashing onto the floor, sending shots of pain through my back. She scooted off of me, scrabbling toward the pitchfork. I turned over and crawled frantically down the aisle toward my rifle while Queenie snarled and held Tricia away from her weapon of choice.

I reached the rifle and grabbed it, using the wall as leverage to get on my feet, and swung around just as Tricia made a final lunge toward the pitchfork. I held the rifle steadily, pointed right at her heart as she leaped upright.

"Drop it, Tricia."

Her eyes flashed. "I don't think so."

"*Drop it.*"

We stood, eyes locked, weapons pointed toward each other. A symphony played on the radio, melodic and aching, the strings crying out. The cows stood quietly, eating, drinking, waiting for their full udders to be relieved. Queenie, knowing a stalemate when she saw one, hunkered down in my sightlines to wait for an opening or an order.

A bead of sweat rolled from my head and down my back, and I blinked away what dripped into my eyes. Tricia didn't move except to breathe, her chest heaving with the effort to calm herself. The air around us hung heavy and still, seeping into my bones as I waited for whatever came next.

Queenie's head jerked up, and her ears rose to points.

My eyes darted to hers. "Go, Queenie."

She jumped up and ran outside.

"It's over, Tricia."

Her face twitched as she held up the pitchfork.

I took a step closer. "Put it down. *Please.*"

"Stella, you still have things to lose. What do I have anymore?"

"Stella?" It was Nick, in the doorway.

Tricia's eyes pleaded with me, but she didn't relax her stance. I really didn't want to shoot her, but one quick thrust from her, and I'd be skewered.

"Nick," I said. "Why don't you go call the cops."

Tricia whimpered. "Please don't, Stella. Please don't do that."

"But Tricia. You're not giving me much of a choice."

The fire grew in her eyes. "You *had* choices. You had them and you chose to turn me in. That's why I can't let you get away with any more!" She poised herself, ready to launch the pitchfork at my face.

And Miranda snuck up behind her, and hit her over the head with a shovel.

Chapter Forty-two

The ambulance showed up with the cops and carried Tricia away. It took them only a few seconds to snip off the cable ties we had locked around her wrists and ankles. I wasn't taking any chances—when she woke up I wanted her trussed up good and tight. She'd shown that even being sick she had the strength of a healthy woman, and if Doug trusted cable ties to protect his milk truck from saboteurs, I'd trust them to keep a crazy woman from impaling me with a pitchfork.

The paramedics wanted to take me away, too, but I wasn't about to go anywhere. My elbow and shoulder were sore, and they'd probably turn stiff and ugly by the next morning, but I hadn't suffered anything time couldn't heal. Tricia would have a good-sized lump on her head, with a headache to match, but Miranda's not so strong she did any permanent damage.

At least, permanent for as long as Tricia had left.

I called Meadows, my new best friend, and he got to the scene before the ambulance left, rolling Tricia's prints right there on her stretcher once the paramedics got her situated. This time I was sure he would get a match with the prints on the shovel. It was over. But for Tricia's family, it was just starting.

Meadows needed to process the scene, since violence did occur, and he did his best to work around the cows, who were finally in the process of being milked. Lucy had rushed over as soon as Nick called, assuring me Lenny and Tess would forgive her for missing this family night out. Meadows took my pitch-fork, but left my rifle with me, seeing how it hadn't been fired and no one was sporting any bullet holes.

Willard had shown up soon after Meadows, dressed casually for the birthday party, and followed Nick, Miranda, and me into the house, where I told my story, the other two filling in details of the last few minutes in the barn. Thank God they'd gotten my voice mail and had immediately come home, leaving their dinners on the table. Miranda was still a bit unnerved, but was feeling pretty proud of herself, too, the way she'd crept up on Tricia and taken her out.

During the interview Willard never once rubbed it in that he'd been right all along—that it had been about the drugs, not about the women. The signs Tricia had made for Dr. Peterson and Katherine had been misleading. She really was mad that they were women, and that they weren't on "her side." But that hadn't been the impetus for the attacks, no matter how the signs had made it look.

Willard listened quietly while we talked, and wrote his notes with the pencil he pulled from his pocket. He didn't bounce it, chew on it, or toss it in the air. Willard, my good buddy, had been shaken.

When he finally left, squeezing my sore shoulders in a bear hug—despite the urine smell—and asking me to please stay home and not get into anymore trouble, *ever*, I stood in the middle of my living room, Nick and Miranda watching me.

"I think," I said, "that I need to take a long, hot shower."

So I did.

The bonfire out back was blazing, and a pot of sausage and veg-etables sat in the midst of it, the smell beginning to filter through the air, taking my salivary glands into overdrive. The past three days had been crammed with filling out police reports, fending off TV interviews, and attending Dr. Peterson's viewing and funeral, where her husband had stood stoically, patting my back, as I'd cried on his shoulder. Katherine called once to apologize for her family's violent intrusion into my life, and while I'd said I didn't blame her, I hadn't heard from her since. The last news I'd had from Ma was that Katherine was going to stick around, her congregation not willing to kick her out for her sister's sins. How very progressive of them.

Sarah had decided to postpone her schooling for a year, choosing to stay home and help her dad take care of Elena, her younger sister, and do whatever she could for her mom. It seemed, she'd said, like the most important thing she could be doing.

Lucy finally declared it was time for an employee cookout to get our minds off of things, and set about planning the whole affair.

Now I was waiting for supper and hanging out with Tess at the calf hutches, where she scratched the nose of Wendy's heifer.

She squinted up at me. "I've picked a name."

I brought myself back from wherever I'd been as I'd gazed into the darkening sky. "Oh, yeah? What is it?"

"Rachel."

Tears welled in my eyes. "That's perfect, pumpkin. And lovely." I laid a hand on the calf's head. "Dr. Peterson would like that."

Tess smiled.

"Everything okay?"

I dropped my hand and turned toward Carla, who stood beside me, her face closed.

"Everything's fine."

"Good."

I looked over my shoulder to see Carla's truck in the driveway, a new Port-a-Vet gleaming in the bed. "Looks good. You enjoying it?"

"Yeah." She crossed her arms and leaned against the calf hutch. "You know, it has some features the old one didn't have. A GPS system. Better gas mileage. A larger refrigerated section in the cap."

"That's nice."

"Uh-huh."

I glanced at Tess, who was down rubbing noses with Rachel, and turned my back on her. "Look, Carla, I'm sorry—"

She waved a hand. "Can we just…not go there?"

I stuck my hands in my back pockets and looked toward the bonfire, where Bryan and Nick were busy stoking the flames and splitting wood, while Lenny sat watching and offering suggestions and drinking a birch beer. You know. Man stuff. Queenie and Concord raced around the yard, stopping only to sniff at trees and water them. It was fun to see the old greyhound stretching his legs.

"You know Bryan's old cross country coach called him?" Carla didn't look at me. "Said some woman with a tattoo on her neck was at the school, asking questions. He couldn't remember her name."

I bit my lip.

"He felt guilty afterward for some of the things he'd told her. And he let Bryan know what all he'd said."

"I—"

"Thanks, Stella."

I blinked. "What?"

"I know you were trying to help. And you actually did. Bryan told me about his dad. And his sisters. His mom. It brought us a lot closer."

"Oh, well, good."

She gave a little smile. "I'm sure that was your intention, and not to prove that he was out murdering women."

I stayed quiet.

"Anyway, do you think you have it in you to give him a chance now? He really is a good guy. And I think I might love him."

Tears pricked my eyes again, dammit. "I will, Carla. I promise. If you love him…"

"Good. Now it looks like Miranda and Lucy could use a little help setting up the picnic table. Want to come?"

We left Tess and the calf getting to know each other and helped Lucy set out a feast. Deviled eggs, baked beans, homemade bread, fresh lettuce from the garden. Carla had called dibs on planning dessert and promised a full ice cream sundae buffet with warm chocolate pudding cake, if we could all save just a little room. I had a feeling she'd save more room than the rest of us.

Zach and Randy were washing the Caddy, which was fresh back from the garage, where the mechanic had replaced a few of the older parts and gotten it back into shape. Until the next part broke. But for now the old car shone with the love and care given by a teenage boy, and it would probably see him through many dates and days out with the guys.

I walked over to them. "You about ready to eat?"

Zach wiped the driver's window before looking up. "I'm starved."

"Randy?"

He was crouched down by the rear tire, where he scrubbed the white walls with a brush. "I can always eat."

I gently took his chin and turned his face toward me. "Looking less black and more yellow. And I can see your eye. That's good."

He smiled. "Yeah. Doesn't hurt anymore, either."

"How about Crystal? Has that stopped hurting, too?"

He glanced at Zach over the top of the car.

I followed the look. "What?"

"Well, actually…"

I waited.

"I met a real nice girl when Zach and I went to the pool the other day…"

I laughed. "So Crystal's history."

"Oh, she is so done."

I let go of his chin and patted his cheek. "Good for you. Now let's go eat."

Dinner was a cheerful affair, the teenagers eating as much as the rest of us combined. Well, the rest of us minus Carla. She held her own. Dessert was overload, but we managed to force it down, and had to sit for a while to let it settle.

Lucy finally got up to take in the leftovers, and I grabbed the empty deviled egg tray and the pot of baked beans and followed her into the kitchen.

"Thanks, Luce. This was…nice."

She got out a Tupperware container and dumped the beans into it, scraping out the good sauce before closing it up. "You're welcome." She hesitated, and turned to me. "You know, Stella, that I'll do whatever I can to help you. To keep things…working here. Whatever you need."

"I know. But thanks for saying it."

She smiled. "Now why don't you go sit down, and I'll take care of the rest of this. Lenny will give me a hand, right, hon?"

He lumbered past me, setting the pot of sausage and vegetables in the sink for Lucy to empty. "'Course. Can't have the boss lady doing all the work."

"And by that," I said, "you mean Lucy."

He raised his eyebrows. "Who else would I mean?"

Lucy laughed and swatted at him with a dishtowel, and I made my exit before they got mushy.

Nick caught me outside the back door, spinning me around and giving me a quick kiss. He held up a blanket. "Can you manage a stroll to our favorite spot?"

I looked toward the campfire. Carla and Bryan were holding hands, looking into each other's eyes. Tess threw sticks for the dogs. And the boys were busy flirting with Miranda, who was much older, and therefore very exciting. It looked like she didn't mind the attention.

"Sure. My foot feels pretty good. Let's go."

He grabbed my hand, and we walked out toward the back field. The corn was the height of our knees, but the irrigation lane was open. The same lane we'd traveled a year ago when he'd questioned my loyalty to the farm. The same lane we'd traveled when he'd questioned my loyalty to *him*. The place I'd come often to be alone, to get away, to have some peace.

We reached the center of the field, and Nick let go of my hand. Together we spread out the blanket and lay on our backs, gazing up toward the sky. The stars were just beginning to come out, and the moon shined brightly, casting shadows of the corn onto us.

"Fun night," Nick said.

"Yeah."

"A lot of your closest friends are here."

"Uh-huh. And then there's your sister."

He grinned. "She'll become one of your friends. You'll see. I mean, she did like you enough to save your life."

I raised an eyebrow.

"Well, she helped, anyway."

I rolled onto my side, my shoulder over its main soreness. "It's important to you, isn't it? That we get along?"

He looked at me, his hands behind his head. "Of course. Just like it's important to Carla that you like Bryan. And to Abe that you approved of him marrying Missy. It hasn't been easy for them to see you questioning their choices."

I dropped back down. "God, I'm a bitch."

He laughed. "Think of it as a strong personality." He rolled over now, looking down into my face. "With all of those people here, don't you think we should celebrate something?"

"We are. It's a Royalcrest Farm employee picnic."

"Sure. Okay. But I had another idea."

"Like what?"

He sat up and reached into his pocket. When he brought out his hand it held a small jewelry box.

My breath caught. "Nick?"

"Go on. Open it."

I sat up, my hands shaking, and took the box. The lid opened easily, looking as I expected, with the velvet cushioning, and the gold-plated name of a jewelry store. What wasn't there was…a ring. Instead, a business card lay on the soft fabric. I pulled it out and squinted at the lettering in the fading light. The card had Rusty Oldham's name on it, a long-time friend, along with his tattooing business' address and phone number. I looked at Nick, confused. "You want to get me a tattoo?"

He smiled and took the box, setting it on the blanket, then held my hand in both of his. "Stella, I know you can't risk stabbing cows or getting a ring caught in conveyor belts or whatever other machinery you use. Lord knows we wouldn't want one scratching your Harley." He kneaded my knuckles. "A diamond, beautiful as it would be, just isn't...*you*. So I would be honored if..." He cleared his throat. "If you would let Rusty tattoo a ring on your finger. I want... Stella, will you marry me?"

A rush of dizziness overwhelmed me, and I closed my eyes. A vision of my farm passed through my mind. My cows, my land, my house, my barns. The friends I had in my little corner of Pennsylvania. The Grangers—the only family I'd ever known. Carla and Lucy and Lenny and Bart. Home. My home for as long as I could remember.

But now...

"Yes, Nick." I opened my eyes. "*Yes*. I would *love* to marry you."

The smile on his face matched the one in my heart, and I reached out and held onto him, wanting never to let go.

But after a minute, he started to squirm. I sat back.

"I think," he said, "that there are some folks back at the farm who would like to hear the news."

My grin felt ridiculous. But oh, so good. "So let's go tell them."

He helped me up, and together we shook out the blanket and folded it. Once he'd tucked it under his arm, he grabbed my hand with his.

"And then," he said, "I need to go back to Virginia and start packing."

I stared at him.

He raised his eyebrows. "You don't expect me to move all the way up to Pennsylvania without bringing my stuff, do you?"

I looked into the face of my beautiful, amazing, *incredible* fiancé. And I laughed with joy, with disbelief, and with a heart full of love.

I was home.

To receive a free catalog of Poisoned Pen Press titles, please contact us in one of the following ways:

Phone: 1-800-421-3976
Facsimile: 1-480-949-1707
Email: info@poisonedpenpress.com
Website: www.poisonedpenpress.com

Poisoned Pen Press
6962 E. First Ave. Ste. 103
Scottsdale, AZ 85251

DATE DUE

OC 29 '10			
DE 1 8 '15			

Demco, Inc. 38-293